BAKED
TO
DEATH

Books by Dean James

POSTED TO DEATH

FAKED TO DEATH

DECORATED TO DEATH

BAKED TO DEATH

Published by Kensington Publishing Corporation

A Simon Kirby-Jones Mystery

BAKED
TO
DEATH

Dean James

KENSINGTON BOOKS
www.kensingtonbooks.com

The medieval re-enactment group and its members depicted in the pages of this novel are a product of the author's imagination and not intended to represent any of the groups or individuals belonging to any existing medieval re-enactment group. Any similarity between the two is unintentional.

KENSINGTON BOOKS are published by

Kensington Publishing Corp.
850 Third Avenue
New York, NY 10022

All Kensington titles, imprints and distributed lines are available at special quantity discounts for bulk purchases for sales promotion, premiums, fund-raising, educational or institutional use.

Special book excerpts or customized printings can also be created to fit specific needs. For details, write or phone the office of the Kensington Special Sales Manager: Kensington Publishing Corp., 850 Third Avenue, New York, NY, 10022. Attn. Special Sales Department. Phone: 1-800-221-2647.

Kensington and the K logo Reg. U.S. Pat. & TM Off

Library of Congress Control Number: 2004110749
ISBN 0-7582-0487-6

First Printing: April 2005
10 9 8 7 6 5 4 3 2 1

Printed in the United States of America

For Nancy Yost
with thanks for a decade
of friendship and hard work.

Acknowledgments

First, thanks to my esteemed editor, John Scognamiglio, and the team at Kensington for all they do so well; second, thanks to Julie Wray Herman and Patricia R. Orr for continuing to read each work-in-progress and offering sage advice; third, to Deborah Howell Patterson, R.Ph., fellow member of the Class of '77, for help with matters pharmacological; and finally, to Tejas Englesmith for constant support and encouragement.

Chapter 1

I haven't been dead all that long, but I'm getting used to it.
In the old days, being a vampire was quite glamorous (just think of Frank Langella as Dracula, and you'll get my drift), but it was also much more dangerous. True, we could shapeshift—though who in his right mind would want to be a bat, I don't know. We were also more likely to end up with a wooden stake through the heart or dragged from our resting places into the noonday sun to be fried into nothingness.

When taking my morning dose, a dandy little pill that gives me the nourishment I need without my ever having to drink blood from a living creature, I often wax philosophical about being a vampire. A couple of these pills every day, and I can pass for a live person.

I can even go out in the sun, provided I'm careful about overexposure to it. This was going to be my first full summer in England since I had taken up residence in Laurel Cottage in the Bedfordshire village of Snupperton Mumsley, and I might have to admit to an allergy to the sun to explain my preference for staying inside during a glorious English summer. Though I had been involved in various village doings over the past nine months, I wasn't ready for a round of garden parties and fetes of the kind that seem endemic to English villages in the summer. Well, I would find some graceful way to do my own thing. After all, we writers are known to be peculiar.

These musings came back to me in force barely half an hour later when my handsome assistant, Giles Blitherington, arrived to begin the day's work and offered me the latest news from Blitherington Hall. In actuality, he was *Sir* Giles Blitherington, but despite his aristocratic look and manner, he generally eschewed use of his title, much to the annoyance of his mother, Lady Prunella. After a hurried greeting, Giles was most impatient to share with me his latest worry.

From behind my desk I regarded Giles with sympathy. "What is the problem now, Giles?"

Giles dropped into the chair across the desk from me. "Oh, Simon, it's this silly medieval 'faire' that's going to be held next week."

I had seen the advertisements for the faire around the village, but I hadn't taken much notice of them. I couldn't see the point in people attempting to re-create life in medieval England, just for the sake of amusement and, more to the point, commerce. Evidently the faire would be host to a number of small businesses that offered all kinds of faux-medieval products: clothing, jewelry, armor, food, and the like. I intended to steer well clear of it.

"What has that to do with you, Giles?" I asked. "I should think you can avoid it completely, so why worry about it?"

"Didn't you pay *any* attention to where the bally thing is being held, Simon?" Giles said. "It's practically in our back garden at Blitherington Hall, and Mummy is beside herself. She thinks all these faire types will be running all over our grounds and making quite a mess."

"No, Giles, I *hadn't* paid much attention to the 'bally' thing, as you call it," I said, a trifle waspishly. "If so-called adults want to run around playing dress-up, it's nothing to do with me. But, frankly, I shouldn't think Lady Prunella has anything to worry about." I paused, frowning. "How did they end up on that land anyway? Doesn't it belong to the manor?"

Giles sighed. "It did, until about a year ago. About that time we desperately needed to raise some cash to do some electrical work at Blitherington Hall. A neighboring landowner had made an offer several times for the land, and finally Mummy and I decided we had no choice but to sell it."

"Pardon me, Giles," I said, "but I still don't quite see the problem."

"The problem, Simon," Giles said, becoming exasperated with me, "is Murdo Millbank, the man who bought the land. He's a businessman from London who rather fancies being a gentleman farmer, or so he said, in the beginning. He told us he intended to keep it as a meadow. He wanted to put some cows on it."

"And I take it his plans have changed?"

"Oh, yes, they've changed." Giles almost spit out the words. "This medieval faire is just the beginning. He kept the meadow as it was until recently, and Mummy and I thought everything would be fine. Now we're told that, after this medieval gathering, he's rented the land out to some music producer, and there's going to be an enormous three-day rock festival in August!"

"Ah," I said. "Now I can see your problem. The folk at the medieval faire might be fairly law-abiding, but if a bunch of rowdy fans are at a rock festival nearby, who knows what might happen."

Giles nodded unhappily. "The whole village will be in an uproar, Simon, and they'll blame Mummy and me because we sold the land to that lying prat." He threw his hands up. "And it's not as if Mummy needs to annoy the village any more than she already does."

I forbore to comment on that last statement. Lady Prunella was a perpetual thorn in the side of the village. She insisted on playing Lady of the Manor because she saw it as her natural role—never mind that the villagers resented her heavy-handed way of interfering in things that were really none of her business.

"It could all be rather frightful, Giles," I said, "but I can't see that there's anything you can do about it. You can't buy the land back, certainly."

"No, of course we can't," Giles replied. "But Mummy has already indulged in one screaming match with Millbank, and I shudder to think what will happen when the rock festival takes place."

I had to make an effort not to smile. The dear boy had a point. His mother had developed a penchant for getting herself into difficult situations.[1] "Then I suppose we shall just have to keep her out of mischief."

"Far easier said than done, Simon," Giles muttered.

"We shall see, Giles, we shall see," I said, trying to comfort him. I decided it was time to shift the subject a bit. "Tell me what you know about this group putting on the medieval faire. Is it the Society for Creative Anachronism, perhaps?" I was familiar with this particular group, which has a good-sized membership in America, but I didn't know whether they had any presence in England.

"No," Giles said. "They call themselves *Gesta Angliae Antiquae.*" He pronounced the Latin name with a frown.

"The Deeds of Ancient England," I translated. "It certainly sounds much better in Latin, doesn't it?"

Giles shrugged. "The whole thing sounds bloody silly, if you ask me. Why sane adults want to sport themselves in medieval garb and pretend not to have heard of bathing once a month, let alone once a day, is beyond me."

"Tsk, tsk, Giles," I said mildly, though I was actually rather annoyed. "Don't tell me you too have fallen for that old canard that no one in the Middle Ages ever took a bath. Surely you know better than that."

Giles opened his mouth to protest, but I cut him off. "And don't tell me that 'everyone knows' that medieval people were filthy, because it just isn't so. Soap was invented in the so-called Dark Ages—a term that I heartily detest, if you'll re-

---

[1] Kindly consult *Decorated to Death.*

member. People washed their hands before and after meals, and most towns of any decent size had bathhouses.

"I suppose," I continued, warming to my theme, "people got the ridiculous notion that medieval folk didn't bathe from the fact that going without bathing was one of the penances people took on to atone for their sins."

Laughing immoderately, Giles held up a hand in submission, and I stopped, a little embarrassed at having rather overdone it.

"*Mea culpa*, Simon, *mea maxissime culpa*," Giles said when he caught his breath, grinning broadly. "I was simply having you on. How could I have forgotten your infamous lecture on medieval fallacies?"[2]

I had to laugh then. "I'm that easy, am I?"

"About some things," Giles said lightly, "but not about others."

"Now, Giles," I said, trying to look stern. Ever since he had come to work for me, he'd been trying to change our professional relationship into something far more personal. While I was not totally averse to the notion, I couldn't in all conscience proceed without first telling him the truth about myself. At that moment I wasn't terribly eager to explain to him that I'm a vampire.

"Yes, yes, Simon," Giles said, "no need to offer me chapter and verse yet again." His tone was airy, but underneath it I could detect the lingering hurt. By then I had little doubt that his feelings for me were sincere—vampires are rather good at sensing and interpreting strong emotion, you see—but I was still uncertain how he would react if he knew the truth. Or, to be perfectly frank, how I would feel if he ran screaming back to Blitherington Hall and wanted nothing further to do with me, once I had Revealed All.

"Getting back to the point," I said, "when do all these *Gesta* folk descend upon Blitherington Hall?"

---

[2] Borrowed with permission from a most gracious medieval scholar, Simon's good friend and fellow author, Sharan Newman.

"This weekend," Giles said. "They'll begin arriving on Friday afternoon, and their gathering will conclude with a big medieval banquet the following Friday night. They usually invite the public to attend the final two days."

"Then you have ample time to prepare for any . . . oddness, I suppose."

Giles shrugged. "No doubt it will all run smoothly, and I'm worrying for no good reason." He stood up. "But I do need to consult our solicitor. I believe there were some restrictions in the deed of sale, and if we have grounds to stop this rock festival, I want to know what they are. I apologize for having to ask so suddenly, Simon, but would you mind terribly if I took a half-day today? The solicitor is in Bedford, and he can see me this morning at ten-thirty. I should be back by one, at the latest."

"It's not a problem, Giles," I assured him. "I shall be quite busy writing while you're away. We can work on correspondence this afternoon. I don't mind putting it off for a few hours." I reached into my desk for my keys. "Take my Jag, if you like."

"Thanks, Simon," Giles said, before blowing me a kiss, the naughty boy. "I shall return as quickly as I can."

I smiled as he departed. Moments later I heard the door close, then the purr of the Jag as Giles headed for Bedford. The car the poor boy runs is a sad rattletrap, and he does enjoy driving my car. I don't mind indulging him, for he is a very good driver. Plus he looks devilishly attractive at the wheel, though I don't tell him that.

Enough of that, I told myself sternly. No use getting sappy when there was work to do. I had recently begun work on a new historical romance, *Perdita's Passion*, and Daphne Deepwood couldn't afford to let her considerable number of eager readers wait too long for the next book. I make quite a tidy sum from the Deepwood books, along with the works of Dorinda Darlington, the name I use for my series about a tough American female private eye.

The current opus featured a heroine caught up in that fifteenth-century drama of Yorkists and Lancastrians, otherwise known as the Wars of the Roses. Perdita was a devout Yorkist whilst her lover was a Lancastrian. There was a lot of turmoil to deal with as I sorted out the differences keeping my heroine and her hero apart.

So engrossed was I in the process that I had quite lost track of time. When the doorbell rang insistently, I surfaced from the fifteenth century and stared at the clock on my desk. I had been writing steadily for several hours, for it was a bit past twelve-thirty. How time does fly when you're having fun giving your characters a hard time.

Frowning, I saved my work on the computer, then left my office for the front door. I wondered who would be calling on me at this time of day. Most folk in the village were aware of my schedule, and they were generally most circumspect about not bothering me while I was writing. Of course, Giles was usually present to deal with anyone who did have the temerity to ring the doorbell during my working hours.

I opened the front door and blinked into the sunshine. Surely I was seeing things.

"Good Lord, Tris," I said. "What on earth are you doing in England?"

"Hello, Simon," said my former lover as he scowled at me. "Lovely to see you, too. And can't we please get inside, out of this beastly sunshine?"

"Certainly," I said, stepping aside to let Tristan Lovelace enter Laurel Cottage. This had been his home once upon a time, but he had given it to me over a year ago.

"That's better," Tris said, as he pulled off his hat and sunglasses and thrust them at me. "It took you long enough to answer the bell, Simon. What were you doing?"

"Writing," I said, placing his things on a table in the hall. "That's how I make my living, if you'll remember."

"Yes, yes," Tris said, "I know that. I've even read a few of your books." He offered me the same vulpine grin that had attracted me the first time I had met him, when I was a fresh graduate student and he was my adviser.

I knew better than to prod Tris for a comment on my books. In his own good time he would tell me his opinion of them. "What are you doing in England, Tris? I thought you weren't coming over until July."

"It's all very last minute. I had an offer for a spot of consulting on a documentary being filmed nearby, something about a group who fancy themselves living in the Middle Ages. I simply couldn't turn it down when I knew it would afford me the opportunity to see you sooner than I had planned."

Tris took a step closer to me and laid his hand on my arm. "I wanted to see you, Simon," he said, "because I haven't been able to get you out of my mind in recent months."

Dumbfounded, I stared at him. Gone were the smile and the joking manner—Tris appeared dead serious (pun not intended). If my heart had still been animate, it would have begun pounding by now. "What on earth are you talking about?" I managed to sputter the words as Tris came even closer.

"This," Tris said before he enveloped me in his arms and placed his lips firmly on mine.

I couldn't help myself. I responded to his embrace as the memories came flooding back.

I'm not sure how long we stood there, locked in each other's arms, but neither one of us heard the front door open behind us.

"What the bloody hell is going on here?"

Chapter 2

Startled, I pushed myself loose from Tris's arms.
Giles slammed the door shut and stood there, glowering at me and Tris.

Before I could say anything, Giles's eyes widened in recognition. "Professor Lovelace? I don't bloody believe it."

"You must be young Blitherington," Tris said, completely unruffled either by Giles's tempestuous entrance or the hostility in his voice. Tris turned to me. "You might have mentioned, Simon, that the boy had grown into quite an attractive man."

This wasn't the first time I had had the urge to slap Tris's face, but I wasn't going to give in to my baser impulses in front of Giles.

"Thank you, Professor," Giles drawled in his insufferably aristocratic tone, the one he assumed when he wanted to be annoying. "I must say that you look rather older than I remembered."

"My, my," Tris said, matching drawl for drawl. "The child has claws and isn't afraid to use them. How frightfully amusing."

Giles reddened, but before he could respond, I hastened to put an end to the bickering.

"As fascinating as this little pissing contest is," I said, my tone deliberately offensive, "I actually find it rather distasteful. It's beneath both of you. You will stop it at once, or I'll ask you both to leave."

Tris simply laughed at me, but Giles grew even angrier. I could feel the waves of emotion simply pouring out of him.

"I'll save you the trouble, Simon," Giles said. Before I could say another word to stop him, he opened the door and pulled it shut with a loud clatter before he stalked away.

I moved forward, but Tris laid a restraining hand on my arm. "Let him go, Simon."

I tried to shrug off the hand, but Tris is a very strong vampire. Even as strong as I am, I couldn't shake myself loose. Then I heard the rattle of Giles's car as he clattered away from Laurel Cottage.

"Are you satisfied?" I demanded, as Tris finally let go of me.

"Not just yet," Tris said, pulling me back into his arms.

After a moment, my lack of responsiveness communicated itself to Tris's overheated libido. He released me.

"You can be excessively tedious sometimes, Simon," Tris complained. He turned and went into what I called the living room, though locals might have referred to it as the parlor or sitting room.

Tris made himself comfortable in the largest chair in the room and reached into his inner jacket pocket for his pipe and tobacco pouch. As I stood there glaring at him, he calmly filled his pipe with tobacco, then proceeded to light it. Aromatic smoke began curling around his head, and he sat and smiled at me while he puffed away.

"You're quite welcome to smoke in my house," I said acidly. I sat down on the sofa across from him. Once again I marveled at his ability to produce smoke in such prodigious quantities. Vampires don't breathe, naturally, but can appear to do so when necessary. Tris had been a dedicated smoker for decades before he became a vampire, and he had kept up the habit in death. As he no longer had to worry about lung cancer, he reasoned, he might as well indulge himself.

"I should think so," Tris said, teeth clenched around the

stem of his straight briar, "especially since this used to be my house, and I gave it to you."

"I'm well aware of that," I said. "I greatly appreciate your generosity, Tris, and I have come to love this place and my existence in this village. If you're having second thoughts about your gift, you need to let me know."

"No, Simon, you're quite welcome to Laurel Cottage," Tris said, waving a hand through the smoke swirling around him. "It's not the cottage I want back."

I almost laughed, but with one look at his face, I could tell he was completely serious. For the moment, I forgot about the problem of explaining all this to Giles and tried to focus instead on what Tris was telling me.

"After what? Nearly three years, you suddenly decide that you want me back?"

"I made a mistake, Simon," Tris said, the very picture of earnestness. "The worst thing I ever did was to let you go."

He seemed sincere, but I had learned not to trust my ability to read him. Vampires can read strong emotion from the living, but with other vampires we simply have to go on instinct and experience. Tris was an Olympic-standard liar when it suited him.

"Pardon my skepticism, Tris," I said, "but this is uncomfortably like a scenario enacted about five years ago. Or have you forgotten?"

"You have every right to be mistrustful, dear boy," he acknowledged, "but even someone as old as I am may learn from his mistakes, particularly deeply regretted ones."

"One would hope," I said, still not convinced.

"I certainly wouldn't expect you to make a decision this very moment," Tris said, waving his pipe about with one hand, "but I did think it fair to let you know that I intend to win you back."

"Since when did I become such a prize?"

Tris smiled at that. "Don't underestimate yourself, my dear Simon. You're well worth having, and I intend to have you. Make no mistake about that."

"Really, Tris," I protested, "you sound like the hero from one of my historical romance novels."

"If the role suits," Tris said, half-bowing from his chair.

"Honestly," I said. I couldn't help laughing at that point, and Tris grinned at me.

Damn the man, but he was just as attractive to me as he had always been. The leonine mane of dark hair streaked with a bit of white at strategic points, the sapphire blue eyes with their roguish twinkle, the handsome weathered face— he could give Sean Connery a run for his money as the sexiest man alive. Or in Tris's case, dead.

"I rather suspect," Tris continued, the corners of his eyes crinkling in amusement, "that I have some competition that I had not considered before. I don't believe you ever mentioned to me, Simon, that young Blitherington is so enamored of you. Had you a boy-toy all this time and not told me?"

His patronizing tone set my teeth on edge, and he well knew it. "Giles and I have a professional relationship, Tris," I said.

"But young Blitherington is hoping for rather more than that, I would say," Tris said, before I could continue my explanation.

"Yes," I said, as evenly as I could. "Giles wants a more personal relationship, but I have thus far refused."

"You're attracted to him, of course," Tris said, a bit too smugly. "And I must say he's a handsome young devil. What's the matter, Simon? Surely you haven't turned celibate?"

"Promiscuity is your game, not mine," I responded with as much acid as I could muster. Tris actually blinked.

"My dear Simon, I see I hurt you rather more than I had guessed," he said, emitting another cloud of smoke, "and that I do deeply regret. The more distant one becomes from the finer human emotions, the more one tends to forget that others might not see things in quite the same way."

"One doesn't have to be *human*," I said, mocking his tone, "to find loyalty a desirable quality in one's lover."

"Touché, Simon, touché," Tris said. "The question remains, however: just how serious are you about young Blitherington?"

Trust Tris to find a sensitive spot and stick a pin in it. I debated briefly whether to lie to Tris, but he reads me far better than I can read him. Lying wouldn't do much good. "I'm very, very fond of him," I said.

Tris laughed. "Ah, Simon, I know you too well, dear boy. That means you're in love with him, but you don't want him to know it. Why? Are you afraid he'll run away screaming if you tell him the truth about yourself?"

"If you must know, yes," I said, wishing that I had never opened my door to him this morning. Then I sat, stunned, because for the first time, I had admitted, aloud no less, to my feelings for Giles. Bloody hell!

"One might as well know what the competition is," Tris said, seemingly unruffled by my admission. He was taking it rather better than I was. "Don't think, Simon, that I'm going to stand aside. I know you still have feelings for me. I'll simply have to work harder to win you back." That vulpine grin appeared once more. "Frankly, I don't fancy young Blitherington's chances of staying the course."

If my blood could have run cold, it would have at that moment. Something about the way Tris spoke that last sentence chilled me to the core.

"You wouldn't dare harm him, Tris," I said, watching him closely.

"Now, Simon," Tris said, "you don't think I would actually resort to physical harm to remove a rival, do you?" He laughed, as if to make nonsense of the notion. "Especially not a human one?"

The trouble was, I did believe it. Tris was completely ruthless when it came to getting what he wanted.

Tris knocked out his pipe in an ashtray on the table beside his chair, stuck the pipe in his pocket, and then stood up. "Now, Simon," he said, "is the guest room habitable? I won't presume to share your bed just yet."

"You'll have to make the bed," I said, glaring up at him. "I'm sure you know where to find the linens. Do make yourself at home, Tris."

He smiled down at me. "Thank you, Simon, I shall. This will be much more comfortable than an hotel, and I can easily pop up to London or drive to Oxford or Cambridge when I need to do research. Being near you, however, is the real attraction."

Whistling jauntily, he left the room and headed upstairs. He could bloody well bring in his own bags, though no doubt he expected me to retrieve them from his car and carry them up to him.

I sat there on the sofa and fumed. I should have told him to get the hell out of my house, that I wanted nothing more to do with him. *So why hadn't I?* I asked myself.

Because, you idiot, I told myself sternly and truthfully, *you've never gotten over the bastard. Not completely.*

The memories came flooding back. Happy memories of times spent with Tris, when I was deeply in love and had no idea how treacherous he could be, how deceiving. I wallowed in the memories for a few moments, then took myself sternly to task. I dredged up the unpleasant ones, forcing myself to acknowledge why I had ended the relationship. The pain was still there, the pain of betrayal and deceit.

Had Tris truly changed? Was he serious about wanting me back? Or was it simply some game he was playing? Why would he want to do that to me?

Then there was Giles. What was I going to tell him? "Oh, by the way, Giles, my former lover is going to be staying with me for a few weeks. Hope you don't mind."

That would go over well. I groaned. Giles had a volatile temper, and I couldn't predict how he would react to the news that Tris intended to stick around for a while. Not to mention the fact that Tris was going to be involved in some way with the medieval faire going on in Giles's backyard, so to speak.

Would he cede the field to Tris and walk away? Or would he stay and fight?

And why did I suddenly feel like the exceptionally dim-witted and totally incapable heroine of the worst kind of romance novel?

Too many questions; not enough answers. The next few weeks couldn't pass by quickly enough for me.

Chapter 3

Giles, when he finally consented to speak to me that evening, took the news of Tris's lodging himself at Laurel Cottage better than I had hoped. He didn't yell at me or slam the phone down in my ear. He accepted my explanation for the embrace he had walked in on yesterday, then calmly announced that he would return to work as usual the following morning.

Annoyed with myself for doing so, and even more annoyed with Tris for my feeling compelled to, I haltingly explained that Tris was sleeping in the guest room.

Giles greeted that particular tidbit with silence. I decided not to tell him about Tris's involvement with the documentary on the medieval faire about to take place in his back garden just yet. He had enough to stew over for now.

"I'll see you in the morning, then," I said, ringing off.

In the meantime, Tris had kept his distance, not trying to force any further physical contact on me. Instead, he concentrated on being the witty charmer he was capable of being, when he so chose. I decided that the simplest thing to do would be to relax and enjoy his company while holding myself aloof from any hint that I wanted anything more than friendship from him. I needed time to sort out my feelings for him and to come to a decision about Giles. If the two of them cooperated, perhaps I could bring the situation to a conclusion without significant trauma, mental or physical, to anyone involved.

I chose to be optimistic, though it was perhaps the more foolish option.

The next morning, I awaited Giles's arrival with some trepidation. Tris was rambling about upstairs, and I was sitting at my desk, fiddling with the computer, when I heard Giles's key in the lock of the front door.

Fixing a bright smile upon my face, I waited.

"Good morning, Simon," Giles said as he walked into my office.

He smiled at my reaction. Perhaps my mouth was hanging open. I don't know. I simply stared.

Well aware of his physical attributes, Giles has always worked hard to maintain them. He spends at least an hour each day exercising and working out. The jeans and casual shirt he wore this morning seemed almost painted on his muscular, hard body. He exuded sex appeal, and I was surprised he had managed to get to Laurel Cottage this morning without being mauled.

While I gaped at him, Giles came around behind my desk and leaned over me. Taking my face in his hands, he proceeded to kiss me. When he finally released me, I didn't dare get up from behind the desk.

Giles sat down in the chair across from me and leaned back, flexing his impressive chest ever so slightly. "What's on the agenda for this morning, Simon? Correspondence? Or do you have some research for me to do?"

Trying desperately to regain some sense of equilibrium, I focused on giving an intelligible answer to his question instead of babbling like an idiot. "I think we had better catch up with the correspondence, Giles."

The words came out a bit rushed, but on the whole, I congratulated myself; I sounded completely professional.

"Certainly, Simon," Giles said. He stretched out his left arm to retrieve a folder from my desk, and a bit of the dragon tattoo that covers much of his chest, upper arm, and back peeked out at me from beneath the sleeve of his shirt. As the arm muscles tensed, it seemed as if the tip of the dragon's wing waved at me.

I brought my eyes back to Giles's face to see him waiting patiently, the hint of a smile hovering around his lips.

Giles had obviously decided to use his most potent weapons in his campaign for my affections. He had youth and beauty on his side, to be matched against Tris's sophistication and experience.

Oy.

From that point I did my best to concentrate on the work at hand and not let myself be distracted by Giles's considerable physical appeal. The few times I glanced directly at Giles's face, I could see that he was making no effort to force the issue. With more patience than I had thought he possessed, he seemed willing to wait to see what developed.

Around noon, as Giles and I were finishing the last bit of correspondence that demanded more immediate attention, Tris knocked firmly on the open door of my office.

I glanced up, startled. Tris was dressed for driving, with hat, gloves, and sunglasses in hand. Good. Having him out of the cottage, even for a short while, would be a relief.

"Off somewhere, Tris?" I said.

"Yes, Simon, I'm off to meet with the man who hired me to consult on this documentary," Tris said. "Afternoon, young Blitherington."

Putting aside the folder of letters, Giles stood up from his chair and turned to face Tris. I had to suppress a smile as Tris got a good look at Giles. I could only imagine the expression on Giles's face.

"Have a safe journey, Professor," Giles said, his voice languid and cool. "Do drive carefully."

Tris began slapping the gloves in one hand against the palm of the other. He appeared unable to stop his eyes from roaming up and down Giles's physique. As I watched, Giles turned his back to Tris, then bent down as if to brush something off his shoe. Tris's eyes widened. Giles stood up, smiling briefly at me, then resumed his seat.

"Well," Tris said, his voice pitched a bit higher than usual. "I must be off."

"Don't let us keep you, Professor," Giles said without turning around. "Shall we expect you back in time for dinner?"

"Yes, most definitely," Tris said. "Simon and I still have much to discuss, dear boy. A pity you can't join us." With that, he whirled and left. Moments later, the front door slammed behind him.

Giles cocked his head to one side and looked at me. "Oh, can't I?" he murmured. "What's this about a documentary, Simon? Something to do with elder care in Britain these days?"

I smothered a laugh. "Er, no, Giles, nothing like that." I assumed a bland expression. "No, it has something to do with this medieval faire. Someone is producing a documentary about it, and he's hired Tris as a consultant."

Giles regarded me in stony silence. When at last he spoke his voice was devoid of inflection. "So, in addition to having these medieval loonies capering about, there will be a crew filming it all as well?"

"Evidently so, at some point," I said. "I'm not certain what it is that Tris will be advising them on, but he has a very distinguished reputation as a medievalist, you know."

"I'm well aware of Professor Lovelace's *reputation*, Simon," Giles said. "No doubt he will advise these people well. I shall hope he is so busy with the loonies that he has little time for other mischief."

He grasped the folder of letters and stood up. "I shall get started on these, Simon, though I might take a short break for a spot of lunch. Fancy a stroll down to the pub with me?"

"Uh, no," I said—though stammered was more like it. "You go ahead. I'm going to work right through lunch. I'm a few pages behind my usual daily quota."

The old Giles would have pouted a bit with me for turning down his invitation, but this new, even sexier, and quite determined Giles merely nodded and offered me a quick smile before he left my office for his own in the next room.

And so was set the pattern of my existence for the next three days. During the day Tris was out on his consulting job, while Giles worked assiduously at any task I might set him to. He even offered to work well into the evening, but I gently refused. Since he had continued to appear daily in attire that left little to the imagination, I needed at least some time free from distraction. My writing was suffering from the tension that I, at least, was feeling.

Neither Giles nor Tris appeared all that affected by their dueling, each perhaps counting on his particular assets to see him through. There was at least one politely bitchy exchange between them each day, but for the most part they remained civil enough to each other.

Though at one level I found the whole situation rather farcically amusing, and more than a bit flattering, on the whole I was annoyed with them both for engaging in such behavior. I had to acknowledge, however, that I bore the greatest share of the blame for not putting an end to it one way or another. The trouble was, I simply found myself in a state of inanition, unable to take decisive action. This was totally unlike me, and therefore a bit disturbing.

As the day approached for the folk of the *Gesta Angliae Antiquae* to descend upon the village, I welcomed the distraction. Once the faire began, Tris would have to spend quite a lot of time away from Laurel Cottage, and Giles would be worried about what was going on in the meadow behind the Hall. Having their attention diverted from their wooing of me would be a relief.

Many of the group began arriving early on Friday afternoon to set up their tents in the meadow. The influx continued on Saturday morning as Tris and I drove the Jag through the village toward Blitherington Hall. There were numerous Land Rovers and other large vehicles with caravans in tow, and it took Tris and me more than twice as long as it should have to reach the forecourt of the manor. We left the Jag and, donning our protective gear, we sauntered across the lawns in the direction of the meadow back of the Hall.

We heard them well before we came in sight of the encampment. Voices rose in song and conversation, and the breeze was already wafting smoke from cooking fires here and there. The noise grew louder the closer we came, and soon we were standing on a slight rise near the edge of the meadow. Just below us a fence and a gate, overseen by a chap in the costume of a soldier, guarded the entrance to the faire.

Everywhere were color, movement, and noise. Tents and pavilions of varying sizes and myriad hues dotted the landscape, many sporting banners with colorful badges flying in the wind. Folk in arcane clothing drifted by, chatting and gesturing. The modern English and variety of accents jarred with the quaintness of their garb and footwear. They looked as if they should be chattering in Middle English or Norman French instead.

Tris turned to me and frowned. "What bloody century are they supposed to be living in? I thought they picked a particular time, and they all went along with it."

I shrugged. "Your guess is as good as mine. Maybe they can pick their century. There certainly doesn't seem to be much agreement." I pointed to a couple of young men digging a pit for a cook fire. "Those two are dressed like common laborers from the early thirteenth century." They sported the simple tunic, worn by both men and women, of that period.

"Yes," Tris said. "And those women at the next tent are dressed like respectable merchants' wives of the fifteenth century." He snorted in disgust. "I can certainly see now why they need the services of a qualified medievalist."

We stood and watched for a few minutes longer, and we continued to see a wide variety in style and century of costume as members of the group paraded past us. Dress ranged from those simple tunics of the thirteenth century to the ele-

gant and decorative styles of two centuries later. The points
on the shoes of some of the men were so long that I wondered how the wearers managed not to fall flat on their bums
or faces every other step. We witnessed the same confusion in
periods of armor sported by some of the more martial-minded
men. Idly I wondered whether there was any kind of tourna-
ment planned, and, if so, how they would fight with their armor
of different centuries. That could be interesting, not to say
amusing.

We walked down to the gate, and Tris explained his iden-
tity to the guard on duty, who consulted a most unmedieval
clipboard and waved us through without comment.

Our arrival had attracted attention. A tall man with regal
bearing stalked toward Tris and me. He came to a stop in
front of us, and I looked up into his face. I am tall myself, but
this man stood a good three inches over me. He was a blonde
with piercing blue eyes and a closely trimmed beard of a
darker hue than the hair on his head. Clad in a red tunic and
a richly purple surcoat, both made of very fine cloth, he also
sported a small crown. The jewels of the crown, mostly mere
flecks of color, sparkled in the morning sunlight.

"I give you good day, gentlemen," he boomed in a deep
voice. "I am Harald Knutson, the sovereign of this small kingdom. As you see, we are still in the process of establishing
our settlement here, and in a few days we shall be delighted
to welcome all visitors. This morn, however, we still have much
to do."

"Knutson, eh?" Tris inquired. "Any relation to good old
Cnut?"

Knutson dipped his head in acknowledgment. "Actually,
yes. I am a direct descendant of the Danish kings of England."

Was this man serious? I wondered. Or was this merely part
of his role as the king of this merry little flock of re-enactors?
Something about the gleam in his eye told me that he wasn't
kidding.

"Your Majesty," Tris drawled, dipping forward into a car-
icature of a courtly bow.

Knutson's mouth turned down into an irritated frown. "I care not whether you scoff, sir. I need not prove myself to the likes of you." His eyes swept over Tris and then me. "Nor to your catamite."

"How clever of you," I said, smiling sweetly. "But how mistaken, Your Majesty." Then my smile turned quickly into a ferocious snarl, and Knutson blinked several times and actually stepped back two paces.

Attempting to recover his dignity, Knutson said, "I will repeat, gentlemen"—and his tone cast doubt on the aptness of that particular word—"if you should desire to visit our settlement in a few days, when the mundane public are admitted to our enclave, you will find a welcome. Today, however, I must ask you to leave."

"I think not, Knutson," spoke a voice from behind us. I turned to see a strange man frowning at the king. Giles stood beside the man, looking about with considerable interest and endeavoring to keep a straight face.

"I beg your pardon, Mr. Millbank?" Knutson frowned.

"I must remind you, Your Majesty," Millbank said, investing the honorific with mild sarcasm, "that your settlement, as you call it, is on my land. Long as you're here, you will be civil to my guests." He had stepped forward to stand beside Tris. "This is Professor Tristan Lovelace, the distinguished medievalist who is advising us on the film. And I presume the gentleman with him is a colleague. Therefore you ought to be respectful. Do you understand me?" His voice held the faintest hint of a Scots burr, but he had worked to overlay it with a more sophisticated Oxbridge accent.

Knutson flushed, and sparks flew from those blue eyes. He was very angry, but he evidently couldn't risk alienating his landlord. "As you wish, Mr. Millbank. Though I must repeat yet again I do not approve of this film and want nothing to do with it. Now, if you gentlemen will excuse me, I must attend upon my court." Without further ado, he spun on his heels and stalked away.

Millbank smiled with great satisfaction. "He's a bleedin'

idjit," he said, "and I take great pleasure in putting him in his place." He laughed. "He might be king in his little world, but this is *my* kingdom."

Giles snorted in disgust, but Millbank paid him no attention. He was a stubby little man, full of self-importance. In his late fifties, he exuded the air of one who was greatly satisfied with life.

"I should think you need the cooperation of the king, Millbank," Tris said, "if you want this film done."

"Oh, he'll cooperate, all right," Millbank responded smugly. "There's a clause in their contract that gives me permission to throw them out afore the week is up, if I find anythin' they do harmful to m'property."

I laughed. "I can't believe they would knowingly sign something of that sort."

Millbank shrugged. "Frankly, I didn't expect that to get by them m'self, but yon King Harald isnae so sharp as he would like everyone to think. I don't think he even read the contract before he signed it, the idjit!"

"Which is exactly why," interposed a strange voice, "his head is about to go on the block!"

Chapter 4

A rich tenor had uttered the harsh threat, and I saw that the owner matched his plummy voice when we turned to greet the man.

He was of more modest height than the man he had just threatened, but he had the breadth of chest and width of shoulders that his erstwhile rival, of reedy build, lacked. Garbed in the sumptuous and elaborate robes of a fifteenth-century monarch, he possessed considerable elán, and the confidence with which he sported his regalia enhanced the image. His flashing dark eyes, tanned face, and luxuriant mane of curly, coal-black hair suggested a Mediterranean origin, but his voice was pure Oxbridge.

As Millbank, Giles, Tris, and I watched, he made a sweeping bow. "Luke de Montfort, Duke of Wessex, at your service, gentlemen."

"Hallo, Luke," Tris said.

The self-appointed Duke of Wessex turned startled eyes to Tris. "My God, Tris. What are you doing here?"

Tris laughed. "I might ask you the same, Monsieur d'Amboise. What are you doing capering about like this? Surely you haven't forgotten your academic training so far as to join in such idiocy."

Tris's tone was deliberately cutting, and Giles and I exchanged amused and curious glances as we waited for the duke's response.

Though his tanned face turned a tiny bit red, Luke de Montfort retained his poise. "I don't consider it capering about, Tris," he said. "Just because I've not isolated myself inside some academic ivory tower doesn't mean I'm not still a serious student of the Middle Ages."

Tris snorted, and before the conversation could degenerate further, I decided to intervene. "I take it," I said, my voice dripping with irony, "that you two are acquainted. Perhaps, Tris, you might introduce us to the duke here?"

"But of course, Simon," Tris said. "I would be delighted. Simon Kirby-Jones, Sir Giles Blitherington, I have the distinct pleasure of introducing to you Luke d'Amboise, a former student, who for some apparent reason now fancies himself as Luke de Montfort, His Grace of Wessex. Luke, *mon vieux*, might I present Sir Giles Blitherington of Blitherington Hall, yon manor up the hill, and Dr. Simon Kirby-Jones, another former student of mine."

Trust Tris to be at his most irritatingly pompous. If I had started batting him over the head, I had no doubt that Giles and Luke would have joined happily with me. Instead of giving Tris the drubbing he deserved for being a twit, I stuck out my hand.

"A pleasure to meet you, Luke," I said. As he clasped my hand in his for a firm shake, I continued, "I gather you too had the misfortune of having studied with Tris."

"Too right," he responded with a cheeky grin, sounding for a moment like an Aussie. He turned to Giles to shake his hand as well. "Sir Giles, I trust you won't be too disturbed by our activities over the coming week."

Millbank laughed loudly. "It doesn't blooming matter, does it? I own the land now, and I can't see as where it's anyone else's business but mine."

Giles flushed in irritation, but he ignored Millbank, choosing instead to offer the faux duke a radiant smile. "I've no doubt, Your Grace, that we at Blitherington Hall will have no cause for complaint."

The sharp twinge of jealousy I felt at those words annoyed me. The fact that the duke continued to hold Giles's hand didn't help, either. I cleared my throat noisily, and the two hands separated, albeit reluctantly, I thought.

"Yes, Simon, Giles," Tris said heavily, "Luke here was once one of my star pupils whilst I was at Cambridge. He could have gone on to a distinguished career as a lecturer, but instead he forsook academia for the pillars of Mammon. And now I find he's mixed himself in with this play-acting rabble."

"Oh, do stop sneering, Tris," Luke said, smiling faintly. "You can be terribly pompous, you know."

I had to laugh at that. I thought I was the only one who had ever dared speak to Tris like that. This Luke character had unexpected depths. But perhaps, the thought struck me, he had a deeper knowledge of Tris than I had anticipated.

Was he a vampire like Tris and me? Was he, indeed, one of Tris's castoffs? I knew I wasn't the first, and it took only one look at the man to know that he was just the type to snare Tris's fancy.

I regarded him more closely, investigating him for the signs of vampirism. He wore no lenses to shade his eyes from the sun, though the rest of him was well covered by his robes. He breathed, deeply and regularly, and his skin had a rich, warm hue to it that betokened the regular flow of blood through his veins. No, he was mortal.

But that didn't mean that he hadn't been Tris's lover at some point. I found that thought vaguely annoying, though when I had become involved with Tris, I was not naive enough to believe I was the first. I had been naive enough, however, to believe that I would be the last.

Tris made no direct response to Luke's teasing reproof. "As touching as this reunion has been, gentlemen," Tris said, his voice deceptively mild, "I am afraid we must cut this short. Millbank and I have work to do. The documentary, you know."

"Yes, I do know," Luke said. "In fact, it was my idea in the first place. Or didn't Mr. Millbank tell you that?" The duke turned to glare at Millbank.

Not in the least ruffled by Luke's hostility, Millbank grinned. "Doesn't matter all that much whose idea it was, now does it, Your Grace?" He laughed uproariously. "It's my money what's bankrolling it, and it won't hurt you to remember that, now will it?"

Luke flushed. "It is your money, Millbank, but it's not your vision, your creativity. That came solely from me."

Millbank sniggered. "Well, now, Your Grace, I've managed to find me a very distinguished adviser in the professor here, and I reckon he's the one we ought to listen to."

"I do not appreciate having someone else, no matter how distinguished, taking charge of my project," Luke said hotly. "Begging your pardon, Tris, but you have no business being here. You're not needed."

"My dear Luke," Tris began, but before he could say anything else, Millbank broke in.

"Now listen here, me fine fella," Millbank said, shaking a finger in Luke's face, "I'm the one bankrolling this film, and I'm the one who says what's what. You just cast your mind back on that contract we signed."

"I do remember the contract, and another pending one as well, even if you seem to have forgotten it," Luke said, slapping Millbank's hand away from his face. "You ignorant prat, I have creative control of this film, not you."

Nursing his hand, Millbank scowled at Luke. "Not if I say you don't, you bleedin' idjit. You should have read the contract more carefully, shouldn't you? I have the final say on anything. You go back to your cooking, and leave the rest to me."

I could feel the rage rising in Luke, and I thought he was going to go for Millbank's throat. Instead, by a supreme effort, he mastered his temper. "We'll see about that, Millbank.

Remember that other, unsigned contract, and remember also that these people here are loyal to me, not you. If we all decide to leave, then you won't have anything to film, will you?"

Judging from the look on Millbank's face, I could tell he hadn't considered that aspect of the situation. I could almost see the wheels turning in his brain as he decided he had to do some backpedaling. "Now there's no need to get so riled up, Your Grace. I didn't say you wouldn't be consulted, now did I? And, after all, you were the one who first mentioned the professor here to me, isn't that right?"

Slowly, Luke nodded.

"And it's not like you don't know the man," Millbank continued. "Surely you two can work together. You're going to have enough to do anyway, and the professor here can lighten the load a considerable bit."

Luke stared at him for a long moment, then turned his head to look at Tris. Tris had remained unusually silent throughout the whole exchange, and I knew he had been embarrassed by the whole thing. He detested any such display of emotion, particularly when he was involved in it by no choice of his own.

"I'm willing to work with Tris," Luke said, "if he is willing to work with me. What about it, Tris?"

Tris cast a baleful eye upon Millbank, and I imagined that Tris was deciding whether to tell Millbank to go to the devil and be done with the whole imbroglio. Then he turned to Luke and smiled. "I think, Luke, that I shall enjoy working with you again. I deplore deeply the fact that Millbank here neglected to inform me completely about the situation, but you and I shan't let that affect us."

Luke inclined his head in a gesture of thanks.

"Come on, Millbank," Tris said roughly. "Let's get on with it. Coming with us, Luke?"

"Not just yet, Tris," Luke said. "I'll catch up with you later on. Millbank can fill you in on the basics in the meantime."

Tris nodded, then grasped Millbank none too gently by the

arm and led him away. Millbank's short legs struggled to keep up with Tris's long strides, and Tris was nearly lifting Millbank off the ground. Giles, Luke, and I all smothered laughs as we watched them.

"Enough of that," Giles said smoothly. "I gather that there is some rebellion in the ranks?"

"What?" Luke said, startled, his attention abruptly drawn from Tris and Millbank. "Oh, you mean my remark when I first approached you."

Giles nodded, and I awaited Luke's response with interest.

His Grace's lips narrowed into a thin line. "Our good King Harald is behaving like the idiot he truly is, and it's about time that the old king was deposed and a new one put in his place."

"That new king being yourself, I take it?" I asked.

Luke smiled modestly. "If called upon to serve, I would certainly do my duty."

"Then it is an elected position?" Giles asked.

"Yes," Luke said. "I doubt you know much about how the G.A.A. is organized, so if you will bear with me." We nodded, and he continued, "There are roughly eight thousand members spread through the United Kingdom, and we are divided into seven great fiefdoms, which are in turn divided into baronies, and so on. I am the leader of the largest of all the seven fiefdoms, that of Wessex."

"So named, I presume, for the ancient ruling house of Anglo-Saxon England?"

"Yes," Luke responded to my query. "I was the founder of my fiefdom, and I chose the name in honor of my hero, Alfred of Wessex."

"Alfred the Great," Giles clarified.

"Exactly so," Luke said. "In the time since I first founded the fiefdom of Wessex four years ago, it has grown to be the largest and most popular among the fiefdoms of the G.A.A." He smiled modestly, inviting us to see that it was all due to his efforts and personality.

"Quite an accomplishment," I said.

"Thank you," Luke said.

"How do you prefer that we address you?" Giles asked. "I take it your real name is Luc d'Amboise, but your name within the G.A.A. is Luke de Montfort."

Luke grinned. "I know it's a bit confusing, but while we are meeting together like this"—he swept a hand through the air, indicating the encampment before us—"I am His Grace of Wessex. Thus you may address me as Your Grace, or Luke, if you prefer."

"Thank you, Luke," I said wryly. Giles could play along and continue to call the man "Your Grace" if he so chose, but I found it all just a bit on the silly side.

"Now, about this Harald character," Giles asked, apparently fascinated by all of it, "is he really a descendant of the Danish kings of England?"

Luke emitted a snort most unbecoming to a duke and would-be king. "Chance would be a fine thing! No, he's just plain Henry Baker from Chester. He likes to pretend he's of royal blood, just to enhance his claim to be our king."

"But it sounds like his days as monarch are numbered," I said.

"They are," Luke said darkly. "He is completely incompetent, and the G.A.A. is being torn apart by his antics. For example, we wouldn't be here at Blitherington Hall at all if he hadn't bungled the lease *and* our relationship with the owner of the land where we have always held our summer gathering."

Giles and I shook our heads in commiseration.

"Furthermore," Luke said, growing more heated, "he should never have signed such an imbecilic contract with Millbank." He grinned. "Nor should I, for that matter. But he should have been more careful in dealing with Millbank. To think that we would have to pack up and leave on a moment's notice!"

"I doubt it will come to that," Giles said.

"I can only hope not," Luke said, his eyes warm. Perhaps too warm, I thought. Luke was definitely interested in Giles, and who could blame him? Probably because he knew Tris and I would appear today, Giles had dressed as he had the last few days, and Luke had not stinted himself of cataloging and assessing every one of Giles's attributes. I had no doubt whatsoever that he approved of everything he saw.

"No," Luke continued, his eyes still on Giles. "If we don't have a change in leadership soon, Harald might just cause a split in the ranks, and we would lose a considerable part of our membership."

"Is there a coup planned for this week?" I asked. I wasn't really that interested in the internal politics of this batty group, but I thought it couldn't hurt to divert his attention from Giles for a few moments.

When Luke grinned this time, he resembled a wolf about to dismember his prey. Suddenly I didn't envy poor old Harald. If he made it through the week with his crown intact, he was far more clever than he appeared.

"I take that as a 'yes,' " I said.

Luke merely continued grinning. I decided to ask him another question, one about which I was truly curious. "One thing I've noticed this morning, Luke, is that there doesn't appear to be any attempt to have the group all existing in the same century." I waved my hand in the direction of the encampment. "From what I've seen, you've got folk dressed in everything from the garb of thirteenth-century common laborers to the robes of a late medieval English king."

Luke frowned. "That's another of the beefs that many of us have with our so-called king. Up until two years ago, we had stuck rather firmly to the late fourteenth and early fifteenth centuries. But ever since Harald was elected king, he has been trying to push us all further back in time."

"Perhaps because of his claim to be descended from the Danish kings?" Giles asked.

Shrugging, Luke said, "Probably. That makes as much sense as any reason he has seen fit to give. There have been enough of the membership to go along with him that it has caused a considerable split between those who want to enact the thirteenth century and those who want to adhere to the original concept of the founding members."

"Quite a kerfuffle in the making," I said.

"It will be sorted out," Luke said in a hard voice. "One way or another, this week Harald will be out of a job."

"Luke! Luke!"

We turned at the sound of a woman's voice, crying out urgently. Moving rapidly toward us, as rapidly as her costume would allow, was a shorter, more feminine version of His Grace of Wessex. From the similarity of her facial features, I knew she had to be his sister.

"Yes, what is it, Adele?" Luke did not mask the impatience in his voice.

"You're needed urgently, Luke," she said, coming to a halt in front of us and puffing slightly. "Harald and Totsye are having another screaming match, throwing things about. Someone has to stop them before one of them is badly hurt!"

Chapter 5

A t those words, Luke de Montfort uttered a curse and strode off to intervene. His sister, with her shorter legs, struggled to keep up as she scurried after him.

I cocked an eyebrow at Giles. "Shall we?"

Giles grinned. "But of course. This is as much fun as a play, don't you think?"

Following at a slightly more leisurely pace, Giles and I made our way through the encampment in the wake of the de Montfort siblings. Word of the imbroglio was spreading, however, and soon we were part of a throng that was making its way to the other end of the encampment.

The closer we came to the scene of the argument, the more easily I could hear the voices of the combatants over the noise of the crowd. The strident soprano of a woman—the aforementioned Totsye, I presumed—soared high above the squeaks of her opponent, Harald Knutson, whose voice had gone up at least an octave since we had spoken with him.

Luke de Montfort had cut a path through the crowd, and Giles and I quickly pushed in behind him. I felt a tug at my elbow and looked down to see Luke's sister trying to get past Giles and me. I moved aside, and with a muttered apology, she slipped through.

The crowd stood in a semicircle around the combatants,

whose simultaneous screaming at each other made their words difficult to understand. Knutson, his head and face smudged black, his crown gone, loomed over the woman by nearly a foot, yet he seemed unable to use this to his advantage. Instead, she was slowly moving him backward, by the sheer force of her personality, toward a smoking mound in the earth behind him.

I eyed the mound curiously. It resembled a medieval oven I had seen in a picture. Evidently this group was very serious about living in the past if they went to the trouble to construct a medieval oven. To me that seemed like much more trouble than it was worth, but I wasn't the one having to tend it.

By now Luke de Montfort had managed to get between the two, and, sticking an arm out toward each of them, he pushed them apart. "That's enough!" His voice was loud enough to rouse the dead down in the churchyard at St. Ethelwold's Church in the village, and I winced from the sheer power of it.

In the sudden stillness that followed, I heard a quickly smothered giggle or two, then no one said a word. I could hear both combatants breathing heavily.

Giles jabbed me in the side. "What is it?" I said.

"It's Totsye Titchmarsh," Giles said in tones of wonder. "She's an old school friend of my mother's. I had no idea she was involved with this group. Mummy will be beside herself when she finds out."

I eyed the woman curiously. She was the same age as Lady Prunella, late fifties, and, again like Lady Prunella, Ms. Titchmarsh had the figure of a pouter pigeon. Her extravagant costume caused her to bulge in odd places, chiefly in the over-large bosom, which now heaved with anger and exertion.

Her clothing drew my attention, for she brought to mind Geoffrey Chaucer's infamous Wife of Bath. Her hose were scarlet, and her hat was large, as was her skirt; the style belonged to the late fourteenth century. I was willing to bet that her name within this potty society was Alysoun something or other. If she were somewhat deaf and gap-toothed, the picture would be almost complete.

"What is all this ruckus about?" Luke said loudly, looking right at Totsye Titchmarsh. Her eyes focused intently on his lips. She must be hard of hearing, then. "And what happened to you, Harald?"

Knutson pointed a wobbly finger at his opponent. "This vicious besom tried to kill me, that's what!"

Totsye screeched back at him, "That's a lie, you knave. I never laid a hand on you! Though if you persist in claiming I did, I very likely will after all."

Knutson stepped back a pace. "Look at me! It's a wonder I wasn't grievously injured. It's only by a miracle that I didn't have all my hair burned off or have my eyes put out by burning coals."

Luke de Montfort breathed deeply in an attempt to keep a rein on his temper. "I will ask you one more time, Harald. What happened?"

Knutson huffily clamped his arms across his chest and stared down at the duke. "I came to inspect the oven. There was no one about, and I knelt down for a closer look. While I was down on my knees with my head near the opening, someone kicked me into the oven." His voice had risen steadily on the last few syllables until he was screeching in fair imitation of Totsye Titchmarsh. "She did it, I tell you! I got myself out of the oven as quickly as I could, and there she was."

"Yes, I was," Totsye said, "because I had been looking for you the better part of an hour." When she spoke, I could see that she was gap-toothed. The Wife of Bath indeed. "I wanted to explain to this poltroon," she said, her voice loud and ringing, "that there is no way we can hold our banquet tonight. The idea is utterly ridiculous. Just as ridiculous as the idea that I shoved his head into the oven."

"Nonsense, you ignorant slut," Knutson shouted, evidently feeling safe with Luke standing between him and the woman he was insulting. Luke automatically thrust out his arm to keep Totsye Titchmarsh from charging forward.

"There is no reason why we cannot have our banquet this evening," Knutson continued in quieter tones. "And if you didn't attack me, who did?" Someone from the crowd stepped forward to hand him his missing crown, and he stuck it on his head at a slight angle.

"Any one of the considerable number of people here who think you're an idiot," Totsye said, and her remark elicited a number of laughs from the bystanders.

"I doubt rather seriously, Henry," Luke said, using the man's real name deliberately, "that Totsye would have attacked you. You probably did it to yourself. We all know how clumsy you are." He laughed, and the crowd laughed with him.

"I'll find out who did it," Knutson said, "and whoever it was will be very sorry indeed." He glared at Totsye, who simply rolled her eyes at him.

"Now, about this idea of having our banquet early," Luke said. "That won't wash. Representatives from several of the fiefdoms won't be here until tomorrow, and we cannot hold the banquet without them."

"Yes, we can, d'Amboise," Knutson said stubbornly. "I am the ruler here, and it is my wish."

Luke shook his head slowly. "Hear me now, Henry, and hear me well. Your days as king are numbered, and you might as well resign yourself to that fact. We will hold the banquet as scheduled, with representatives of all the fiefdoms present, which is according to the rules of our society. You're trying to maneuver the election so you won't be defeated, but it won't work."

"Exactly," Totsye Titchmarsh said in ringing tones. "I told the fool that, but he's too stupid to see when he's licked."

"This is not over just yet," Knutson promised them. "I'll see you both in Hades before I give up my crown." He turned and pushed his way through the crowd. There was considerable tittering amongst those assembled, and it seemed to me old Harald didn't have much support left. He was fighting a losing battle, and rather than accept defeat gracefully, he intended to go down swinging.

Luke clapped his hands peremptorily. "Everyone back to your tasks! We still have much to do."

Slowly the muttering crowd began to drift away, back to their tents. Adele de Montfort went forward and tucked her hand in the crook of her brother's arm. "Poor Luke," she said. "The sooner that idiot Harald is drummed out of the society, the better. You'll make a much better king than he ever did."

"What's that you say?" Totsye Titchmarsh leaned forward, trying to hear what Adele was saying.

"My sister," Luke said, enunciating clearly and slowly, "is simply saying that I'll make a good king."

"Indeed, indeed," Totsye said, beaming at him. As I watched, I got the strongest feeling that Ms. Titchmarsh was deeply in love with the handsome duke. The love and longing fairly poured out of her. Poor woman! She wouldn't be the first woman to fall hopelessly in love with a gay man.

"Miss Titchmarsh," Giles said loudly as he strode forward, "I'd like you to meet a dear friend of mine."

Her head turned at the sound of Giles's voice, and she beamed in recognition. Luke and Adele watched in amusement as I took in the full glory of Miss Titchmarsh's get-up at close range.

"Giles, dear, how lovely to see you," Miss Titchmarsh said. "I haven't had the chance yet to visit dear Prunella, but tell her I shall attend upon her soon."

"Certainly," Giles said. He motioned for me to come forward. "Miss Titchmarsh, allow me to present a very dear friend, Dr. Simon Kirby-Jones. He's a medieval historian."

"How do you do, Miss Titchmarsh," I said. "Though I suspect you have rather a different name among this society."

She giggled loudly. I tried not to wince. "But of course, Dr. Kirby-Jones. And I am quite certain you can tell me just what my name is, you being a medievalist and all."

I bowed slightly, then began quoting, in the original Middle

BAKED TO DEATH 39

English, "A good wif was ther of biside Bathe, But she was somdel deef, and that was scathe."

Again she giggled. "Alysoun of Bath, at your service. How clever of you, Dr. Kirby-Jones."

And how unoriginal of you, I thought. If people were going to play at these games, surely they would have more imagination.

"Would you mind, Simon, translating for those of us who aren't *au courant* with Middle English?" Giles said in a slightly acid tone.

"There was a good wife from near Bath, but she was somewhat deaf, and that was unfortunate."

Totsye giggled again. The woman was old enough to know better. Girlish giggling at her age. Honestly.

"Most impressive, Simon," Luke de Montfort said. "You should think about joining us. You certainly have the background, and we can always use someone of your credentials." The way he was eyeing me, I didn't think it was my academic credentials he was after.

"Thank you," I said. "I'll certainly keep that in mind." Until I had met some of these re-enactors face to face, I'd had no intention of having anything to do with such a group. But I was beginning to find myself oddly intrigued by the whole thing. There was an added bonus as well. It would drive Tris utterly mad. I smiled at the thought.

"Giles, Simon, this is my sister, Adele," Luke said, patting the hand tucked into the crook of his arm. He continued the formal introduction.

Giles and I both inclined our heads, and Adele curtsied to acknowledge the introduction. "You certainly must prevail upon both Giles and Simon to join us, Your Grace. They would make such a handsome addition to our court." She leered briefly at Giles and me, then turned to her brother with a demure smile.

He frowned down at her. He apparently detected some sting in those words that escaped the rest of us. "Thank you, sister dear," he said. "I will certainly keep that in mind."

"Oh, you should join us," trumpeted the wife of Bath. "We have a merry old time, and I must say you would both be quite striking, properly dressed."

"Thank you," Giles said, speaking for both of us. "But I'm afraid neither Simon nor I has the appropriate clothing."

Totsye giggled, yet again. Why someone hadn't stuffed her in the oven for that blasted giggling, I had no idea. "Nonsense, Giles, dear. I'll just take you along to Master Anselm Webster. Besides weaving the most divine textiles, he keeps quite a number of ready-made garments for sale. No doubt there will be something suitable for both of you."

"Well," Giles said, unsure how to decline such an invitation gracefully.

"We shall certainly make a visit to Master Webster," I said smoothly. "But first, good Alysoun, you must tell us about yon oven."

Totsye, Luke, and Adele all turned to the oven. "We're quite proud of that," Luke said. "It's only in the last couple of years that we've had a functioning medieval oven during our gatherings." He looked about, seeking someone. He caught the eye of a rotund man garbed in sweat-stained workman's clothes, overlaid with an apron. "Ælfwine," he called. "You are needed."

"Yes, Your Grace," the man said as he ambled over. His rolling gait was that of a sailor, but judging from his girth, he was an expert trencherman as well. His florid face perspired in the heat of the midsummer sun, and occasionally he would flap his apron about in an attempt to generate a breeze.

I too was beginning to feel the heat of the day. After a quick look at the oven, I'd be ready to seek cover from the sun.

"These gentlemen are interested in your oven, Ælfwine," Luke explained.

The baker beamed at us. "Ah, gentlemen, we're all very proud of our oven. Come closer."

We stepped nearer the oven, and Ælfwine launched into a technical explanation of the oven's construction. The salient point was that they chose this particular type of oven, based on a twelfth-century example found in an excavation in York, because it could be constructed and fired fairly quickly. The base was between four and five feet square, and, hemispherical in shape, it looked rather like half a large and lumpy beehive.

The brick with which it had been constructed, Ælfwine explained, was regular building brick, and it was covered with ordinary daub—that is, clay mixed with straw, a common building tool of medieval times. A wooden door with a metal handle covered the opening, and wafts of smoke and steam escaped here and there.

"It's been firing for about fifteen hours now," he said. "We arrived early yesterday afternoon so's we could get it going. By this evening we can start baking bread in it." He paused to wipe his dripping brow with his apron. "You can see there are still a few leaks in it, but we'll just keep putting on the daub until they're sealed." He pointed to a bucket of the material sitting near the oven.

"Fascinating," Giles said heartily, and Ælfwine beamed proudly. The oven was interesting, but mostly it made me thankful that I didn't have to tend to it. Before the week was out the portly baker would have sweated away a few pounds of his excess flesh.

"Thank you, Ælfwine," Luke said. "I shall send over some of my special bread loaves this afternoon for you to start baking." Then he frowned. "Where were you, Ælfwine, when someone allegedly attacked the king?"

The master baker shrugged. "I had need of a privy, Your Grace, and I had stepped away but for a moment. No one else was about when I left, but when I returned, all I saw was the two of them arguing."

"Was the oven damaged?" Luke asked.

"No, Your Grace," the baker replied with a wide grin. "The oven is in fine shape."

"Thank you, Ælfwine," Luke said. Then, as if dismissing the incident to be of no further importance, he started forward, his sister still attached to his arm. "Now, gentlemen, if you'll excuse me, there is business to which I must direct my attention. Should you be interested in visiting me, anyone here can point out my pavilion." He and Adele swept regally away.

A deep sigh sounded from behind us. Totsye Titchmarsh was not in the least bit subtle about her admiration for her would-be king.

"Miss Titchmarsh," Giles said, arching an eyebrow at me, "perhaps now you would be so good as to show Simon and me to the tent of Master Webster?"

Collecting herself, Totsye gathered her skirts in her hands, lifting them from the grass of the meadow, and tottered forward on her heels and pointed toes. "Certainly, Giles, dear. Follow me."

I cast one last glance at the oven. It was properly several feet from the nearest tent, but close enough to the one that was apparently serving as a kitchen. They had obviously given some thought to fire prevention. The tent next to it proudly proclaimed itself as a pub—The Happy Destrier. I thought that naming the pub for a warhorse was an odd choice, but then, most everything about this group was a bit on the odd side.

I trailed behind Giles and the tittering, chattering Totsye. Several women cast admiring glances in Giles's direction, as did one or two men. I frowned. I couldn't believe that Giles was actually serious about wanting to play dress-up, but I decided I might as well go along with it, at least up to a point.

Totsye seemed little the worse for her confrontation with Knutson. I strongly suspected that she *had* kicked the royal derriere, forcing the royal head into the oven. Why she had such animus against Knutson, or what she hoped to gain by such a potentially dangerous prank, I had no idea, but it might bear discreet inquiry.

We came at last to the tent of the weaver, Master Webster, and Totsye Titchmarsh introduced us to the man. His eyes brightened at the thought of sales. "Certainly, gentlemen," he said, eyeing us both up and down like an expert tailor, "I've no doubt I can find appropriate raiment for each of you." He threw out an arm in an expansive gesture, indicating the array of cloth on a table nearby, as well as ready-made garments hanging from pegs and rope strung around the tent.

As Totsye urged Giles forward to examine some of the clothing, I moved to one side of the tent and peered out from behind a concealing flap. I had spotted something interesting going on across the way, between two tents opposite that of the weaver.

Harald Knutson stood in the shadows between the tents, talking to two thuggish-looking brutes dressed as foot soldiers. Broad and burly, they looked more like rugby players than medieval soldiers. They watched the king intently as he talked and gestured at them.

I focused my hearing to tune in on what they were saying. One of the advantages of being a vampire is that one's hearing becomes much keener than it was in life, and I have had a number of occasions to be grateful for the change.

I filtered out the noise of the encampment around us and homed in on Harald's voice. "I assure you, if you do this for me, you'll both have what you want."

One of the thugs grunted. "It's worth a knighthood to me, sire," he said. "And Guillaume here will go along with what I says."

Guillaume nodded. "Me, too, sire. I fancy being Sir Guillaume."

"And so it shall be," Harald promised them. "Just get it done, and make sure no one sees you. He has to be stopped." With that, he slipped away behind the tents.

What little plot had the king just hatched?

Chapter 6

I watched for a moment longer, but the king's two conspirators didn't linger in the shadows between the tents. They strode off in the opposite direction from that taken by the monarch himself. Frowning, I turned my attention to what was taking place inside the weaver's tent. I had no doubt that whatever Harald Knutson was planning, it boded nothing but ill for Luke de Montfort. Perhaps I should warn him.

"What do you think of this, Simon?" Giles asked, his eyes bright with mischief and amusement.

He held up in one hand some brightly colored hose, which would no doubt mold themselves to his shapely legs and hips. One leg was scarlet, the other navy blue. They looked suspiciously like modern, mass-produced tights, but I supposed one could not expect 100 percent authenticity. In the other hand he clutched a navy blue houppelande with red sleeves, elaborately embroidered with silver and gold geometric patterns. The houppelande was a dresslike garment worn by both sexes in the late Middle Ages. They were usually ankle length, but the one Giles had chosen was a knee-length tunic. He didn't want to miss an opportunity to show off his nether parts.

"Very nice, Giles," I said. "The colors are quite flattering to you, and you'll cut quite a dash. But of course you need some sort of headdress." I turned to Master Webster. "No doubt you have something suitable?"

Anselm Webster beamed at me. "Certainly, good sir." He turned to a table behind him and selected a low-crowned black hat with an upturned brim. "Begging your pardon, sir," he said as he reached forward to set the hat gently on Giles's head.

Giles grinned at me. I thought the medieval garb would suit him just fine. It was definitely more extravagant-looking than his usual wardrobe.

"Now it's your turn, Simon," Giles said.

"Very well," I said, giving the appearance of bored reluctance, but seeing how attractive Giles looked made me curious to try it for myself. I had never worn any kind of medieval costume, and now here I was, preparing to play dress-up for the first time since childhood.

I examined Master Webster's wares and finally settled on a full-length houppelande of a deep green, embellished with rich embroidery. It was split in front and back and would flap about a bit as I walked, allowing my hose to be seen. I found a black hat with a large brim, along with some black hose. I fingered the latter. As I had suspected, these were simply tights and none too authentic. Giles and I each picked out shoes, his red and mine black, to match our costumes, and of course we had to have leather belts. Giles again chose red while I found a black one. Now that we seemed to have everything we would need, I asked Master Webster just how much all of this finery cost.

My eyes widened slightly at the price he named, and Giles made a move as if to put his selections back. "No," I said, "this is my treat, Giles. We'll mark it down to research expenses." I reached into my jacket pocket for my wallet. I had enough cash to pay for our clothing.

Master Webster beamed even more widely as he watched the pile of fifty-pound notes growing in his palm. "Thank you most kindly, noble sir," he said when I had finished. He turned to tuck away his money into an ornately carved wooden box he retrieved from under one of his tables.

"Master Webster, I must speak with you," came a strident voice from behind us. "We must stop those idiots Knutson and de Montfort before they ruin everything." Giles, Totsye, and I turned to behold a man of enormous girth waddling into the tent.

Perhaps the newcomer fancied himself as Henry VIII, for his features and size were reminiscent of that much-married monarch. His costume was the most elaborate I had seen this morning. He might have been one of the king's chief courtiers for all the elegance and extravagance of his headdress and his houppelande. The points of his big shoes stuck out a good twelve inches, and he looked a bit like a medieval duck as a result.

Totsye Titchmarsh sniffed loudly in distaste. "Bugger off, why don't you, Sir Reginald."

Thus addressed, Sir Reginald paused to cast an evil eye on Totsye, Giles, and me. The eye did indeed seem evil, because his left eye moved while the right one didn't. Perhaps the right one was glass, I speculated. His inspection of us seemed comically sinister because of the unmoving eye.

"Well, well, if it isn't the Whore of Bath," he said. "I see you've found a couple more sodomites to mince about with you." He sniffed loudly. "As if mooning constantly over that bugger de Montfort isn't embarrassing enough."

Master Webster clucked anxiously behind us. I laid a restraining hand on Totsye's arm, because I could feel her about to launch herself at Sir Reginald. The woman certainly had a temper. Though I wouldn't have minded seeing him brought to his knees by this whirling dervish, I really didn't see any need for blood to be shed on my account.

Instead I stepped forward until I had trod upon Sir Reginald's extravagant shoes, immobilizing him. I stared down at him, ignoring his outraged sputters. "Really, Sir Reginald, you do have the most appalling manners. I should think it ill behooves anyone who obviously eats like a pig at a trough"—I pointed to the numerous stains on his gown—"to cast aspersions upon anyone else. I believe an apology to Goodwife Alysoun is in order, don't you?"

Sir Reginald's one good eye rolled around as he nervously contemplated what might happen if he refused to do as I had requested. I took a step back, releasing him, and he drew a deep and shuddering breath. "My apologies, Alysoun," he at last mumbled.

"Accepted," Totsye said, almost growling out the word.

"There, you see, Sir Reginald," I said, beaming at him, "good manners will always be appreciated."

Behind me, Giles and Master Webster were trying, not very successfully, to suppress their laughter. Sir Reginald's face grew even redder.

"Come along, Sir Giles, Alysoun," I said. "No doubt Sir Reggie has business of grave import to discuss with Master Webster, and we should let them get on with it." Clutching my costume in a bag provided by Webster, I stalked out of the tent. Giles and the Wife of Bath were right behind me.

The sky had clouded over, and I was grateful for some respite from the sun. We walked a few paces away from the tent before I stopped to question Totsye. "Just who was that prat?"

She made a moue of distaste before responding. "Sir Reginald of Bolingbroke, he calls himself."

I groaned. "Don't tell me. Another pretender to the throne." Otherwise, why would he have chosen the family name of Henry IV, who had wrested the throne away from Richard III in 1399?

"Exactly," Totsye said, nearly spitting. "He despises both Harald and Luke, and he fancies he has the qualities that will make him a good king."

"And do others of the group share this delusion?"

Totsye laughed. "Oh, Reggie has a few adherents, but only

a few. Both Harald and Luke would have to be completely out of the running before Reggie stood a chance at being chosen king."

"It sounds as if this is going to be quite an interesting week," Giles said.

Totsye sighed deeply. "But not interesting in the right way. Ever since Harald became king, our society has become increasingly divided. He has not been the kind of leader we had hoped for, and the sooner he is dethroned, the better. The leaders of the great fiefdoms are not happy with him."

"I would say that Luke de Montfort is quite determined to see Harald dethroned," I said.

Totsye's face brightened. "Dear Luke, such an intelligent man. And he has such presence as well. He looks like a king, unlike Harald."

I couldn't disagree with her, but I didn't see any point in continuing the discussion at present. "Is there somewhere nearby that Giles and I might change into our new clothing? We could go back to Blitherington Hall, but if we don't have to, that would be most helpful."

"But of course," Totsye said. "You may use my pavilion, dear sir. Please, follow me."

She strode forward, and Giles and I followed. After a few paces she turned from the main lane of the encampment down one of the side paths. We passed several large tents until we came to hers. Made of canvas like most of those we had passed, but dyed a rich gold, it was a large structure and must have taken some time to erect. She waved us inside, explaining that the pavilion had two chambers.

"The front is my sitting room, more or less. There, behind that curtain, is my sleeping chamber." She demonstrated how to let the flap down so that the opening was covered. "When you're done, you may pin the flap back open again. You're most welcome to leave your mundane things here, if you like. No one will bother them, I assure you."

"Thank you," I said, and Giles did the same.

I let the flap down behind her, then turned to find Giles regarding me with considerable amusement.

"Why are you suddenly so bent upon taking part in this play-acting, Simon? I believe that's what you called it earlier."

I shrugged. "It *is* much more interesting than I anticipated, I must admit. I don't see any harm in having a bit of fun with it, do you?"

Giles laughed. "No, I suppose not, Simon. I'm game if you are."

"Thank you, Giles. Besides, I must admit to considerable curiosity about what is going on here. All this internecine struggling over the monarchy"—I couldn't help laughing over it—"might lead to something most interesting."

"Surely not another dead body, Simon," Giles said, his mouth twisted in distaste.

"You never know," I said. "Some of these people are a few cards shy of a deck as it is, and they all seem to take this pretty seriously. Whether they take it seriously enough to commit murder over, I don't know. But let me tell you what I overheard." As I spoke I had begun removing my clothing, and Giles, seeing me disrobe, began to do the same.

I related to Giles the conversation I had heard between Harald Knutson and the two soldiers, and he frowned in response. "There's definitely some plot in the works," he said, his voice a bit muffled as he pulled his tight shirt over his head.

"Yes, something's up," I agreed. I turned my back to him. I didn't want him to think I was going to stand there and ogle him while we dressed. I also didn't want him staring at me in the nearly altogether.

It took us a few minutes to dress ourselves in the unfamiliar clothing, but when we were both finished, I was satisfied with the results. Giles was most handsome in his costume, and his hose molded themselves quite attractively to his muscular legs. I moved around a bit, letting the houppelande flap about me. I caught a glint in Giles's eyes, which told me my own costume was flattering.

"Now for the hats," I said, fitting mine upon my head and appreciating the protection from the sun it offered. Giles's brimless hat sat atop his curls at a jaunty angle. He could easily pass for a medieval lordling about to stroll through the village in search of mischief. He flashed me a saucy grin.

"What now, Simon? I've no doubt you've hatched some plan yourself."

"As a matter of fact, Giles, I have," I said, unruffled by his playful tone. "I would like you to wander about the encampment, chatting with folk, trying to get a feeling for what people think about this struggle over who's going to be king." I paused. "And about this film as well."

"Very well, Simon," Giles said. "I wouldn't mind having a look round. Particularly in The Happy Destrier. I'm more than a trifle peckish, not to mention thirsty."

"Certainly," I said. "And you can tell me about the food later. I'm curious to know what kind of medieval fare they're offering here."

"And what will you be doing?" Giles asked as I pinned the tent flap open again.

The sky was still cloudy, I was relieved to see. I had tucked my sunglasses into my houppelande, along with my wallet and my pills. If the sun came out again, I'd have to don the glasses, even though they would be out of place. I had noticed a couple of the encampment folk wearing them earlier, so I wouldn't be the only walking anachronism.

"Me?" I asked. "I'm going to find the would-be king and tell him what I overheard. If he's the target of the plot, he ought to be warned, don't you think?"

"Certainly," Giles said, "but perhaps I should tag along, just to make sure you're safe. What if those thugs should attack him while you're with him?"

"Thank you, but no," I said, mistrustful of the jocular tone in which he had spoken. "I'll be perfectly fine, Giles, and you needn't worry that I'm going to throw myself at the handsome duke."

"Perish the thought," Giles said, his voice dripping with sarcasm.

"Be on your way," I said, and he laughed as he turned and walked away. "We'll chat later," I called after him. He waved to acknowledge that he heard but did not slow down.

I looked around for a moment. There were people in several of the tents nearby, but I didn't think any of them had overheard the exchange between Giles and me. They were all busily engaged in various tasks.

I approached a woman a couple of tents away who was sitting on a stool in the opening, plying a needle and thread to what looked like a pair of men's braes with a frayed hem.

"Pardon me, good lady," I said, and she looked up at me.

"How might I help you, sir?" she said, her hands stilled in her lap.

"Could you point me in the direction of the tent of His Grace, the Duke of Wessex?"

"Certainly, sir," she said, pointing down the alley to her left. "Follow the path between these tents to the end, then turn to your left. You will see his pavilion a few paces away, off to itself. There will be a banner flying from it if he is within."

"Thank you, madame," I said, bowing slightly. She nodded, then bent her head once again to her work.

I ambled down the lane between the tents and soon came to the end. Turning to the left, I could see the pavilion she had described, about thirty yards away. It sat off by itself at a short distance from any of the others. It was the largest I had yet seen, of a rich and most definite royal purple. A banner flew from a flagpole stuck in the earth near the front of the pavilion.

Striding across the rough ground of the meadow, I thought about what I would say to de Montfort about what I had seen and heard. As I approached, I could hear voices, raised slightly in anger, coming from within. Nearing the side of the pavilion, I slowed my steps and moved cautiously around the side until I was a couple of paces from the opening at the front.

"Don't be so hasty, Tris," Luke de Montfort was saying. "Did I threaten you? Surely you can't think that."

"How else," Tris's voice was low and deep, indicating his fury, "am I to interpret your remark just now?"

Luke laughed. "Dear Tris, always expecting the worst. Could it be because you have such a guilty conscience over your own behavior? You treat others badly, and naturally you assume they will act badly as well."

"Stop playing these little games with me," Tris said. "I warn you, Luke, you will regret ever crossing me if you follow through with your little threat."

"Dear, dear Tris," Luke said, his tone mocking, "you really do think I'm afraid of you, don't you? Despite your rather special . . . abilities, shall we say, I'm not frightened of you in the least. You won't dare do anything. You're the one who would lose."

Should I intervene? I wondered. Tris had quite a temper when roused, and he might easily hurt de Montfort if he were goaded enough. Before I could decide, however, I heard a crash as something heavy hit the ground.

Chapter 7

———●———

That seemed as good a cue as any. I rounded the side of the tent just in time for Tristan Lovelace to barrel into me. Had I been mortal he would have knocked me onto the ground, such was the force with which we collided. Instead we bounced apart, both still on our feet.

"Get the bloody hell out of my way!" Tris snarled at me, his face clouded with anger. He started to brush me aside, but then he realized who I was.

"What are you doing in that bloody get-up, Simon?"

"So kind of you to notice, Tris," I said coolly. "Don't you think it flatters me?"

"If you want to waste your time playing dress-up, that's your choice," Tris said, "but I find the whole thing utterly ridiculous."

I looked past Tris to see Luke de Montfort surveying the damage Tris had wrought in his pavilion. A large wooden table lay top down on the ground. Some of the crockery and pewter drinking vessels that had been atop it were now shattered or bent out of shape from the force of the table's falling on them.

"I should think you're the one who's ridiculous," I said, waving my hand toward the mess, "if you're responsible for that. You still have your nasty temper, I see, Tris."

Luke de Montfort guffawed, and Tris spun around. "Be glad it's not you under that table, Luke."

De Montfort shook his head. "Oh, Tris, you are priceless. Luckily I can afford to replace what you've destroyed by your childish outburst."

Tris made a step in Luke's direction, but I placed a restraining hand on his arm. He shook it off, but he stopped. "You'd best keep out of this, Simon." He turned back to glare at me.

"And I think you had better calm down," I said in a low voice, "and consider very carefully what it is you're doing here."

Tris blinked at me. I could feel him struggling to control his rage at Luke, and as I watched him with concern, I saw that he was quickly getting his temper under control. After a moment, he turned back to Luke.

"Let me know how much the damage is," Tris said gruffly, "and I shall reimburse you. Now, if you'll both excuse me, I have other things to do." He pushed past me and strode off across the meadow, disappearing into the encampment.

I watched him for a moment. What had set him off like that? I had rarely seen him so angry.

"Would you mind lending me a hand, Simon?" Luke's voice recalled me from my reverie.

"Not at all, Luke," I said, stepping over to help him right the heavy oaken table. Once the table was again in place, we both stared down at the mess of pottery shards and dented pewter. "How much will it cost to replace all this?"

Luke shrugged. "A hundred pounds or so. It's really not that important. I can easily replace them."

"Shall I help you clear it away?"

"No," Luke said, "I'll have one of my servants take care of it. They'll be returning soon from their errands. Just ignore it for the nonce." He gestured toward the other side of the tent, where several chairs stood around a small table. "Might I offer you some mead?"

"None for me, thanks, but go right ahead." I sat down in one of the chairs, a heavy oak affair with a broad seat and low back and arms. Luke sat across the table from me and poured himself a beaker of mead from a pitcher he had placed on the table.

"Now, Simon, to what do I owe the pleasure of this visit?" Luke regarded me quizzically as he sipped at his mead.

I decided for the moment to pretend no interest in Luke's little altercation with Tris. I would come back to that when he seemed more relaxed, less on guard.

"I have come across some information today that I thought might be of interest to you," I said. "Goodwife Alysoun escorted Giles and me to the tent of Master Webster where, as you can see, I purchased some of his wares."

"A most excellent choice," Luke said. His eyes expressed an even warmer sentiment, but I pretended not to notice.

"Thank you. As I was standing in the opening of the tent," I explained, "I happened to witness Knutson speaking with two scruffy-looking soldier types." I repeated what I had heard.

De Montfort did not appear in the least troubled by my report. Instead, he laughed. "That's good King Harald for you, Simon. He loves his grubby little plots, and he's always getting someone else to do his dirty work for him."

"Then I gather this is not the first time he has done such a thing."

"No," Luke said. "At our past two gatherings he has done his best to make my participation as uncomfortable as possible. My servants are harried needlessly by his minions, things disappear from my pavilion, and such. All petty irritations, but nothing I and my retinue cannot withstand." He grinned. "Besides, I have a spy in the king's camp, and the king doesn't know it."

"A bit of medieval espionage, as it were?" I smiled. "Is there no recourse to justice within the rules of your society, without having to resort to such tactics?"

"Certainly," Luke said, "and the king will be facing the consequences of his little campaign against me this very week. When the heads of all the fiefdoms gather in a few days' time at our banquet, Harald will find himself handing over his crown." He drank deeply from his mead. "Most of the society are aware of the shabby little games Harald plays, and his popularity has eroded drastically as a result. I have nothing to fear from him, particularly since I will have a witness from within his own little coterie who can corroborate my charges."

"It seems a particularly unintelligent thing for him to do," I said.

Luke shrugged. "Once upon a time, Harald wasn't so bad. But that was before he decided he wanted to be king. Do you know, I really think sometimes he believes he *is* a king. He's become quite potty in the last two years."

"I wouldn't argue that with you," I said. "But there's something else I perhaps ought to mention. While we were in Master Webster's tent, we also had the great misfortune of meeting Sir Reginald Bolingbroke."

Luke barked with laughter. "And no doubt Sir Reginald was fussing and flapping on about his own campaign to be elected king."

"More or less," I said.

"The man's a cretin," Luke said. "And a homophobe to boot. He is beside himself with rage because I am far more popular than he is, not to mention the fact that he is nobly born and I am not. He quite fancies himself as a ladies' man, you know." Luke shuddered in distaste. "Though what woman would so demean herself as to have anything to do with him, I cannot imagine."

"He is rather an unprepossessing specimen, I grant you," I said. "But how serious a threat is he to your bid to be elected king?"

Rolling his eyes, Luke said, "Oh, Reggie has a few followers in his camp, but they're just as demented as he is. Fortunately for the rest of us they are a very small minority." He slapped his hand against the table, and the pitcher of mead skittered slightly. "I have nothing to fear from the likes of him either. No, I am fairly certain the results of the election are a foregone conclusion."

"Then might I offer my congratulations, Your Majesty?" I tried to keep any note of sarcasm out of my voice.

De Montfort inclined his head in a gesture of graciousness. "Thank you, Simon. Now, have you given any thought to joining our society? The duchy of Wessex would welcome you, I can assure you of that, and no doubt I could find you a suitable title."

"That is most kind of you, Your Grace," I said, playing along with him. I wondered just what I might have to do to gain that "suitable title." "I will give your kind invitation all due consideration. I must admit that, when I first heard of your society, I was rather dubious about what you are doing." I shrugged. "But now that I have had a chance to see the group in action, I do admit that what you're doing is of some interest. Living history, as it were."

"Exactly," Luke said. "I know there are many who believe we are crackpots, but we are all brought together by a sincere interest in the Middle Ages." He grinned, and he was really most attractive when he did so. "I grant you, there are those among us who *are* crackpots, most notably our king, but the vast majority of us are quite sane, I can assure you."

"And would weeding out the crackpots, as you call them," I said, "be one of the goals of your kingship?"

"Exactly," Luke said. "We have procedures for dealing with those who violate the rules of the society, and from time to time we have had to expel a few members. I don't say that we will actually come to the point of throwing Harald out altogether, but if he doesn't accept his defeat graciously, he might just find himself kicked out."

"He might be a bit on the barmy side," I observed mildly, "but that doesn't mean he's stupid. He might be a tougher opponent than you credit him."

Luke scoffed at that. "Harald is mostly blather rather than action. He might resort to a few underhanded tricks, but he doesn't have what it takes to challenge me effectively. He's a piss-poor fighter. If I wanted to end this quickly, I would simply challenge him on the battlefield, but there's no need. The election at the banquet will suffice."

"Then perhaps you really have nothing to fear from that quarter. Or from Sir Reginald." I paused. "But I must admit, when I was nearing your tent, I couldn't help but overhear some of your argument with Tris."

"So?" Luke said, his eyes wary.

"I gather you know Tris pretty well," I said, "so you know that he can be an implacable enemy. Are you entirely certain you want to be on his bad side?"

Luke waved his hand in the air, as if to dismiss the whole matter. "Nothing but the proverbial tempest in the teapot," he said. "We had a disagreement, nothing more. Tris will come round, I've little doubt."

I regarded him for a moment. He seemed completely confident.

"I haven't seen Tris quite that angry before," I said. "I would be very careful, if I were you. If you push him too far, you might not like the consequences."

"Tris will do nothing to harm me," Luke said. "He wouldn't dare. He knows that trying to do so will only result in problems for himself. Problems that he would not want to have to deal with."

"Whatever it is you're trying to blackmail him over," I said bluntly, "I hope you understand just what you're dealing with yourself."

"All this concern on your part is quite touching, Simon," Luke said mockingly, "but quite unnecessary, I do assure you. Apparently you know Tris as well as I do, and thus you know that there are things he would not wish brought to the attention of his university colleagues."

"Then, if I may be so bold as to ask," I said, "what the bloody hell do you want from Tris? What is it you want so badly that you're willing to blackmail him for it?"

Luke laughed. "Oh, Simon, surely you can't be that dense!" He laughed again, and I could feel my own temper beginning to flare.

"I want to be a vampire, just like you and Tris."

Chapter 8

There seemed little point in pretending ignorance. Luke apparently knew too much for me to offer a convincing denial.

"Why are you so eager to become a vampire?" I asked, ignoring his taunt.

"Why not?" he returned flippantly. "I spent enough time with Tris when I was at university and he was my tutor to see just what it was all about. I know it's not like the old days." He bared his teeth in a menacing grin. "Though I wouldn't have minded the old ways all that much."

I didn't attempt to hide my distaste, but he appeared not the least fazed by my reaction.

"I've no doubt that Tris made it all seem glamorous and thrilling," I said.

"And sexy," Luke added. "Don't forget that part." He leered at me. "Though I surely don't have to remind you of that."

"That really is none of your business."

Luke threw back his head and laughed. "My, my, Simon, you are quite prim and proper, aren't you? Whatever did Tris see in you in the first place?"

I refused to be drawn into a catfight. I stood up. "I rather think you should ask Tris that, if you really want to know."

"Now, now, Simon," Luke said, "don't go away angry with me. I apologize for being so bitchy. Please, sit down."

What did he want from me? I wondered as I resumed my seat. *Why was he attempting to be conciliatory after being quite offensive?*

"I suppose I got a bit carried away with myself, Simon," Luke said earnestly. At least, I believe he hoped I would think he was sincere. I rather doubted he was. "Please don't hold it against me. What I said was inappropriate, and I do apologize."

"Accepted," I lied.

"Thank you," he said, affecting not to notice the brusqueness of my response. "Tris told me he is staying with you while he's in England, Simon. I would be most grateful if you would consider putting in a good word for me, try to make Tris see he's really being unreasonable in resisting me."

"What makes you so certain that I disagree with Tris and agree with you?"

"But why could you possibly object, Simon?" Luke said. He appeared truly puzzled. Then his face cleared. "Oh, I see. You must be jealous. You think I want Tris back. But I can assure you that is not the case."

I bit back the first retort that sprang to my lips, and then it hit me. Luke had hit the nail on the head, at least partially. I was a bit jealous, I had to admit. *How bloody silly!* I told myself. Why should I be jealous of Tris's relationship with Luke? Even if Tris did decide to accede to Luke's request, what business was it of mine?

"Tris and I no longer have that kind of relationship, Luke," I said.

Luke grinned. "Yes, I know. Tris told me. He also told me that he's not happy about that. He made it perfectly clear that he's not the least bit interested in me. The only man he wants is you."

I said nothing, and Luke regarded me with amusement for a moment.

"I see, Simon," he said. "You can't quite make up your mind what you want, is that it?"

I stood again. "At the risk of being boringly repetitive, Luke, that really is none of your business. Now, if you will excuse me, I have things I must attend to."

His mocking laughter followed me out of the tent. I strode a few paces away, furious that I had allowed him to get to me. Then I stopped and fumbled for my sunglasses. The clouds had disappeared, and the sun was once again radiant and hot in the summer sky.

With my eyes protected, I resumed my progress back into the encampment. Time to find Giles and see what he had managed to find out. Judging by the sun's position, it was a bit past the noon hour. No doubt I would find Giles near the cook tents or in the pub.

Reaching the main lane of the encampment where all the various shops were located, I turned toward the end where the oven and The Happy Destrier both stood.

I found Giles at the pub, just finishing up some sort of stew. He mopped out his pewter trencher with a bit of coarse bread, then looked blearily up at me. I could tell from the expression on his face that he had drunk a bit more mead than was good for him.

He grinned tipsily at me. "H'lo, Simon. How are you?" He burped, then reached for his tankard. He drank noisily, then set the tankard down with a thump.

"Quite well, thank you," I said, stepping into the shade inside the tent. "No need to ask how you are, Giles; I can see for myself."

He burped again. " 'Scuse me, Simon. Have some of the stew. I c'n recommend it." He burped once more. "The mead, too. Damn good."

Giles was not much of a drinker, so I reckoned it hadn't taken much of the powerful mead to get him quite happily drunk. His face was flushed, and his eyes had a bit of a glassy stare to them. I thought I had better get him home so he could sleep it off.

"Come on, Giles," I said. I grabbed hold of his arms and pulled him up out of his chair.

"Wanna dance, Simon?" he said.

"No, Giles, I don't," I said as patiently as I could. "I think it's time for you to have a bit of a rest. Come with me." I turned to the man who seemed to be in charge of the pub. "Have you been paid yet?"

"Yes, sir," he said, grinning. "The young lordling paid me straightaway. I warned him about the mead, sir, but he quite liked it."

"I can see that," I said, putting one arm around Giles and beginning to lead him away.

"Come again, sir," the man called after us.

"Really, Giles, why on earth did you drink so much mead?" I muttered as we stumbled out of the tent. I was strong enough to carry him, if need be, but that would have been a pretty spectacle. If his mother happened to see him like this, she would be mortified. I thought that perhaps I shouldn't take him home after all. I decided instead to take him to Laurel Cottage, and Lady Prunella need never know what happened.

Giles was singing in an undertone. It sounded like an old ballad, but it wasn't one I could readily identify.

This was most aggravating. I really should have collected our belongings from Totsye Titchmarsh's pavilion, but I didn't want to drag Giles all the way there and then on to where my car was parked. Our things should be fine there until later on. Once Giles had slept it off, we could come back. So deciding, I half-dragged Giles down the path toward the entrance to the encampment.

Ignoring the good-natured chuckles and sniggers from passersby, we made steady progress. Once I had Giles a little way up the hill, out of sight of the encampment, I picked him up in my arms and cradled his head on my shoulder. He smiled and flung an arm around my neck, then started trying to nuzzle me.

"Giles, stop that immediately, or I'll dump you on the ground," I said, exasperated.

"C'mon, Simon, be a sport," Giles said, then giggled. But he stopped trying to kiss my neck and in moments was snoring loudly in my ear. I put on a burst of speed and in moments had rounded the corner of Blitherington Hall onto the fore-court where my Jag was parked. I hoped no one could see us from inside as I maneuvered Giles into the car.

He kept up the snoring on the short drive to Laurel Cottage, but he roused long enough to walk, with my assistance, into the sitting room. I got him situated on the sofa, found a thin blanket to cover him with, then left him to snore and sleep it off.

"What on earth is that noise?" Tris asked from behind me.

I turned. "Giles had a bit too much mead, and I brought him here to sleep it off."

Tris's mouth twisted in distaste. "The young blighter. He shouldn't drink if he can't hold his liquor. You should have dumped him at Blitherington Hall, where he belongs."

"He's not used to strong drink," I said, holding on to my temper. "I doubt he realized just how strong the mead was. And I brought him here so he wouldn't have to deal with his potty mother. She'd have a fit if she saw him like this."

"And I see you've appointed yourself his minder," Tris said nastily.

"If you like," I said. "Though what business it is of yours, I haven't the least idea."

"I wouldn't put it past him to have done this on purpose, just so you would look after him."

"Oh, Tris, don't be so bloody silly," I said, tired of both of them suddenly. I brushed past him and stalked into my office.

Tris followed me. "I'm sorry, Simon," he said, and he sounded as if he really meant it. He sat down in the chair across from my desk and regarded me with a sober gaze. "I'm not used to being jealous of a boy like that, and I suppose I am behaving rather childishly."

"Yes, you are," I said, too annoyed with him to be anything other than blunt.

"I suppose you're enjoying having the two of us competing for your attention?" Tris gave me an arch smile.

"No, I'm not," I said. "If you must know, I find the whole thing tedious."

"I'm sorry, Simon," Tris responded. "But if you didn't matter so much to me, I wouldn't be behaving like this, I suppose. I hadn't thought you would replace me in your affections so quickly."

"I suppose you thought I would swoon with delight the moment you said you wanted me back?" I couldn't keep the bitterness from my voice. I knew him well enough— that's exactly what he *had* thought. Tris had a colossal ego.

At least he had the grace to appear abashed. "I realize I took a number of things for granted, Simon. But I promise you I shall never do that again. Please, forgive me."

By now my fit of pique had begun to wear off, and his contrition, very real as far as I could judge, affected me more strongly than I would have guessed. "It's okay, Tris," I said, my voice gruff. "Let's just forget it for now, okay?"

"Fine," Tris said. He started to rise from his chair, but I waved at him to remain where he was. He sat down again. "What is it, Simon?"

"I need to talk to you about Luke de Montfort," I said. "Or Luc d'Amboise, if you prefer."

"What about him?" Tris held himself very still.

"He told me what you were arguing about," I said. "And he even tried to enlist my aid in persuading you to grant his wish."

"The bloody idiot!"

"Yes," I said, "no doubt he is, in some ways. But why won't you grant his request? Surely it can't matter all that much to you."

"Have you forgotten what it entails for one of us to bring someone across, as it were?" Tris frowned at me.

I thought back to my own experience with Tris. To "bring me across," as he called it, he had had to stop taking his pills for two months and revert to the old ways long enough to be able to drain me almost completely of blood. Then, at the very brink of death, I had drunk from him and become a vampire. The experience had been fairly easy for me, but now that I thought about it, I could understand Tris's reluctance, up to a point.

"Yes," I said. "It's rather uncomfortable for you, and more than a bit messy, but you've done it before."

"I have," Tris said, "but at a considerable cost."

"What do you mean?" I asked, completely puzzled.

Tris looked away from me. "You don't realize, Simon, what it's like, tasting the blood again. You never really became accustomed to it, because you were able to start taking the pills after a couple of days. I, on the other hand, remember all too well what it was like before the pills." He paused for a moment. "It's intoxicating, incredibly pleasurable, even more than the best sex you've ever had. It's addictive, too."

"And you're afraid of that feeling, aren't you?" I asked.

Tris returned his gaze to mine, and his eyes burned with lust. Not lust for me, but for blood. "Yes, Simon, I am," he said simply. "And I don't want to risk it, ever again. You never realized it, but after I brought you across, I had a devilish hard time going back on the pills."

"Tris, I had no idea," I said, feeling suddenly, and horribly, guilty. "And there's no reason you have to give into Luke's demands. Just tell him to piss off."

Tris snorted with laughter. "I tried that, Simon, but you've talked to Luke. You could see how determined he is. I can tell you from past experience, Luke is rarely thwarted from getting what he wants."

"Are you afraid of his attempting to blackmail you?"

"What's to stop him?" Tris said. "He thrives on power, or hadn't you noticed that? That's what this playing at medieval dress-up is all about. Luke fancies himself as a monarch, and being part of that loopy society is all the means to an end. I don't think he's completely rational any longer. He's just as barmy as that fellow Knutson, if you ask me."

"Then what are you going to do to stop him?" I asked. "Short of killing him. And you can't do that."

Tris didn't answer. He simply sat and stared at me. For the first time since I had become a vampire, I was afraid.

Chapter 9

"You can't kill him, Tris," I said, when I could trust my voice not to quaver. "Surely there has to be some other way out of this."

"There is another way," Tris finally spoke. His voice was so dead it chilled me even further, if that were possible. "I could fake my death and disappear, and start over somewhere else. I've done it before."

"That's drastic," I said, wincing as I realized the inanity of what I had said. It wasn't so drastic as killing someone.

Tris laughed, but there was no mirth in the sound. "I confess I have little liking for either option, Simon, but if Luke gives me no choice, I can't answer for what I might do. I like my existence as it is, and I have no wish to jettison it all because I refuse to give in to his wish to become one of us."

"I can't blame you for that, Tris," I said, "but maybe there *is* a way out of this after all." An idea was taking shape in my mind. It just might work.

"What, Simon?" Tris demanded when I fell silent.

"What if you went to Luke and told him that you were willing to fake your death and disappear, rather than give in to his demands?"

"Call his bluff, you mean," Tris said. "I've thought of that, Simon, but you don't know Luke as well as I do. He's vindictive. He would 'out' me just for the hell of it. He'd throw my bluff right back in my face."

"Maybe," I said, unwilling to concede my plan. "Why don't you at least talk to him about it?"

"Simon," Tris said, "if I have to talk to him again, I can't answer for what I might do. But that might be the simplest, most efficient thing to do. Wait until late tonight and visit him. I could be in and out of his pavilion quickly, and no one would be the wiser. I could snap his neck, and he would never know what hit him."

I couldn't believe I was hearing Tris discuss murdering someone so calmly. He was dispassionate, as if he were talking about the weather.

"You wouldn't betray me, Simon, would you?" Tris's eyes bored into mine, and I was transfixed, unable to look away.

"Tris, you can't be serious about this. You can't kill him. I won't let you," I said, desperately wishing I could dissuade him, if he had truly made up his mind to do it.

"My dear Simon," Tris said, "there's really nothing you can do about it. But I haven't decided on my course of action yet. I might try your plan, though I have little faith it will work."

There was no use in my continuing to argue with him about it, I thought. Tris was implacable, and at the moment, I had no idea what I could do to resolve the situation without murder.

"In the meantime," Tris said, "I need to do some research for this asinine film Millbank is making. I'm hoping you have some of the books I need to consult, Simon. That would save me a trip to Cambridge."

How he could switch so easily from talking about murder in one breath to doing research in the next was beyond me. I couldn't afford to let him rattle me, however. "What books do you need, Tris?"

"Books on medieval cookery," he said. "Do you have an edition of Hieatt's *Pleyn Delit* or Henisch's *Fast and Feast*?"

I got up from my chair and faced the wall of books behind

me. I reached up to a shelf near the top and pulled both books down, along with Maggie Black's *Medieval Cookbook* and Madeleine Pelner Cosman's *Fabulous Feasts*. I turned and handed them to Tris.

"Ah, excellent, Simon," Tris said, smiling. He took the books and wandered out of my office. I slumped back in my chair and stared into space.

What on earth was I going to do about Tris and Luke? I could go to Luke myself and try to persuade him that Tris would simply disappear rather than grant Luke's request. I could even go so far as to tell Luke that Tris was willing to kill him if he persisted in his demands and threats. Would Luke back down? Tris seemed to think not.

Based on my experiences today, I would have said that Knutson was the true nut. But if Tris were right, Luke was just as dotty in his way as Knutson. Luke had seemed perfectly reasonable to me, if a bit caught up in playing his role as the Duke of Wessex and pretender to the throne.

I stood up, feeling as if I should do something, anything, and I remembered that I was still wearing the medieval garb I had bought this morning. While the houppelande was actually pretty comfortable, I decided to change into my ordinary working togs. Maybe if I focused on work for a while, the effort at creativity would stimulate ideas to resolve the Tris–Luke situation.

From the smell of pipe smoke wafting about in the hall, I deduced that Tris must be in the kitchen. I hoped he'd stay there for quite some time. Giles was still snoring softly on the sofa as I went upstairs to change.

Once back in my office, I turned on the computer and tried to direct my thoughts to my work in progress. It took a few minutes to get my mind to focus on the task at hand, because visions of Tris standing over Luke's lifeless body kept intruding. By sheer force of will I banished those thoughts and concentrated on my book.

A couple of hours later I was still immersed in my work

when the phone rang. Absentmindedly I reached out a hand for it and picked up the receiver. "Laurel Cottage," I said.

A woman's voice barked into my ear so loudly I almost dropped the receiver. "Is that you, Dr. Kirby-Jones?" Gingerly I held the earpiece away from my head, but I spoke slowly and clearly into the mouthpiece. "Yes, Miss Titchmarsh, it is, and please, call me Simon." I really wished the woman would get herself a hearing aid. It would be an anachronism while she was playing at being the Wife of Bath, but at least it would make communication easier.

"I'd be delighted, Simon. So charmingly American of you. You must call me Totsye. I looked around for you," Totsye said, "for quite some time, then someone told me you had left with Giles. He appeared to be a bit under the weather." She brayed with laughter.

"Er, yes," I said, trying not to wince at the assault on my eardrums. "He had a bit too much sun, so I brought him home to rest and recover."

"Sun, eh?" Totsye laughed again. "That's not what we called it in my day! But I suspect you were just trying to keep Prunella from hyperventilating."

"Ah, yes," I said. "Just out of curiosity, Totsye, where are you calling from?"

"On my mobile," she said. "Many of us have them, just in case. You never know what might happen."

"Certainly," I said, though I had to smile at my sudden mental image of the Wife of Bath chatting away on a mobile phone.

"I'm calling, Simon," she said, "to invite you and Giles to dinner this evening in my pavilion. Seven o'clock. I've spoken with Prunella, and she's coming as well. And bring along that handsome Professor Lovelace if you like. Plenty of good, old-fashioned medieval grub for everyone." She cackled again. "Besides, you need to collect your things."

I had planned to go back sometime that evening to the encampment anyway, so I thought I might as well accept. "Thank you for keeping our things for us, Totsye. Giles and I will certainly be there. I don't know whether Tris will be available, but I'll ask."

"Ask me what?" Tris said from the doorway, his pipe clenched between his teeth and smoking away.

I motioned for him to be quiet, and I concluded my conversation with Totsye Titchmarsh. I set the phone back in its cradle, then explained the invitation to Tris.

He strode forward and dropped the books he had borrowed onto my desk, then sat down in the chair across from me. He removed the pipe from his mouth and said, "Why not? Could be amusing. I haven't seen the fair Prunella in quite some time. Is she still as bloody annoying as ever?"

I felt unaccountably irritated on Lady Prunella's behalf. Yes, she could still certainly be annoying, but Tris's tone was altogether too condescending. My voice was a bit stiff as I replied. "Lady Prunella has her moments, Tris, but actually she's rather a nice old thing, some of the time, anyway."

"I see," Tris said, examining me shrewdly. "You've somehow managed to get her to lower her guard. Don't count her as a loving mother-in-law just yet, Simon. I haven't given up, you know."

I had no answer to that. Tris had spooked me badly over his talk about killing Luke de Montfort, and I had tried not to think about how I felt about him now. Like Scarlett O'Hara, I wanted to think about it tomorrow.

"Speaking of food," I said, wanting to change the subject a bit, "what's with the interest in medieval cookery? I suppose it's something to do with this film you're advising on."

"Yes," Tris said. "Partly that. But Millbank has some other ideas, and he asked my opinion on some of them." He paused to relight his pipe. After he had it going again to his satisfaction, he continued. "What I'm going to tell you, Simon, is strictly *sub rosa* for the moment. Millbank is working on a deal, and he doesn't want it to go public until he's ready."

"Fine," I said, shrugging. "I can't see myself running about, shouting the details of Millbank's business doings to all and sundry."

Tris cocked an eyebrow at me. "You haven't heard what the deal is, Simon."

"Well, what is it?" I said, trying to remain patient. "I won't go bruiting it about, Tris. Either tell me or forget it."

He laughed. "Very well, Simon. I'll tell you. Millbank wants to make this medieval faire a semipermanent installation on his property. He thinks it would bring in a lot of tourist money, particularly in the summer, when so many Americans are visiting England."

"There are a number of such faires in America," I said, "but as far as I know, they only run a few weeks a year. I can't see one being economically viable year-round."

"No," Tris said, "but Millbank isn't proposing that the faire itself run year-round. That would be mostly in the summer. But he does want to build a restaurant, a kind of medieval banqueting hall, and serve medieval food and period-style entertainment. He thinks it would be a big draw in the area."

"It could be," I said, "and the people in the village might welcome some new jobs. But I don't think Lady Prunella and Giles will be too thrilled to have all that going on in their backyard, so to speak."

"I rather doubt there's anything they can do about it," Tris said, exhaling smoke as he talked. "They sold the land to Millbank, and now he can do whatever he likes with it."

"Wouldn't he need planning permission before he could develop this scheme of his?"

Tris laughed. "Millbank is a very shrewd businessman, Simon. He's already approached the members of the planning commission, and he's confident that getting approval won't be a problem."

"Very well," I said, though I was uneasy about keeping this news from Giles and his mother. I knew they would be very unhappy about the scheme. "But what about the members of the G.A.A.? Surely some of the success of this scheme depends on their cooperation?"

"Yes," Tris said. "It does. Tell me, Simon, do you have any idea what it is Luke does when he's not prancing about, pretending to be a medieval nobleman?"

"Haven't a clue," I said, "though I suppose it's some kind of business."

"He's a very successful restaurateur," Tris said. "His family have been in the business for generations."

"And so he's in cahoots with Millbank to bring this all about." I laughed. "It all becomes clear now. I'm sure Harald Knutson would be opposed to the idea if he knew, which is another reason that Luke wants to replace him as king of the G.A.A. Am I right?"

Tris shrugged. "Very likely. Millbank despises Knutson, that I do know. Thinks he's a complete idiot. But Luke has the experience he needs if he's to make his restaurant scheme work."

A loud yawn from behind Tris alerted us to Giles's presence in the room. Waving his hand in front of his face to dissipate some of the pipe smoke Tris was emitting, Giles advanced farther into the room.

"What are you talking about, Simon? What restaurant scheme?" Giles yawned again.

I looked at Tris, and he merely shrugged. I took that as permission to tell Giles what Millbank had planned.

Briefly I outlined the proposed scheme. Giles's face grew increasingly dark as I talked. "Bloody hell!" he said when I had finished. "Just what we need at Blitherington Hall. A bloody restaurant at our back door. Mummy will have a stroke."

"So there is a positive side to it, Giles," Tris drawled, deliberately offensive.

Giles ignored him. "Millbank assured us when we sold him the land that he intended to keep it undeveloped. This is intolerable!"

"I can understand your concern, Giles," I told him, doing my best to calm him a bit, "but you might want to wait and talk with Millbank first, before you get too excited. See exactly what his plans entail, and if you foresee significant problems, talk to him about a compromise."

Giles ran a hand through his hair. "I suppose you're right, Simon, but I had better talk to him before Mummy gets wind of this. Maybe if I go back to the encampment now I might find him." He turned as if to go.

"No," Tris said, "you won't find him there this afternoon. He was off to London for a meeting with one of his partners in the scheme. He won't return until the evening."

"Just as well," I said. "That will give you time to think this over a bit, Giles. Besides, we have an invitation for dinner." I told him about Totsye Titchmarsh's call.

"Very well," Giles said, his face evincing his worry. "Do you have anything for a headache, Simon? My head is pounding." He rubbed the top of his head gingerly. "I had no idea that mead was so powerful."

Trying not to smile, I directed him upstairs to the cabinet in the bathroom.

When he was out of earshot, Tris spoke again. "Don't get his hopes up, Simon," he advised me. "Millbank isn't going to alter his plans a jot just because Giles and his mother raise a fuss. He's a very determined little bugger."

"That will have to sort itself out," I said, dismissing the problem for the moment. I had a deeper concern in mind. "Tris, what are you going to do about Luke? Have you reconsidered my idea?"

Tris stood up. "Don't worry, Simon. I will take care of the situation, and you needn't concern yourself with it any longer." He tapped out his pipe and stuck it in his jacket pocket. "I have an errand to run. I'll meet you at the encampment in time for Miss Titchmarsh's little soiree."

With that, he walked out, and I sat there, staring into space and worrying.

Chapter 10

Giles decided to remain with me at Laurel Cottage until it was time to leave for Totsye Titchmarsh's dinner party. He wanted to delay having to talk to his mother as long as he could. Besides which, he was still feeling the effects of his hangover, despite the dose of aspirin. Between groaning over his aching head and mumbling over the perfidy of Millbank, he was rather miserable company. Finally, in exasperation, I gave him a few bits of research to do and sent him to his office while I attempted to focus once more on writing.

Without Tris in the cottage and with Giles at last occupied by something other than complaints, I applied myself to writing. By the time I emerged from the fifteenth century and the perils of Perdita, my latest heroine, it was after six o'clock. Shutting down the computer with a sigh, I got up and stretched muscles grown stiff from my having sat hunched over the keyboard for so long.

"Giles," I called. "It's time to get ready for dinner."

Hearing no response, I walked out of my office to the next room, which served as Giles's office space. It was actually little more than a glorified closet, but it was large enough for a desk, a computer, and a couple of shelves. Giles was sound asleep and snoring softly, his head cradled in his arms atop the desk.

I reached forward and gently shook him awake. "Giles, wake up," I said. "Time to stir. We need to prepare ourselves for dinner."

Giles sat up and turned around in his chair, rubbing his eyes like a schoolboy. I resisted the impulse to smooth the tousled hair back from his forehead. He smiled warmly at me as he came more fully awake. "What time is it, Simon? I'm sorry I fell asleep. I don't think I got much work done."

"That's quite all right, Giles," I said. "It's a bit after six, and we're supposed to show up for dinner at seven."

Giles glanced down at his rumpled clothing. He groaned. "If I appear looking like this, Mummy will think I went on a bender for sure."

I laughed. "Well, you did, in a way, Giles. Not much of one, but enough for you. Why don't you run up and have a hot shower, and hang your clothes in the bathroom while you do it. The steam will get rid of some of the wrinkles, and you'll feel much better yourself."

Grinning, Giles stood up. "A capital idea, Simon. I could do with a bit of freshening up, and a shower sounds jolly good." He moved past me, then paused at the foot of the stairs, just outside his office door. "I don't suppose you'd care to join me?"

I was sorely tempted, I must admit, but I knew that if I did, things might go too far too fast. Instead, I smiled and said, "Thank you, Giles. Perhaps another time."

He didn't sulk, as once he would have. Instead, he merely grinned again and said, "I'll hold you to that, Simon."

"Be off with you, varlet," I said, and I watched him appreciatively as he moved up the stairs away from me.

I waited until he was safely in the shower with the water running before I too ascended the stairs. In my bedroom I changed back into my medieval clothing. Fully dressed, I surveyed myself critically in the mirror on the inside of one of the wardrobe doors. (Sorry to shatter the illusion, but, yes, we can see ourselves in the mirror. That we can't was just a myth invented by Hollywood.)

Actually, I thought I looked quite dashing in the arcane clothing. The colors flattered my dark complexion, and when I assumed an austere mien, I appeared quite like a medieval nobleman. Then I laughed at myself. It wouldn't do to take this dressing up too seriously. I couldn't envisage myself becoming a regular member of the G.A.A., no matter how good I looked in this outfit.

By the time Giles reappeared downstairs, refreshed and ready to go, it was a few minutes before seven. We would arrive only a bit late. I let Giles drive us through the village, and we parked in the forecourt of Blitherington Hall. The late evening sunshine was still warm as we ambled down to the meadow toward the encampment. The sun wouldn't set until around nine-thirty, but the intensity of the light had lessened, thankfully for me.

The guard posted at the entrance simply waved us through. I supposed he figured if we were dressed appropriately, we had legitimate business here, or else someone—Luke, probably—had put us on the list to be admitted freely.

All around us, the members of the G.A.A. were relaxing after a long day's work. Here and there groups sang as they sat in front of their tents, quaffing beverages that would no doubt make them even merrier as the evening—and the drinking—wore on. As Giles and I turned down the lane leading to Totsye Titchmarsh's pavilion, an ill-mannered brute brushed hard against Giles. He glared at Giles as if it were his fault, then stomped off.

The rag-mannered ruffian was none other than Sir Reginald Bolingbroke, erstwhile pretender to the throne. I resisted the urge to call after him. "Bloody idiot!" Giles said, rubbing his arm.

"Yes," I said. "I wonder what put him in such a foul mood." We continued our progress down the lane.

As we reached Totsye's pavilion, Harald Knutson barreled out, straight into me. Close on his heels was one of his henchman, the one called Guillaume. Knutson glowered at me. "Get out of my bloody way," he barked.

"Why don't you watch where you're going, you prat." Giles was angry now and spoiling for a fight.

Knutson paid no attention and strode off down the lane, his companion right behind him.

"What is wrong with these people?" Giles shook his head.

"Perhaps they equate living in the Middle Ages to acting in a boorish manner," I said. "After you, young sir." Giles grinned and stepped into the pavilion.

Inside stood a large table, set to accommodate eight and lit with candles. Totsye was scurrying about, setting pewter cups at each place. A young woman dressed as a servant was carefully placing what looked like pastries at each place.

"Good evening, Dame Alysoun," I said loudly, and Totsye paused in her work to beam a smile of greeting upon us. She set the last cup at one end of the table and came forward with outstretched hands.

"Good evening, gentlemen," she said. "I am delighted that you could join us tonight."

"Thank you for inviting us," Giles said, doffing his hat and bowing.

She tittered with delight as she curtsied in return.

"Your mother will be most impressed, Sir Giles," she said, a little breathless from merriment.

"Has my mother arrived yet?" Giles asked.

"Oh, yes," Totsye said. "She's here, in the other chamber of the tent. She'll be out in a moment." She turned to check on her serving girl and nodded her approval. The girl curtsied, then disappeared into the back of the tent.

I turned to grin at Giles. Evidently Totsye had prevailed upon her old school chum to dress up, too. The thought of Lady Prunella garbed as a medieval lady amused us both.

"We ran into the king as we arrived," I said. "He seemed to be in quite a hurry."

Totsye snorted. "I should think so. I put a flea in his ear. As if I would switch allegiances, especially after he accused me of attacking him earlier today. He's quite deluded, poor man." Then she smiled. "I seem to be quite popular tonight. Not only

Harald, but poor Reggie Bolingbroke as well, one right after the other. Both petitioning me. I must have more influence than I thought."

Evidently Totsye had sent Reggie away with his own flea, which explained his ill humor. Such drama!

While we waited for Lady Prunella to appear, I stepped forward to examine ornate cards laid at each place at the table. I picked one up, because the writing was too cramped to read without holding the card closer.

Adele de Montfort's name was inscribed across the top of the card, in spiky calligraphy. Below the name was tonight's menu. I frowned as I read. This would be a rich meal, and I would have to nibble carefully. It doesn't take much food for a vampire to feel stuffed, and I would have to take care not to offend my hostess. Tonight we would be offered:

LAMB STEW
BRAISED SPRING GREENS
MUSHROOM PASTIES
HADDOCK IN TASTY SAUCE
FRIED FIG PASTRIES
ALMOND MILK
MEAD

"Quite an impressive menu, Dame Alysoun," I commented, setting the card back in its place. "You must have been working all afternoon to prepare such a feast." At each place was a small dish of pastries, two each per person. The fried fig pastries, I cleverly deduced.

"I'm very fond of cooking," Totsye said, smiling, "but I can't claim credit for having prepared everything for tonight's festivities. I must confess that I ordered some of the dishes from one of the best cooks in our society."

"Let me guess," Giles said, frowning a bit. "The person who cooked this is no doubt someone who would be working in the restaurant that Millbank is planning to build here."

"Why, yes, very possibly," Totsye said, startled. "But how did you know about that?"

"I'm afraid the secret is out, Dame Alysoun," I said. "Professor Lovelace let it slip earlier today when we were chatting. You'll find that Lady Prunella and Sir Giles are not keen on having a restaurant in their back garden, as it were."

Totsye's face mirrored her considerable distress at this news. She held out a hand impulsively to Giles. "My dear boy, I had no idea you would find the plan so repugnant." She frowned. "In fact, I would swear that Murdo Millbank told me you and dear Prunella had been apprised of the plan and were not in the least bothered by it."

"Then Millbank has misled you completely," Giles said, taking her hand and patting it.

"Oh, dear, oh, dear," she said. "Prunella will never speak to me again."

That was of course the cue for Lady Prunella's entrance.

"Why shouldn't I speak to you, Totsye dear?" Lady Prunella trumpeted. "Good evening, Giles, Simon. My, how positively *medieval* you both look tonight."

"And you as well, Lady Prunella," I said, sweeping forward into an extravagant bow. She giggled and grasped the skirts of her substantial houppelande in her hands and almost pranced about with glee. She was like a giddy schoolgirl going to her first grown-up party.

"Mother, you do look lovely tonight," Giles said. "Your dress is most becoming." This was no mere filial flattery, I noted. The deep claret of the houppelande, trimmed with black silk, highlighted the vivid coloring in Lady Prunella's hair and cheeks. A simple headdress complemented her robe, and she could easily have taken her place at the royal court.

"Thank you, dear boy," she said. "How handsome you both look. And what a handsome *couple*." She tittered.

I glanced at Giles, who turned an innocent gaze to meet mine. What *had* he been telling his mother?

"Certes, milady, you do us both great honor," I said, offering her another bow.

Once she had recovered from her merriment, Lady Prunella turned once more to Totsye. "Totsye, my dear, why *shouldn't* I speak to you? Have you done something *naughty?*"

Totsye twitched about, refusing to meet Lady Prunella's eye. "Now, *Prunie,*" she said, and Giles and I avoided looking at each other, "please don't be angry with me. It's none of my doing, I assure you, and had I known the truth about how you feel, I would never have encouraged the idea."

"What idea?" Lady Prunella said, all trace of amusement gone. She had assumed her fiercest lady-of-the-manor glare, and Totsye withered from it.

Giles laid a warning hand on his mother's arm. "Now, Mummy, do think of your blood pressure. It won't do to upset yourself." He paused for a long breath, and Lady Prunella made a visible effort to calm herself. Giles continued, "Murdo Millbank is planning to build a restaurant here, a sort of medieval banqueting hall."

Lady Prunella blinked rapidly as her mind struggled to cope with the news. Finally she found her voice again. "That's outrageous! A *commercial* establishment in our back garden. Preposterous! What is the man thinking?"

"Oh, Prunie, I'm sorry," Totsye wailed.

"Nonsense, Totsye," Lady Prunella replied. "It's not your fault that that vulgar *businessman* wants to destroy our peace and quiet."

"I beg your pardon," came a huffy voice from behind us.

We all turned to behold Murdo Millbank, simply dressed in a peasant's tunic and cap. I was mildly surprised, for I would have expected him to choose something more ornate and lordly.

Before anyone could respond to him, Luke and Adele de Montfort arrived, and Millbank stepped aside to allow them entrance to the pavilion. The siblings sported extravagant, richly colored garments suitable for the most important of state occasions, making the rest of us feel sadly underdressed.

"Good evening, everyone," Luke said, echoed by his sister.

"Good evening, Your Grace," Totsye said, dipping into a curtsey. Lady Prunella stared at him, open-mouthed. He did cut an imposing figure, not to say a very handsome one. Lady P was ever one to appreciate a handsome man, and evidently she had not laid eyes on the would-be king before now.

Giles watched his mother in amusement, then before the pause could grow more awkward, he stepped forward to introduce her to the duke and his sister.

Lady Prunella, the complete snob, could not resist a duke, even a make-believe one, and simpered accordingly as Luke clasped her hand. Her curtsey was so deep she almost went on down to the ground, but Luke held on to her hand as she righted herself, blushing mightily.

Millbank had waited impatiently until the social niceties were observed. Now he pushed himself forward. "What were you saying as I arrived, Lady Prunella?"

"You *common* little man," she said, all thoughts of flirting with the duke pushed out her head by her anger, "how *dare* you spoil the area around my home with your *vulgar* commercial enterprise. It's bad enough having *hundreds* of people capering about, attracting all sorts of *undesirable* elements, but the thought of a *business* in my back garden! It's insupportable."

Millbank had taken a step backward, as if to shield himself from Lady Prunella's verbal assault, but he found his voice again. "Now just a bloody minute!"

Luke de Montfort stepped between them, his face dark with anger. "Millbank, I cannot believe you lied to me. You told me your scheme had the complete approval of the landowners here. God's blood, man, why did you lie to me?"

"My, my, what a dramatic little gathering this is." The cool amusement in the newcomer's voice startled everyone. Tristan Lovelace, dressed in the black robes of a Benedictine monk, strode forward into the pavilion. Though he had not had himself tonsured to complete the effect, Tris made an imposing figure as a monk.

Several voices rose at once, and the resulting din made my head ache. Lady Prunella was screeching at Millbank, and Luke added his voice to her complaints. Millbank, beleaguered on two sides, tried to compensate by raising his voice to drown out both of theirs. Adele de Montfort clutched her brother's arm, babbling away, as if she feared he would strike someone. Indeed, he did appear angry enough to do violence to someone.

I looked at Tris, a question in my eyes. He nodded and held up three fingers. On the count of three, we thundered in unison. "Quiet!"

Our combined voices were so loud I swear the table rattled, but we achieved the desired effect. The quarreling ceased.

"That's better," I said. "None of you will solve anything by this screaming at one another. Either you all sit down to dinner and behave in a civilized fashion, or take it elsewhere." I took turns glaring at Millbank, de Montfort, and Lady Prunella. Even Luke quailed slightly at the scowl on my face.

Totsye stepped forward and in a quivering voice asked everyone to be seated. Wonder of wonders, no one left. All the combatants meekly found their places and sat down. Totsye dithered about the table, pouring mead for everyone. She held a cup up at an angle, then tilted the pitcher to fill the cup. She called out for someone named Adelisa as she worked her way around the table, but there was no response.

"Where can that girl be?" Having finished pouring the mead, Totsye went to the door of the pavilion and peered out. "Well, drat the girl, she's disappeared."

"Who could blame her?" Tris said to me in an undertone. "She probably heard all the yelling and decided she wanted nothing to do with this farce."

I nodded to Tris but got up from my place next to him and went to Totsye, standing indecisively in the opening of the tent.

"We shall have to serve ourselves," Totsye said, turning to me with a frown. "That girl! I suppose she was frightened."

"No doubt," I said, "but it's no matter. We're perfectly capable of serving ourselves. Where is the food?"

"The dratted girl was supposed to deliver it with the help of a couple of men, but they're nowhere in sight." She wrung her hands. "Oh, dear, what shall we do?"

I was just about to offer to go in search of the missing food, when a scream from behind us startled us both.

Adele de Montfort was on her feet, staring down in horror at her brother, writhing on the ground. "Luke! Oh my God, somebody help him!"

Chapter 11

Everyone stared at the stricken man clutching his stomach as he twisted and turned on the ground. He wheezed and gasped for breath.

His sister continued to scream, until we all snapped out of our shock and began moving in to help. Lady Prunella and Totsye took hold of Adele and moved her out of the way. Tris got down on his knees beside Luke and attempted to help him, but Luke kept twisting and turning, then he vomited. Tris jerked aside barely in time to avoid getting splattered.

"He's been poisoned," I said to Giles and Murdo Millbank. "Is there a doctor anywhere in the camp?" I raised my voice, and Totsye heard me.

"Yes," she said. "I'll get her at once." She pushed Adele into Lady Prunella's arms and darted through us and out of the tent.

"Tell her he's been poisoned," I moved quickly to the opening to call after her. She raised a hand and waved to acknowledge me as she bustled away.

"Giles, help your mother," I said, coming back to the table. "Millbank, do you have a mobile with you?" He stared at me uncomprehendingly for a moment, then nodded. "Call for an ambulance, then," I snapped at him. He pulled out his phone and punched in the numbers.

I joined Tris on the ground with Luke. He had ceased writhing and now lay still, except for his labored breathing. I felt completely helpless. "What do you think, Tris?"

Tris stared bleakly down at his former protégé. "He was poisoned," Tris said, "and I'd be willing to bet it was digitalis. I've seen it before." Something in his expression warned me not to question his knowledge. I shivered.

"What can we do for him?" I asked.

"Not much," Tris said. "We need to try to keep him breathing, keep his throat from becoming constricted. He's already vomited a bit, at least. We can't do much without a doctor. If she doesn't have some potassium chloride or some form of atropine, I don't know if he can survive long enough for us to get him to a hospital."

Tris and I tended Luke as best we could while we waited for help to arrive. Tris held Luke gently while Luke vomited up what looked like the remains of one of the fried fig pastries Totsye had set at each place. Not a pleasant sight, but it did give me pause for thought. Frowning, I got up and looked at the table.

I quickly found Luke's place at the table, and there was just one complete pastry on his plate. He had eaten one, then been overcome. How could the fig pastry have been poisoned? Were both of the pastries on his plate poisoned?

Before I could contemplate the question any further, a tall, very young woman dressed in simple robes came running into the tent, toting a hefty Gladstone bag. The doctor had arrived. Breathing heavily from exertion, Totsye came in almost on the doctor's heels.

The doctor, who seemed barely old enough to have qualified, knelt beside Luke and commenced examining him, checking his vital signs, while Tris tersely explained his theory about digitalis poisoning. The doctor listened to his heart beat, then checked his pulse. She opened her bag and rummaged until she found a small bottle of some solution and a needle. Without being prompted, Tris held one of Luke's arms and pulled the sleeve of his gown up to give the doctor access to a vein.

The injection ready, the doctor stuck the needle into Luke's arm. We all watched in horrified fascination. Would what the doctor just injected help Luke? Was it some kind of antidote?

"An ambulance is on the way," Murdo Millbank announced into the tense silence.

Adele de Montfort broke out into fresh, loud sobs, and Totsye and Lady Prunella tried to comfort her. The doctor watched her patient, who had grown very still. Tris looked up, and I met his eyes. They held no hope for Luke's recovery. Tris bent his head again, and I speculated. Was this his doing? Had Tris poisoned Luke?

Tris seemed awfully certain about the poison. How did he know so much about poisons? He seemed to know more than the doctor, at least. Had he used poison in the past to rid himself of someone causing a problem like the one Luke had posed?

No, surely Tris wasn't the poisoner.

If not Tris, who? Was it someone in the tent with us now? I concentrated and tried to get a reading on the various emotions emanating from the people around me. I could feel fear and horror, and even pity, but from nowhere could I get any sense of satisfaction, no feeling that someone here was happy over what had occurred.

That made me nervous. Surely, if one of the persons in this tent had brought this about, he or she would be feeling quite happy over Luke's condition. But if it were Tris, then I wouldn't be able to read him. Another vampire could successfully hide his emotions from me, unlike the humans around us. Unless they were extraordinarily skilled at hiding their feelings.

Uneasy, I stared at Tris. For a moment, he held my gaze, and I had the strangest feeling he was assessing me. Surely he couldn't think that I had poisoned Luke. The idea was ludicrous.

I had never seen Tris look at me like that. Perhaps he thought I had poisoned Luke to protect him from Luke's blackmail scheme.

No, that was too absurd. Even with his colossal ego, Tris couldn't think I would kill someone for him, at least not for such a reason. He knew me better than that.

We all became aware of commotion outside the tent. Eager for something to do, I moved to the doorway and looked out. A crowd had gathered, and the babble of excited voices was growing louder by the moment. I was just about to shush them when Harald Knutson pushed through the crowd to stand in front of me.

"What the devil is going on in there?"

"Luke de Montfort has been taken ill," I said, choosing my words carefully. I didn't want to cause any kind of panic or start rumors flying just yet. Time enough for that later. I raised my voice. "The doctor is with him, and an ambulance has been called."

In an undertone, I continued, "Come on, man, use whatever authority you have, and get these people to disperse. They're not doing anyone a bit of good milling about like this."

Knutson stared at me as if he would object to my giving him orders, but then he turned to face the crowd around us. He held his hands up, and quickly the throng fell silent. "Everyone, please go back to what you were doing. The Duke of Wessex has fallen ill. All is well in hand here, and we need to make room for the emergency team."

Almost upon the words, we heard the ululation of the siren as it approached. Knutson continued to exhort the excited crowd, and slowly they began to trickle away.

I stepped back inside and moved to stand near Tris and Luke, still recumbent on the ground. Eyeing him critically, I could see that he was still breathing, shallowly. The doctor watched him with considerable anxiety. No one else in the room moved or said a word as we waited for the emergency personnel to arrive.

Time seemed to hang suspended, but it really was perhaps only two minutes later that the cavalry arrived. Everyone except Tris and the doctor left the tent, to give the EMTs plenty of room to work. A tense silence had fallen over the area immediately around Totsye's pavilion as we waited.

Moving quickly and efficiently, the EMTs brought Luke out on a stretcher. One of them held an IV bag, and the doctor from the encampment scurried along with them as they moved the patient through the grounds. Adele de Montfort, still sniveling, went with them, and the doctor reached out a comforting arm to her as they disappeared through the tents. A couple of minutes later, we heard the siren once more as the ambulance began the journey to the nearest casualty center in Bedford.

"Did anyone call the police?" I asked, turning to Millbank.

He blinked at me. "When I called, I told them it was suspected that the poisoning was deliberate. The operator said he would inform the local constabulary."

That meant my friend Detective Inspector Robin Chase would likely get the call, unless he were off duty. I hoped that Robin did come, because I respected his intelligence and professionalism. I also appreciated his willingness to listen to my ideas and to accept my assistance. He might take exception, however, to finding me at the scene of yet another potential murder.

"You did this!" The screech of Totsye Titchmarsh's accusation startled all of us. I turned to see to whom it was directed.

Totsye had advanced upon Harald Knutson, who was standing just inside the doorway of the tent. He stepped back against the canvas to the side of the opening in reaction to Totsye's onslaught. "Did what? What are you talking about, you harridan?"

Totsye got right up in his face and shook a finger at him. "You poisoned Luke, that's what you did! You knew he was going to defeat you, and you took the coward's way out."

A slap rang out, and Knutson slumped hard against the side of the pavilion. For a moment I feared he might pull the whole thing down on top of us all, but he righted himself quickly.

The pavilion shivered from the impact but otherwise remained sturdy.

"You're a lunatic, Totsye," Knutson said, rubbing his cheek. "I did not poison Luke, and I'll see you in court if you persist in such irresponsible talk."

"It's exactly the kind of cowardly thing you would do," Totsye said, her anger undiminished. "Sneaky, underhanded, devious. Coward!"

"Don't be ridiculous, woman," Knutson said, raising his voice. "And just how would I have poisoned Luke? It was *your* tent he was dining in, not mine. How do we know that *you* didn't poison him yourself? Who had a better opportunity to do it than you?"

"That's utterly ridiculous," Totsye sputtered back at him. "Everyone knows in what high regard I hold Luke. Why should I want to poison him?"

"High regard," Knutson said in a sneering tone. "That's a laugh, that is! You're besotted with the man, that's what you are. But you don't have the sense to know that he's never going to return the feeling. He's a ponce, for god's sake. He doesn't like women!" He hooted with laughter. "You're a laughingstock, because you keep chasing after a man who'd never want you in a million years. I daresay you finally got fed up and decided to do away with him. He turned you down one too many times, didn't he?"

Totsye had grown increasingly pale as she stood before Knutson, listening to his venomous attack. "That's not true," she said feebly. "It's not true. It's not!"

Sobbing now, she turned away, and Murdo Millbank was there, surprisingly, offering her his shoulder. He tucked an arm protectively around her and patted her awkwardly with his other hand. She cried so hard his robe would be soaked in no time.

"You're a prat, Knutson," Millbank said in fierce tones. "I had no idea just what a wanker you are, but now I see with me own eyes just what everyone else has been telling me."

"Correct me if I'm wrong, Knutson," I said, stepping forward, "but weren't you and one of your henchman here in this very tent, speaking with Totsye, when Giles and I arrived earlier this evening?"

He looked blankly at me.

"Surely you remember," I said. "The two of you almost knocked me and Giles down, you were in such haste to leave."

"What of it?" Knutson replied, his eyes narrowing in suspicion.

"I'm just saying that you, or your lackey perhaps, did indeed have an opportunity to poison the duke."

"Ridiculous! I did no such thing, nor did Guillaume."

"I didn't say you actually did it, Knutson. I merely observed that you had the opportunity." I smiled at him. "And I'm certain that the police will be following up on that when they investigate."

"Yes, we will," observed a cool voice from the opening of the tent. Detective Inspector Robin Chase stepped into view, and behind him I could see several other police personnel.

"Good evening, everyone," Robin said as he moved further inside the tent. "Professor Kirby-Jones. How unusual to find you here."

"Evening, Detective Inspector," I said. No doubt the others around me heard the irony in Robin's voice as he greeted me, but that didn't bother me one whit.

"I'm afraid I must ask you all to vacate this tent," Robin continued. "In situations such as this, we must investigate, and we'll need to secure the scene of the unfortunate event."

Two of his men held open the tent flaps, and slowly the entire dinner party, plus Knutson, moved outside. Robin addressed us again once we were outside. "Please remain nearby for the moment. I shall need to speak with each of you, and I will endeavor to do so in as timely a manner as possible."

Without waiting for our assent, Robin turned back into the tent. Moments later, in the quiet around us, I could hear the chirping of a mobile phone. Robin answered and spoke in low tones, so low that even I couldn't make out his words.

Robin now came to the door of the tent. He regarded us solemnly. "I regret to inform you that Mister d'Amboise has died."

Making a small sound of distress, Totsye Titchmarsh slipped from the shelter of Murdo Millbank's arms and crumpled on the ground in a faint.

Chapter 12

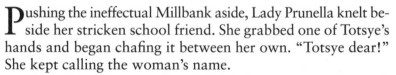

Pushing the ineffectual Millbank aside, Lady Prunella knelt beside her stricken school friend. She grabbed one of Totsye's hands and began chafing it between her own. "Totsye dear!" She kept calling the woman's name.

After a minute or so, Totsye slowly began to come around. "What happened?" she inquired in a weak voice. As I watched, I could see the memory of what had caused her to faint come back to her. Lady Prunella and Millbank helped her to her feet, and she leaned heavily on Lady Prunella.

"Oh, dear, what shall I do?" Totsye said, looking piteously about her.

"There's nothing to do, Totsye dear," Lady Prunella assured her kindly. "We must find you a place to rest. You have had quite a shock, my dear."

"Oh, yes," Totsye replied, almost whispering. "Poor, dear Luke. Whatever shall I do?"

She was acting more like a bereaved spouse than a friend. Had she really deluded herself to that extent? Had she truly believed that Luke returned her feelings?

Across the way, a woman called out, "Please bring the poor dear in here. I've a place for her to rest."

Lady Prunella and Totsye hobbled gratefully into the tent, away from the prying eyes of the encampment. The crowd had gathered again, but they were quiet, perhaps in respect for the fallen Duke of Wessex. Judging from their faces, I figured the news had spread rapidly through the encampment.

Many eyes were fixed on the king, and I wondered whether he would make some sort of announcement, now that official word had come of Luke's death. As I watched, Knutson opened his mouth to speak, but Robin Chase interrupted him before he could utter a word.

"Ladies and gentlemen," Robin said, projecting his voice to reach all those now gathered around Totsye's pavilion, "I regret to inform you that a tragic accident has occurred. Mr. Luc d'Amboise has died, and since the circumstances of his death are somewhat uncertain, we must investigate." Robin went on to introduce himself and his men, then concluded with, "We will endeavor to disrupt your proceedings as little as possible, but I would remind you that we will need to gather information, and your cooperation will be greatly appreciated."

There arose quite a bit of murmuring at the end of Robin's speech, and Robin once again raised his voice. "Ladies and gentlemen, for now you can assist us by going back to what you were doing. As we need information we will come to you. At the moment, I will ask only those who were present at the dinner party to remain here." He asked the guests to join Lady Prunella and Totsye in the neighbor's tent, and everyone but me complied with his request. Giles cast me an interrogative look, but I winked. Shaking his head, he followed Tris into the tent. I turned back to watch.

Slowly the crowd dispersed, and Harald Knutson tried to sidle away with them. "Oh, no, buddy boy, you're not going anywhere," I said to him in an undertone as I strode forward to grab his arm.

He turned to glare at me and attempted to shake his arm loose from my grip, but when I tightened my hand, he whimpered. "I think you should stay and talk to the nice policeman, Your Majesty."

I dragged a protesting Knutson none too gracefully toward

the front of Totsye's pavilion, where Robin Chase regarded me with an unreadable expression in his eyes.

"Assisting the police with their inquiries again, Dr. Kirby-Jones?" he asked. His question lacked its usual irony.

I eyed him warily. "Just trying to do my civic duty, Detective Inspector. Surely you would expect no less of me."

Knutson mewled in distress, and I let go of his arm. He stood there rubbing it, shooting daggers at me with his eyes. I ignored him after one glance to assure myself that he wasn't trying to sneak away again.

"I think you will find it helpful to question the king, Detective Inspector," I said, relishing the expression of incredulity on Robin's face.

"King of what, might I ask?" Robin said, his eyes moving back and forth between Knutson and me.

"I am the duly appointed monarch of this realm, Detective Inspector." Knutson had drawn himself up to his full height and did his best to appear regal, but he couldn't quite pull it off. The fear evident in his face quite ruined the effect.

"And what realm is this, Your Majesty?" Robin said, with nary a flicker of an eyelid.

Knutson launched into a rambling explanation of the G.A.A. Robin's eyes quickly glazed over, and he held up a hand to stem the flow of Knutson's babbling. "I think I get the picture now," Robin said. "Could you explain to me then why Dr. Kirby-Jones insisted that you remain here? Were you not one of the guests at the dinner party?"

Sniffing angrily, Knutson replied, "No, I was not. I know nothing of what happened to the late Duke of Wessex, nor do I particularly care. The man was pestilence personified, and if anyone asks me, I'll say he's no great loss."

"Is that so?" Robin asked. "Perhaps you would care to tell me, Your Majesty, *why* you disliked the deceased so much?"

Belatedly, Knutson realized the hole he had just dug for himself. "Detective Inspector, you mustn't misunderstand. I didn't like the man, but I would never do anything to harm a rival. I had no need."

"Rival?" Robin asked.

Really, the man was a fool. No wonder the late duke had been so impatient to wrest the kingship away from him.

"Would you care to explain what you meant by 'rival,' Your Majesty?" Robin spoke a bit sharply when Knutson failed to respond to his first question.

Blinking rapidly, Knutson hastened to explain. "Mine is an elected position, Detective Inspector. The Duke of Wessex intended to challenge me for the kingship, but I had no reason to fear a challenge from him. He wasn't nearly as well liked as he wanted to think, I can assure you of that!"

"Really," Robin said. "Were there others who despised him as much as you seem to have, Your Majesty?"

Knutson goggled at Robin. He hemmed and hawed for a few moments but was able to produce only one name. "Reggie Bolingbroke, Sir Reginald, that is. He hated Luke, really hated him."

I distrusted Knutson's surge of relief at naming his other rival for the kingship. Was he telling the truth, or merely trying to divert suspicion from himself? Then I recalled my own meeting with Sir Reggie. Knutson might not be lying after all.

"Reggie hated Luke," Knutson said. "Anyone can tell you that, Detective Inspector, I assure you. Reggie is a raging homophobe, and Luke made little secret of his, um, his proclivities." Knutson pronounced the word as if it were a profanity. I figured ol' Reggie wasn't the only homophobe in camp. "If you ask me," Knutson's tone grew more confidential, "Reggie is hiding something. Don't they say that the men who are the most homophobic are the ones who are denying their own tendencies?"

Robin did not respond to that last query. "I shall speak to this Sir Reginald Bolingbroke later. But now, if I might return to a previous point. Why, Your Majesty, was Dr. Kirby-Jones so insistent that you should remain for questioning? Other than your position, of course."

When Knutson failed to answer, I could control my exasperation no longer. "Because, Detective Inspector, Knutson was in the tent this evening, just before we all arrived for the dinner party."

"I see," Robin said. "I think that will be all for now, Your Majesty. I shall no doubt have further questions for you, after I know more about what occurred here this evening."

"Certainly, Detective Inspector," Knutson said with patent relief. "Anyone can direct you to the royal pavilion. Simply ask." He almost scampered away.

Robin stood staring after him, a bemused expression on his face. Then he turned to me. "These people are really serious about this stuff, aren't they?"

"Apparently deadly so," I said.

Robin ignored my attempt at a bit of black humor. "What's your take on it, Simon? Accident or murder?"

I shrugged. "It could be an accident, but somehow I doubt it. There's a lot of animosity here among the rival factions for the kingship, and I think the late duke's chances of being elected were pretty strong. Maybe someone decided to put him permanently out of the running."

"The present king certainly made little secret that he was glad his rival was out of the way."

"He certainly did," I said, chuckling a bit. "King Harald is a bit dim, isn't he? He handed you a motive, clear as day."

"One that I would quickly have heard from other sources, no doubt."

"That's true," I conceded. "So perhaps it was a pre-emptive strike. If so, that means Harald is brighter than I give him credit for. But somehow, I don't fancy he's all that good at chess."

Robin allowed a small smile. "Now, Simon, tell me what happened in there." He gestured toward Totsye's pavilion. I could see his crew at work inside. There was yet a good hour and a half until sunset, and the soft evening light lingered.

I glanced over my shoulder to espy Tris and Giles standing at the opening of the tent belonging to Totsye's solicitous neighbor across the way. Tris could hear every word I said to

Robin because of his acute vampire hearing, but Giles was having a harder time of it. I flashed them both a quick grin. Giles rolled his eyes in response, but Tris remained impassive. I wished I could read him. Perhaps then I could dismiss my suspicions of him.

Turning my back on Giles and Tris, I stepped closer to the opening of Totsye's tent, forcing Robin to follow me. He laid a hand on my arm to stop me from entering, then withdrew the hand quickly, as if he had been burned by the touch.

Under my quizzical gaze, Robin flushed slightly. He stroked his moustache, a nervous tic of his that seemed to occur whenever he was around me for very long.

Taking pity on Robin's discomfiture, I ignored it and launched into a summary of the evening's events. I took care to include a description of the behavior of King Harald and his henchman, Guillaume.

Robin studied the ground carefully and continued stroking his upper lip while I spoke. When I had finished, he finally looked me in the face. "There seems little doubt that he was poisoned, and by your description, I would say that whatever it was, it was in one of those fig pastries."

"Yes," I said. "There were two of those pastries at each place, and one of them was gone from Luke's plate. When he vomited, it was obvious that he had recently eaten a fig pastry. Ergo, the poison was probably in the pastry."

"There was still one whole pastry at his place?" Robin asked.

"There was, when I looked right after Luke was taken ill."

"Please stay here for a moment, Simon," Robin said before striding inside the tent.

Trying not to appear too obvious, I looked into the tent, trying to see the top of the table. Robin and one of his crew, however, blocked my view. Frustrated, I turned instead to see what Giles and Tris were doing.

I almost did a double-take. Tris and Giles were standing close together, and Tris had one hand resting in a proprietary manner on Giles's neck. As I watched, Tris stroked the side of Giles's face with his thumb. It was an intimate gesture, one that infuriated me. What the hell was Tris playing at?

More to the point, what was Giles doing flirting so blatantly with Tris?

I was all set to charge across to the other tent and demand to know what the hell was going on when Robin spoke at my side.

"Simon," he said, "I need you to look at something."

"What?" I said, bewildered. "What do you want?"

"Is something wrong, Simon?" Robin asked, concerned. Then he looked past me, and his eyes widened. "Uh, Simon, I really need you to look at something."

Turning my back on Giles and Tris, trying to quell my flare of temper, I said, "What is it, Robin?"

"It's important, Simon," Robin said, responding to the tone of my voice. "Step inside the tent here and have a recce at the dinner table."

Now curious, trying to push aside thoughts of what was going on behind my back, literally and figuratively, I moved closer to the table.

I frowned. Something was different. What was it?

Then I had it. The plate at Luke de Montfort's place was empty. What had happened to the second pastry I had seen there earlier?

Chapter 13

I scanned the table once more to be sure, but at Luke's place there was not a single fig pastry. Every other place had two, though some of them had a bite or two missing. I shut my eyes and concentrated on the table as it had been after Luke became ill. I was certain that there had been one pastry, and I was certain also that no one had, in the interim, switched the place cards.

During my rapid cogitations, Robin had waited patiently. "What is it, Simon? What is different?"

I pointed to Luke's place. "When I examined the table after Luke became ill, there was one *whole* fig pastry at his place. Now there is none." Anticipating Robin's next question, I continued, "And, no, the place cards have not been switched. I am positive of that."

"What is the point of taking a pastry away?" Robin asked in a tone indicating he was thinking aloud.

"Someone is playing a twisted little game here," I said. "I'm not certain exactly what, but for some reason, the murderer didn't want you to have the second pastry. When it was taken, I don't know, it could have been any time after Luke collapsed, but you'll have to ask whether anyone noticed anything."

Robin nodded. "Sounds plausible. Now we'll have to search

for the second pastry, or traces of it." He called one of his men over and issued some instructions.

"Now, Simon," he said, "you realize this is just a formality, of course, but would you mind letting one of my men search you?"

I thought about it for a moment. After all we had been through together, surely Robin didn't consider me a suspect? No, I reasoned, he probably didn't, but he couldn't afford to neglect any possibilities.

"No, Robin, of course not. Anything to help, as I always say." I grinned at him. "But why don't you perform the search?"

His cheeks grew the slightest bit red. "I think that is a task better left to one of my men, Simon." He called a name, and after a moment, one of his staff, a grizzled veteran, came from the back of the tent.

I waited patiently while my examiner patted me down. At least Robin had let the tent flap down, so no one outside was treated to the sight of me being frisked.

After a thorough search, which included a close look at my hands, the policeman reported to Robin that I was clean. Robin thanked him and sent him back to his previous task. He opened the tent flap again, for which I was thankful. The atmosphere inside the tent was oppressive.

"Now that that is out of the way, Robin, what's next?"

"I will continue pursuing my inquiries, Simon, as you know very well. One of the priorities will be to determine how the poison was administered." He shook his head. "Nasty business, poison."

"Yes, poison is a devious means of killing someone, don't you think? Surely the postmortem will reveal something about how long the digitalis had been in his system before causing that collapse."

As soon as the words were out of my mouth, I realized I had erred. Robin didn't miss a beat when he asked, "And just how do *you* know it was digitalis, Simon? If indeed it was."

A curse word of supposedly Anglo-Saxon origin came to

mind, but I was too genteel to utter it aloud, particularly in the presence of a police officer. Instead I smiled as sweetly as I could at Robin. He blinked. "I don't *really* know that it was digitalis, Robin. But it certainly seems plausible, given Luke's symptoms, don't you think?"

Should I grass on Tris to Robin? If I didn't mention it now, surely someone else would. Oh, what the heck. "Actually, Robin, it was Tristan Lovelace who first mentioned digitalis."

Robin wasn't taken in by my feigned innocence. "And just what does Professor Lovelace know about digitalis poisoning? I thought he was an historian specializing in the medieval period, like you." When I didn't reply immediately, Robin went on, "Do both of you make a habit of studying poisons, Simon? Does Professor Lovelace also stumble over dead bodies as frequently as you?"

"You'll have to ask Professor Lovelace that for yourself, Robin," I replied in frosty tones. Really, the man was being unnecessarily sarcastic, I thought. "He was the one who mentioned that Luke's symptoms were like those brought on by digitalis poisoning."

"I certainly will ask him about that, Simon," Robin said. "In fact, if I can peel him away from young Blitherington, I'll ask him right now."

Robin had been facing the opening of the tent, and I had momentarily forgotten the flirtation I had witnessed minutes earlier between Tris and Giles. Robin's rather catty remark brought the memory, and my anger, flooding back. I whirled around, and, sure enough, Tris and Giles were still standing there, much too close together.

I marched out of the tent and over to them. I tapped Tris on the arm. Actually, I thumped him, but to him it felt no more than a tap. "Yes, Simon, what is it?" Tris drawled at me without taking his eyes from Giles's face.

I poked him again. "Detective Inspector Chase wishes to speak to you, Tris, if you can tear yourself away from this tawdry little scene you're enacting. Now!"

From behind me came the sound of a clearing throat.

"Professor Lovelace, I would like to speak to you for a few minutes, if you don't mind."

Tris took his hand away from Giles's neck and turned to regard both Robin and me. Tris's eyes held a faint glint of humor as they met mine. Then he focused on Robin and let the poor man have the full force of his dazzling smile. When I glanced back at Robin, he was stroking his moustache so furiously I thought he might actually rub it off.

Tris stepped past me and followed Robin back to the opening of Totsye's pavilion. I turned my back at them to glare at Giles.

"And just what was all *that* about, I'd like to know?"

Giles blinked at me. He had the appearance of a man who had been in a trance but was now slowly coming back to the present. "What was *what* all about, Simon? What are you talking about?"

"That rather intimate little tête-à-tête you were having with Tris," I said, watching him uncertainly. "You know, when he had his hand on your neck and was gazing deeply into your eyes?"

Giles's right hand went to his neck in an involuntary gesture. He frowned. "Really, Simon, are you sure about that? I remember talking with Professor Lovelace about something, I'm not sure what, but that's all."

My gaze bored into his, and I focused all my senses on him to get a reading of his emotions. He gave off an aura of confusion, not of deceit. He wasn't lying to me.

This was very odd. I had thought that vampires on the pill, like me, weren't able to "put the glamor" on anyone the way they could if they were still bloodsuckers. I certainly wasn't able to do it. But Tris had followed the old ways for much of his existence as a vampire, since the convenient pills had been invented only about twenty years ago. Perhaps because he had been a bloodsucker for so long, he still had the power to hypnotize people with his eyes, for that's all that the "glamor" really was.

"Perhaps I was mistaken, Giles," I said, "but it did look for a moment there like Tris was flirting with you and you weren't doing much to resist."

Giles hooted with laughter, causing his mother to turn admonishing eyes on us. She pointed to the still recumbent Totsye and then made a shooing gesture with her hands. Giles laughed again, but then put a hand on my arm and drew me a bit away from the tent.

"Really, Simon, this is too, too delicious," he said with a wicked grin. "The tables are well and truly turned if you've started imagining that Professor Lovelace has designs on me, when it's you he's been all hot and bothered about. That really is quite amusing."

I started to protest that it was anything but my imagination, but an explanation would entail more information than I was ready to impart to Giles. "Perhaps I was mistaken then."

"I should say so," Giles responded. "I grant you, Simon, that Professor Lovelace is a very attractive man. I have always admired older men, as you well know." Here he fluttered his eyelashes at me. "But, really, Simon, the handsome professor is rather a bit *too* old for me, don't you think?"

Little did Giles know. Try two hundred years too old. But of course I couldn't tell Giles that.

"Unlike someone else I could name," Giles continued. "You need not worry, Simon. I have no designs on the professor, and I rather doubt he has designs on me."

Before I could frame a reply to that, Lady Prunella's trilling voice interrupted us. "Simon, dear boy, come speak to Totsye. The poor lamb wants you."

Stepping past a smiling Giles, I entered the tent and squatted beside Totsye Titchmarsh. She held out a trembling hand, and I clasped it, patting it reassuringly with my free hand.

"You've had quite a shock," I said in tones of gravest sympathy.

"Oh, Simon, I still can't take it all in," Totsye said, her

voice barely a whimper. "Can it really be true? Is my darling Luke really and truly dead?" The tears flowed down her face, and her skin grew splotchy.

"I'm afraid it is," I said.

"How could someone do such an evil thing?" Totsye moved restlessly on the divan where she lay. "It had to be that horrible idiot, Harald. Who else would want to harm poor darling Luke? That man ought to be drawn and quartered for doing such a thing."

The virulent spite in her voice took me a bit aback. She was even angrier with the man than she had been earlier in the day, when I had first met her. "You may rest assured, Totsye, that Detective Inspector Chase will soon sort all this out, and whoever did this will be charged accordingly."

"He won't have to look very far," Totsye said, letting go of my hand and attempting to sit up. Her enmity toward Harald Knutson was apparently reviving her. "Harald did this, or else he talked one of his minions into doing it for him. Either way, he's guilty. Guilty, guilty, guilty."

"Totsye, dear, don't excite yourself." Lady Prunella fluttered around. "It's not good for you, my dear."

"I'm perfectly fine, Prunie," Totsye snapped at her friend. "Suddenly I feel reinvigorated. Luke's death must not go unavenged. I will see to that." She stood up.

"I wouldn't do anything rash," I told her as I too stood. "Detective Inspector Chase won't thank you for disrupting his investigation."

"You should know," Giles murmured behind me.

I ignored him. "Totsye, the best thing you can do is to tell Chase the truth. Tell him what you know, even what you suspect, and let him sort out the truth."

Totsye frowned. "I suppose you're right, Simon. But you'll never convince me that Harald is innocent. No one else would have any reason to harm poor, dear Luke." The tears began to flow again, and she collapsed onto the divan. With a reproachful glance at me, Lady Prunella once again assumed her role as chief comforter to the bereaved.

Though I knew Robin would castigate me for it later, I decided to brave his wrath and ask Totsye a few questions. "Totsye, I know how distressed you are, but would you mind if I ask you a few questions?"

Lady Prunella started to protest, but I held up a hand. Miraculously, she shut up.

"I suppose so, Simon," Totsye said, sniffling into a handkerchief. "What do you want to know?"

"I wanted to ask about the menu for tonight's dinner," I said. "How many people knew in advance what you would be serving?"

Totsye frowned as she put the handkerchief aside. "One other person, at least. But, really, Simon, it was no great secret. It is a favorite menu of mine, and I often serve the very same dishes at the little dinner parties I give during our summer meetings."

"Would everyone in the encampment know, then?"

"Not everyone, I would say," Totsye answered after a few moments' thought. "But the various guests I have had over the years would certainly know. Poor dear Luke and Adele, naturally, because I could not think of having a dinner party without inviting them both." She grimaced. "Even that prat Harald, because once upon a time, if you can believe it, he was actually a friend of mine. Before he became so unspeakably horrid."

That was interesting. Totsye and Harald had once been friends. I wondered what he had done that made him "so unspeakably horrid." Had he become jealous of Totsye's fascination with Luke? I'd have to investigate that further.

"Was there any particular significance to any of the menu choices?" I tried to ask this in an offhand manner so that Totsye wouldn't attach any particular significance to the question.

Frowning, Totsye thought about that. "The only thing I can think of, I suppose, is that the fig pastries are always popular. I love them myself, and poor Luke was quite addicted to them." Her eyes widened in shock as that hit home. "Oh, no. Don't tell me the poison was in one of my fig pastries."

"I really don't know. We'll have to wait for the postmortem results to tell us." Robin would have to be the one to tell her about the fig pastries, if he so chose.

At the word *postmortem,* Totsye went into hysterics, saving me the trouble of dodging any further questions about the pastries. Muttering "sorry" over and over, I moved away as Lady Prunella sniffed and harrumphed and tried to soothe Totsye.

Deciding that my presence in the tent was no longer welcome, I went outside and stood a few feet away from the entrance. Giles remained inside, for which I was grateful. I had no particular wish to speak to him at the moment.

The sunlight was beginning to fade as sunset rapidly approached. I welcomed the coming night. All that sunshine made me tired.

As I watched Totsye's pavilion across the way, Tris strode out and made his way to the opening of the tent behind me. He summoned Murdo Millbank to speak with Robin, then came to stand beside me.

I glowered at him, and he raised an eyebrow. "And what, pray tell, is the matter with you, Simon?"

"As if you didn't know, Tris."

"Please, dear boy, let's not start that tired routine." Tris was being deliberately patronizing. He knew how it annoyed me.

"What the hell were you doing, trying to hypnotize Giles?"

Tris laughed. "Really, Simon, you can be so very amusing."

"Tris! Don't play innocent with me. I know what you were trying to do." I almost stamped my foot at him in frustration. He could make me angrier than anyone I had ever known.

"And what would that be?"

"Really, Tris, you can be so very amusing," I said, throwing his words back at him. "Any schoolboy could see through what you're trying to do."

When he made no reply to that, instead merely continuing

to regard me with that supercilious look of his, I wanted to strike him. I knew, however, he would take great satisfaction in such a display of anger on my part.

"I see, Simon," Tris said. "You're afraid that your boy-toy's affections aren't sincere and that I will steal him away from you. How very delicious."

His mocking laughter rang out as I turned and stalked off.

Chapter 14

I was so angry with Tris I wanted to smash something, but as I stomped my way through the encampment, my wrath spent itself in the physical exertion. By the time I had reached the entrance to the encampment, I had begun to feel more than a bit foolish. I really shouldn't let Tris rile me this way.

Standing in the rapidly deepening shade of an ancient oak near the guard post, I tried to compose my thoughts. Behaving like a jealous lover wouldn't do anyone a bit of good. I had to examine the situation rationally and try to understand what was motivating Tris's extremely odd behavior.

Could it have something to do with Luke's murder? With a shudder I recalled the look on Tris's face when he had talked of putting a stop to Luke's plan for blackmail. Tris hadn't wanted to make Luke a vampire, but neither had he wanted to face exposure if Luke carried through his threat to reveal the truth about Tris.

Given that difficult situation, had Tris taken the devious way out and used poison to rid himself of the problem? Tris obviously had knowledge of digitalis and its toxic effects. I suspected that, even if Tris hadn't used it on Luke, he had at least used it on someone in the past. Tris was also definitely crafty enough to poison Luke and get away with it. I was the only one aware of Tris's motive for murder, and no doubt

Tris would count on the fact that I wouldn't grass on him to the police.

That thought brought me to a most uncomfortable question. If I had proof that Tris had poisoned Luke, would I tell Robin Chase? The nightmarish aspects of that scenario made me want to run screaming away from this place. "Outing" Tris as a vampire would mean outing myself as well, because how would I be able to convince the police if I didn't tell them everything?

If, that is, Tris were the murderer.

I had to hope someone else was guilty, otherwise I faced a thorny moral dilemma. My conscience would not let me keep silent if I knew, beyond the proverbial shadow of a doubt, that Tris was the murderer.

Why the bloody hell hadn't Tris stayed in Houston? Why had he come back to England? Was he really serious about his feelings for me and his intent to win me back?

If so, what was he doing playing mind games with Giles? I couldn't fathom his motives in hypnotizing Giles, but I was sure that's what he was doing. But why? Was he trying to distract me so that I wouldn't delve too deeply into his role as a murderer?

I could find no sensible answer to that question. Tris was playing games with both Giles and me, and I didn't like it one little bit. If he thought he would win me back with such dirty tricks, he was sadly mistaken.

If he did anything to harm Giles, he would regret it deeply.

The strength of my emotion as that thought hit me settled any doubts I might have had about what, and whom, I wanted.

Tris wasn't the only one who could play devious games, however. On that thought, I pushed myself away from the old oak and started walking back into the encampment. Torches were being lit as dark descended, and for a moment, I had the oddest feeling I had stepped back in time a few centuries. I shook my head to clear it. No time now for such fanciful thoughts.

Instead of heading for the crime scene, I veered off in an-

other direction, another goal in mind. Robin would be livid
when he found out what I was planning to do, but I would
deal with that later.

Master Ælfwine was tending his oven, as I had hoped.
"Good evening, Master Ælfwine. How does your oven?"

"Splendidly, sir, splendidly." The master baker beamed
proudly as he gazed on the device.

The fragrant odor of baking bread wafted on the evening
air, and I sniffed appreciatively. Even though I ate very little,
I could still enjoy the olfactory pleasures of food. "That
bread smells wonderful," I said.

Ælfwine nodded. "I can assure you it tastes every bit as
wonderful as it smells, sir," he said, with the air of a salesman
making a pitch. "Mistress Maud, the bread maker, has quite
the knack. Her loaves are much in demand, this year as ever."

"Does she make other things besides bread?"

"Oh, my, yes," Ælfwine said. "Her pastries are highly prized
as well. In fact, they are in such demand that she cannot make
enough of them here. She brings many with her to the gathering that she has made ahead of time in the mundane world."

"I had a quite delicious fig pastry this evening," I lied. "It
must have been one of Mistress Maud's."

"No doubt, sir, no doubt. No one else has the hand with
pastries that she does, and she has standing orders for them
every gathering." A shadow crossed his face. "The late Duke
of Wessex was one of her best customers. Alas, poor fellow,
he'll enjoy no more fig pastries."

"Yes, the poor man. Quite shocking, isn't it?" I made
noises of commiseration for the man's obvious grief. "Tell
me, though, was it well known that the late duke had a fond-
ness for these pastries?"

Ælfwine laughed sadly. "Aye, sir, it was well known. I
have seen him eat as many as six or seven at a sitting." He
patted his ample stomach as he continued, "Even I, stout
trencherman that I am, could never manage more than two,
rich as they are."

That answered one important question, why a fig pastry

had been chosen as the medium of delivery for the poison. Luke's greedy appetite for the pastries was well known. Another question had also been answered. Thanks to the culinary talents of this Mistress Maud, an ample supply of the pastries was available. Anyone could have bought one, laced it with poison, and slipped it to the victim.

"Tell me, sir," Ælfwine said. "Were you there when it happened?"

The man was saddened by what had befallen the late duke, yet he wanted to hear the details. I thought it couldn't hurt to give him a brief recounting. Perhaps that way the story wouldn't get exaggerated and embellished beyond reason. Master Ælfwine gave the impression of an amiable gossip, and no doubt my tale would soon be spreading through the encampment.

If the master of the oven were disappointed in what I told him, he at least had the manners not to let it show. Taking my leave of him, I inquired where I might find Mistress Maud.

"Why, in our shop, sir," Ælfwine said, smiling. "I have the great good fortune to call the lady my wife." Raising an arm, he pointed to a nearby tent. "You'll find her there, sir."

I thanked him, then made my way to his tent. As I approached, a tall, stoutly built woman emerged from the opening and began to spread a thin cloth over the baked goods displayed on the racks outside. "Good evening, Mistress Maud," I said. "If I might trouble you, good lady, before you close up for the evening?"

"Why certainly, sir," she said, turning a rosy, smiling face to me. " 'Tis never too late for good custom." She twitched back the cloth to reveal a tasty array of baked goods. I moved closer to examine them.

Thankfully for my purposes, several fig pastries remained. "I'll take those," I said, pointing to them.

Mistress Maud smiled even more widely. "An excellent choice, sir, and you have just bought the last of the batch. I must make more tomorrow."

"Then I did indeed come in good time," I said, withdrawing my wallet from inside my tunic. I handed over the money, my eyes widening a bit at the price. Mistress Maud's wares did not come cheaply. "After having sampled these delightful pastries at a dinner party, I decided I must have some to take home with me."

"They are quite popular," she said, cheerfully taking my money, before handing me the pastries wrapped in paper and stuffed into a paper bag.

She had no idea how popular they would be with the police, but it was not my place to enlighten her. Instead I said, "Yes, I have heard that. Apparently the late Duke of Wessex was one of your best customers."

Mention of the deceased brought a frown to her face. "Yes, the poor man. I brought along five dozen for him alone." She shook her head. "No one else seemed to enjoy them the way he did."

"That must be why Dame Alysoun arranged to have them for her dinner party this evening," I said.

"Ah, yes," Mistress Maud replied. She cut her eyes back and forth to see whether anyone else was in hearing distance. "The poor lady. She was a one to believe that the way to a man's heart is through his stomach, I'm here to tell you. But how she deluded herself with that one." She shook her head in sorrow. "All her persistence availed her nothing."

Mistress Maud was every bit as amiable a gossip as her husband, it seemed. "She is deeply grieved by his most untimely death. Just as his sister must be." I paused. "But I gather there are others who will actually rejoice in his death."

"The idiot who fancies himself our king, you mean. I've a good mind to sell him no more of my fine goods. He can look elsewhere for his pastries. What he bought today will be the last he'll have from me. I'll just tell him I've run out of figs." Her lips compressed themselves into a prim line for a moment. "And that goes for that slimy little toad, Sir Reggie, too. He's just as obnoxious as Harald, though he has spent many a shilling here. Live and let live, that's what I say. But Reggie despised Luke for being what he was. The blighter didn't have the wit to realize that very few of us cared who Luke slept with. He was a better man than Reggie any day." Tears misted her eyes. "No more of my fine pastries for him either."

"I have distressed you, Mistress Maud," I said, "and for that I beg your pardon most humbly." This was beginning to sound like the dialogue from one of my own historical romances. Forsooth!

She waved away my apology. "You need not worry, sir. I have not taken it amiss. 'Tis common knowledge, after all."

"The police will surely be quite interested to hear all this," I said. "Especially that both the king *and* Sir Reginald bought fig pastries from you today. If I understood you correctly, that is."

"Aye, they did." Mistress Maud's eyes narrowed. "Surely, though, it was just some sort of accident, sir?"

I shrugged. "That is what the police must determine."

"I see."

And indeed I could see. The wheels in her mind had begun to turn busily, and no doubt she would soon come to the conclusion that Luke's death was no accident. I had better move along before she started asking questions I didn't want to answer.

"Thank you, Mistress," I said, patting the bag in my hand. "I will enjoy these. And now I must bid you adieu." Bowing slightly, I then took my leave.

I could hear her muttering to herself as I strode away. Without asking her directly, I had discovered that my two chief suspects, Harald Knutson and Reggie Bolingbroke, were customers of hers. They had both bought fig pastries from her today, and they had both been in Totsye's tent shortly before the dinner party. Either of them could have put a poisoned pastry on Luke's plate. If, of course, they knew which plate was his.

Then there was the question of the poison. Was it digitalis that killed Luke? If so, what was the source? It could be someone's heart medication, but that would be too easy to trace.

Foxglove shouldn't be that difficult to find. Gardens all over England were full of it. In fact, I fancied I had seen it growing on the grounds of Blitherington Hall, just up the hill. An enterprising killer could have taken some from there and made his or her own little batch of deadly digitalis.

The police would be better equipped to discover the source of the poison, once of course they knew for sure just what poison it was. That would be the key, along with opportunity.

When had Luke eaten the poisoned pastry? And who'd had the opportunity to give it to him?

I mulled over these questions as I made my way back to the crime scene. As I neared Totsye Titchmarsh's pavilion, Robin Chase came out. Catching sight of me, he changed direction and strode forward to meet me.

"And where, might I ask, have you been, Simon?"

From the tone of his voice I could tell he was rather annoyed with me.

I held up the bag of pastries. "Just looking for something to eat, Robin. After all, our dinner *was* interrupted."

His eyes narrowed in suspicion. "If I didn't know you better, Simon, I would believe you." He raised an eyebrow. "But I do know you, and I rather doubt it was food you were after. Hazarding a wild guess, I'd say there are fig pastries in that bag."

"Touché, Robin, touché," I said. "It's a fair cop."

He ignored my witticisms. "Why must you always stick your nose into my investigations, Simon? You have been of considerable help in the past, I will admit, but this is becoming rather tiresome."

I affected a hurt look. "Why, Robin, I'm beginning to get the idea you don't like me after all. I should think you would be pleased to have the willing assistance of a member of the interested public."

Robin snorted. "Come off it, Simon. Liking has nothing to do with it. Your name keeps cropping up in the reports of my murder investigations, and my superiors aren't too keen on that."

It was my turn to raise an eyebrow. "Then why mention my name, Robin? I'm perfectly happy for you to take all the credit."

"That's not what I mean, Simon, and you know it. I've kept your name out of things as much as I can, for your sake as well as my own. But people are beginning to notice that you're always around when there's a dead body somewhere."

"I'm just an innocent victim of Jessica Fletcher Syndrome, Robin."

"And what is that when it's at home, might I ask?" Poor Robin was looking increasingly frazzled.

Laughingly, I explained. "She was a mystery writer in a popular American television show, and in every episode she found another dead body, or two or three. She couldn't help it that, everywhere she went, people died."

"At the rate you're going," Robin said, sarcasm dripping from his voice, "they'll soon be calling it Simon Kirby-Jones Syndrome instead."

I smiled.

Robin closed his eyes, obviously counting to ten before he spoke again, but before he could say anything, someone else spoke.

"You're needed in here, guv." One of Robin's men was calling from the opening of Totsye's tent.

Frowning, Robin said, "We'll finish this later, Simon." He turned and walked away.

He didn't notice that I was following him. He stopped just inside Totsye's pavilion to examine something one of the crime scene boffins was holding in a latex-gloved hand.

"What do you think of this, sir?" the man asked.

"What is it?" Robin said, still not having realized that I was practically peering over his shoulder. "It's some kind of plant, but what is it?"

"I think it's foxglove," I said.

Chapter 15

———◆———

Robin stiffened, no doubt about to offer a rebuke for my sticking my nose in where it wasn't wanted. Perhaps because he had a witness, however, he contented himself with a loud, exasperated sigh.

"I think he's right, guv," the boffin said, not batting an eyelid at Robin's obvious irritation.

Moving to stand beside Robin, I peered more closely at the bell-shaped, tubular flowers attached to the stem. Three of the five crimson blossoms had been slightly crushed.

"Why are you so certain it's foxglove, Simon? I had no idea you were an expert horticulturist."

"I'm admittedly no expert, Robin," I said, "but I do have a garden at Laurel Cottage. I did have some foxglove growing there, but I had it taken out several months ago." *Along with a few other plants of a similarly harmful nature*, I added silently. I hadn't even thought about it until now, but Tris had obviously been interested in poisonous plants. But had he used his knowledge to do away with Luke?

Robin nodded, accepting my statement, at least for the moment. "Where did you find this, Haines?" he asked.

"Under a pile of pottery in the back of the tent, guv. There's a pot with a bit of liquid in it, and we've bagged it, just in case."

"There are no leaves on this stem," I said.

"Your point being?" Robin asked, his temper under tight rein.

"I believe it is the leaves one uses if one wishes to extract digitalis from the foxglove plant," I said, "and not the blossoms." I had done a bit of reading on each of the plants before I'd had them removed from the garden, and I still remembered bits of what I had read about them.

"Thank you, Professor," Robin said dryly. "Now, Haines, I think I had better have a look at that pot."

"Right away, guv," the man replied. He was back very quickly with the pot and extracted it from its evidence bag. He held it in his gloved hands, and Robin peered inside. He sniffed at the contents.

"A bit of a strong odor," was Robin's comment.

"Then it's probably distilled from the foxglove leaves," I said, dredging more facts from my memory. "The leaves have a bitter taste and pungent smell, from what I read about foxglove."

"Thank you, Haines," Robin said, and Haines went back to his work, taking the pot and the foxglove with him.

"That seems a bit too obvious, don't you think, Robin?" I said, when I thought Haines was safely out of earshot.

"Why are you still here, Simon?" Robin asked.

My, my, his patience with me really had worn thin. I was not in the least offended, however. "Just doing my bit to help," I said, smiling brightly.

Robin simply grunted at that.

"Very well, Robin," I replied, "have it your way. I'll go away now, but if I discover anything of use to you, I'll let you know."

"Simon, there are limits," Robin began, then threw up his hands. "Oh, what's the bloody use. Nothing I do or say will stop you, even if I threatened to arrest you, so you might as well bloody get on with it." He stomped off toward the back chamber of the tent where his boffins were still working.

Suppressing a smile, I left the tent. The sun was waning in

the sky. There was less than an hour of light left. Still plenty of time to nose around a bit further.

Now, where could Giles and the others have got to? I peeked inside the tent of the solicitous neighbor, who informed me that Lady Prunella had taken Totsye with her to Blitherington Hall when the police had finished questioning them. She had no idea where Millbank, Tris, or Giles had gone. I thanked her and withdrew.

Giles might have gone home with his mother, but he might still be around the encampment somewhere. I walked back down the lane toward the main thoroughfare and glanced into the various shops as I moved along.

My search led me eventually to The Happy Destrier pub, and upon entering, I found more than I wanted. Giles and Tris were seated at one of the tables, and from the looks of things, Giles had imbibed a bit more mead or ale than was good for him. Yet again. When would the dratted boy learn that he couldn't hold his liquor?

Tris, of course, merely pretended to drink. Even as I watched from the opening, I saw him surreptitiously pour some of his drink onto the ground beneath the trestle table. This really was the limit.

My temper rising with every step, I moved through the crowded tent and sat down next to Giles on the bench. "Really, Tris, when you have to get them drunk, it doesn't speak well for you, now does it?"

"Shall I order you a saucer of milk, Simon?" Tris said, then laughed at his witticism.

Ignoring him, I turned to Giles, who was trying vainly to focus his eyes on my face. "Giles, I thought you had learned your lesson earlier. Why are you drinking so much?"

Giles frowned in concentration. "Dunno, Simon," he said. "Bloody thirsty, that's what. Still thirsty." The rest of what he said was lost in a mumble. He tried to get up from the bench with his tankard in his hand, but he was tottering so, I had to catch him to keep him from falling and hitting his head on the next table. I grabbed the tankard away from him once I had him seated safely beside me again. He leaned tipsily against my side.

"Tris!" I practically hissed at him. "This is ridiculous. What have you done to him?"

"Just a little sport to pass the time, Simon," Tris said. "Don't be so wet."

"Whatever you've done to him, Tris, you undo it *now*." A red haze seemed to alter my vision. My right hand squeezed the pewter tankard, and I could feel it crumpling. "Don't make me any angrier."

Either Tris had tired of his prank or he didn't care to push me any further, for after rolling his eyes, he muttered, "Very well, Simon." He leaned across the table and took Giles's head in his hands. Gazing into Giles's eyes, he stared deeply into them for at least a minute, perhaps more. Then he released Giles and sat back.

Giles shook his head. He turned slowly to look at me. His eyes were clearer, but he was still under the influence of the drink. "What's going on, Simon? Where are we?" He caught sight of Tris. "And why is he here?"

Before I could respond to any of these questions, Giles got unsteadily to his feet. "Going to be sick," he said as he stumbled out of the tavern. Moments later, I could hear him retching in the alley between the pub tent and the next.

"This is the absolute bloody limit," I said to Tris in an undertone, ignoring the amused and interested stares of those around us. "What the bloody hell are you playing at, man? Why are you doing this?"

"Because I can," Tris said coolly. "But if you're going to overreact like this, I'll leave the boy alone. Really, Simon, you are becoming too, too tedious."

I made a concerted effort to rein in my temper. There seemed little point in continuing this discussion. Besides, I was more concerned at the moment with Giles's welfare. "We will continue this discussion later." I stood up. "I have some questions for you, and you will bloody well answer them. And you can pay for that tankard I ruined."

Without waiting for a reply, I turned my back on him. I pushed my way through the crowd to the bar and asked the tavern keeper for two cups of water. With those in hand, I left the tent. I found Giles in the alley, sitting on the ground with his head between his knees. I squatted beside him and touched his arm.

"Giles, are you all right?"

He raised his head to look at me. "I'll be fine, Simon. I think I rid myself of most of whatever it was I was drinking." He managed a weak grin. "Though I pity the poor person who stumbles through this alley." He nodded his head sideways to indicate the patch of grass onto which he had heaved up the contents of his stomach.

"Yes, well," I said, wrinkling my nose in disgust, "I'll see if I can't find someone to take care of that." I handed him the first cup of water. "Here, take some of this, and clean up a bit."

"Thanks, Simon," he said. He rinsed with a mouthful of water first, spat that out in the grass, then repeated the process. He poured the remainder of water in the cup into his hands, then splashed his face. I gave him the second cup, and he drank it down. He set this cup on the ground next to the first one.

I stood up and held a hand out to him. "Now let's get you on your feet."

Giles clasped my hand and pulled himself up. Without my realizing what he intended, he pulled me into an embrace and rested his head, his face still slightly damp, on my shoulder. In the shadows between the tents, I doubted anyone could see us that clearly, but I kept my back to the lane to shield us from view.

"That's much better, Simon," Giles said, his voice muffled. "I feel better just being with you."

I tightened my arms around him. His warm breath tickled my neck. He raised his mouth to mine, and we kissed. Then he tucked his head back into my neck again and sighed with contentment.

We stood that way for a few moments longer. I wished the rest of the world would go away for a while, but the sounds of the encampment around us intruded on our privacy. Reluctantly, I pulled Giles loose from me. He grinned sleepily up at me. "Time to go," I said gently. "But you wait here for a moment."

After retrieving the empty cups, I stepped inside the tavern, where it took a moment to catch the eye of Mine Host. I explained about the mess in the alley and handed across the cups and a fiver, and he promised to take care of it. As I turned to leave, I espied Tris, still at his table, now chatting up an attractive young man in soldierly garb. That should keep him busy for a while.

Giles was steadier on his feet now, and he fell in beside me as we walked toward the entrance to the encampment. "I think you had better go home and get some rest, Giles," I said.

"Not a bad idea," he said, yawning. "This day has rather taken it out of me." He yawned again. "But would you first mind explaining to me what it was that happened to me back there? I have no memory of going into the tavern with Professor Lovelace. The last thing I remember is being dismissed by Chase and seeing my mother off with Totsye."

I was half hoping that Giles would forget about asking me for an explanation. What could I tell him that would sound reasonable?

"Simon," Giles said, prompting me when I had remained silent too long.

"It was Tris's idea of a prank, Giles," I said. "He fancies himself as a hypnotist, you see. Merely a parlor trick, but he does it to amuse himself. I'm sure you'll suffer no ill effects from it, and I'll see to it that he doesn't try it with you again."

"I should bloody well hope not, Simon," he said, but without much rancor.

"Whatever you do, just don't gaze into his eyes again for

more than a second or two," I said, trying to make light of it. "He's like a little boy, he can't resist temptation."

"And I suppose I make rather an easy target for him," Giles said. He tucked his hand into the crook of my arm. "But if I do any more soulful gazing into someone's eyes, Simon, I promise they will be yours."

"Yes, well," I said, not wanting to encourage the drift of this bit of conversation. I decided to change the subject. "Tell me, Giles, what do you know about Totsye Titchmarsh?"

"What do you want to know, Simon? She and my mother are old school friends, and she has visited us at Blitherington Hall two or three times over the years. I can't say, however, that I know her that well."

"What does she do? How does she afford to take part in all this?" With a sweep of my arm, I indicated the encampment around us.

"She's actually a well-known gardener and herbalist," Giles said. "She even had her own gardening program on the telly a few years ago."

That was certainly interesting. As an herbalist, Totsye would know all about foxglove and digitalis. Could that be the answer? Would it were so simple. Totsye the herbalist used foxglove to poison Luke de Montfort.

No, that seemed *too* simple. It looked a bit too much like a frame-up job to me. But Totsye would most definitely bear further investigation.

"Why are you so curious about Totsye, Simon?" Giles asked.

By this time we had reached the entrance to the encampment, and I waited until we had passed through the guard post before I answered. "It could have some bearing on Luke's death, Giles. If he was poisoned with digitalis as Tris suggested, Totsye very well could be a suspect, thanks to her knowledge of plants and herbs."

"But why on earth would *she* want to kill him?" Giles asked. "She was plainly barmy about the man."

"That might be it exactly," I said. "King Harald could be

right. She could be so insanely jealous she decided that, if she couldn't have him, no one would."

"I can't quite see that," Giles said. "She didn't seem *that* barmy."

"Maybe not," I replied. "But it's a possibility we can't ignore."

Just ahead, coming down the hill toward us, ambled Adele de Montfort and Murdo Millbank. Millbank had an arm around Adele and was leading her carefully to the encampment.

I stopped walking, and Giles halted beside me. When Millbank and Adele were close enough, I said, "Adele, I'm so very sorry about your brother. This has all been a terrible shock."

"Oh, yes, Simon, it has," she said, her voice breaking. "Poor, dear Luke. I just can't believe he's gone."

"There, there, lassie," Millbank said, his Scots brogue becoming thicker as he spoke. "Don't distress yourself, now. You need to rest."

Adele patted his hand, the one tightly clasped to her shoulder. "Thank you, Mr. Millbank. You're being so kind." She looked at me with tears glistening in her eyes. "Mr. Millbank came to fetch me from the hospital to bring me back here. And he said he would help me take care of Luke's . . . arrangements." Her voice again broke on a sob.

"There, there," Millbank said. "We must get you back to your tent, lassie. I'm sure you gentlemen will excuse us."

"Of course," I said. "And if there's anything either of us can do, Adele, please let me know."

"Yes, certainly," Giles said. "Your servant, ma'am."

Adele smiled prettily, if sadly, at Giles's courtly bow, then allowed Millbank to lead her slowly on to the encampment. Giles and I resumed our walk up the hill.

"He's being quite the solicitous attendant," I said.

"He is that," Giles agreed. "If I were of a suspicious nature, I'd say he has an eye on Adele's share of the family business."

"What do you mean, Giles?"

He laughed. "Surely you've realized by now who Adele is, Simon. She's the sole owner, I expect, of the d'Amboise chain. You know, the 'Cuisine d'Amboise' French restaurants. They're everywhere. She must be worth millions now."

And well worth killing for, I reflected.

Chapter 16

A fter seeing Giles safely to the front door of Blitherington Hall, and after a few more kisses, I headed home. I had much to think about, not the least of which was the motive behind the poisoning of Luke de Montfort, alias Luc d'Amboise.

Tris had mentioned that Luke came from a family of well-known restaurateurs, but I hadn't made the connection between Luke and Adele and a chain of high-priced French eateries. Like most vampires, I was not overly concerned with haute cuisine, so I rarely paid much attention to where the elite went to eat. There were some among us, however, those moving in the highest social circles, who were often to be seen in such establishments. The hoi polloi like me rarely entered them.

If Adele were the sole heiress to the family business, that certainly made her worth courting, at least to a venal businessman with an eye to the main chance. I suspected that Murdo Millbank very much fit the profile. Could he have poisoned Luke to get him out of the way, thinking that Adele would be easy prey? From what I had seen of Adele thus far, she hadn't impressed me as being a particularly strong or forceful personality, but beside her brother, almost anyone would fade into the woodwork.

Adele herself, tired of always being cast in the shade by Luke despite her obvious physical charms, might have decided to take a rather drastic way out of her dilemma. She could easily have poisoned Luke, more easily than anyone else, in fact. They shared a tent, and she would have known his habits better than the other suspects.

One of the crucial questions to be answered was when Luke was given the poisoned fig pastry, if indeed that was how the poison was administered. The rich, sweet taste of the pastry would mask the taste of the digitalis, and given Luke's well-known predilection for the delicacy, it seemed perfect for the task. But confirmation would have to wait, until the results of the postmortem. I would winkle the information out of Robin Chase somehow.

At the very first opportunity, I would try to get Adele alone and question her, as delicately and discreetly as possible. Robin would not be happy with me, but she might speak less guardedly with me, particularly if she had had a hand in her brother's death.

At home in Laurel Cottage again, I undressed and put away my medieval dress. I would have to don it again tomorrow, to blend in more readily as I went nosing about the encampment, and so I spent a few minutes brushing away some of the dirt and grass that had clung to it here and there. By the time I had finished, I was just on the point of going downstairs when I heard the front door open and close. Tris had returned.

I moved to intercept him before he could retire for the evening. I was determined to talk to him and get some answers, one way or another.

Downstairs I found Tris in the sitting room, comfortably ensconced in a chair. Puffing away at his pipe, he was reading the *Times* as if nothing untoward had occurred this day.

"Found anything of interest, Tris?" I said as I sat down on the sofa across from him.

The paper came down, and Tris regarded me with a sardonic gleam in his eyes.

"So you *are* speaking to me, Simon," Tris said, his pipe clenched between his teeth. He looked every inch the professor about to dress down one of his recalcitrant students. "Lucky, lucky me."

I snorted. "Don't try that tone with me, Tris, it won't work."

The paper went up, and smoke streamed from behind it.

"Put down the bloody paper, Tris. I want to talk to you."

A heavy sigh issued forth from behind the newsprint. Tris folded up the paper and put it down on the table between us. "Very well, Simon, what is it you want?"

"I want an explanation for your behavior today, Tris. I have known you to be many things. Rude, insensitive, selfish, to name but a few. Rarely have I seen you be deliberately cruel, though, picking on someone who has done nothing to you. Furthermore, someone who has no defense against you."

"I gather, Simon, you are speaking of my little joke with young Blitherington?" Tris arched one eyebrow.

"Don't play coy with me, Tris," I said, endeavoring to hold on to my temper. "It doesn't become you in the least. Of course I'm talking about what you did to Giles. That really was beneath you, Tris. Why should you pick on Giles like that?"

"All is fair in love and war, they say," Tris replied. "One has to get the measure of the enemy, so to speak."

"If you are truly trying to win me back, as you claim, you have a bloody funny way of showing it," I said. "First you play a reprehensible trick on Giles, and then, right in front of me, you flirt outrageously with a handsome young man. And I have little doubt that you didn't stop at a mere flirtation. Past experience has taught me that much."

Tris remained unruffled. "Why, Simon, you sound like a

jealous spouse. How flattering. I was beginning to think you no longer had any feelings for me." He smiled smugly.

I glared at him, momentarily speechless.

"I had forgotten how chivalrous you can be, Simon," Tris mused. "Yes, it might be no more than that. Your sense of fair play is outraged because of the trick I played on young Blitherington. After all, if I considered him to be a worthy rival, I could end this contest very quickly and very simply."

The room threatened to spin around me as the full implications of what Tris had said began to sink in. This was no time for dithering. I had to make a quick decision, and I did.

I laughed, and I hoped it was convincing. "Really, Tris, now I am the one feeling flattered. You would put Giles permanently out of the way, just for me? Perhaps I've underestimated the strength of your devotion to me after all."

Tris's eyes narrowed. "I rarely fail to get what I want, Simon. I would remind you of that."

"I know it well, Tris," I said, forcing myself to relax. I leaned against the back of the sofa and struck what I hoped was a seductive pose. "But you certainly can't blame me for being a bit cynical where you're concerned. The problem is, what you want seems to change on such a regular basis." My left hand caressed the empty spot on the sofa beside me.

Tris ignored my invitation. "I can't dispute that, Simon. I wouldn't be foolish enough to try." He paused to relight his pipe. "But perhaps I have finally realized that some choices are more important than others."

I felt a noose tightening around my neck. If I rejected Tris completely, there was no telling what he might do in retaliation. He disliked being thwarted whenever he wanted something, and I had no desire to see Giles pay the price for my turning Tris down flat. I had to continue to appear undecided until I could think of some safe way out of this dilemma.

"You have a very forceful way of getting what you want," I said. "I am faced with quite a dilemma, Tris. Power, strength, experience, confidence, on one hand. On the other, youth, beauty, enthusiasm, devotion. Sometimes making a choice can be difficult."

"You're forgetting one thing, Simon."

"Oh, what's that?"

"I won't run screaming in the other direction because you're a vampire." Tris had never sounded so smug.

I refused to let him rile me. "True. But I know Giles far better than you, Tris. I rather doubt he would react in that way."

"So you say, Simon, but you can't count on that, now can you?" Tris laughed. "Far better to rid yourself of him now and not let this foolish flirtation of yours go any further."

"Why, Tris, how tiresomely mean-spirited of you," I said mockingly. "I was quite enjoying the thought of two very attractive men vying for my affections, and here you want to spoil it all by eliminating your competition. That isn't quite cricket. Certainly not what I would expect from a true gentleman." Indeed, if what Tris had once told me was true, he had been born an aristocrat, the youngest son of an earl, albeit more than two centuries ago.

The slight emphasis I placed on the word *true* had hit the mark with Tris. He shifted slightly in his chair.

"I'll leave young Blitherington alone, at least for now," Tris said, well upon his high horse. "Heaven forfend I violate your absurd notions of fair play, Simon. Really, you are beginning to sound like one of those dim-witted women in those historical novels you write. Men vying for your affections, indeed!"

I saw no further need to press my advantage. I would have to keep on my toes, though, to stay a move or so ahead of Tris in this bizarre little game.

"As much as I do love talking about myself," I drawled, "I must change the subject for a moment, Tris, if you don't mind."

"And what subject would you like to discuss now, Simon?" Tris said warily. "The price of tea in China?"

I laughed as if I found that inane little sally amusing. "Ah, Tris, such a ready wit you have. No, I have no interest in the price of tea. But I am rather curious about whether you might have murdered Luc d'Amboise. Tell me. Did you poison him?"

"What would you do if I told you that I had, Simon?" Tris said. "Would your notions of chivalry demand that you hand me over to that rather handsome young policeman? Chase, isn't that his name?" He offered a wolfish grin. "Not that I would mind spending a few hours gaining a closer acquaintance with him, you understand, but I have no intention of being arrested and tried for murder."

"You haven't answered my question, Tris," I said. "Not, I suppose, that I really expected you to. But you can't ignore the fact that the man was murdered, and you *were* rather quick off the mark with the idea that he had been poisoned with digitalis. How could you have known that, I wonder?"

"I told you," Tris said in a bored tone, "I have seen the results of digitalis poisoning before."

"I've no doubt that you have. You certainly had a nice little collection of noxious plants here at Laurel Cottage. At least, before I had them taken out."

Tris made no reply.

"The question about the poisoning remains. Was it by your own hand," I asked, "or by someone else's? I really am rather curious to know, Tris."

"I find it rather amusing, Simon, to leave you wondering," Tris said. "Frankly, I don't care whether Luke was poisoned with digitalis or with something else. My problem has been dispensed with, and thus ends my interest in the subject."

"I don't really care whether you poisoned the man, Tris," I said, hoping that Tris would not be able to detect the lie, "but if you didn't do it, someone else did. And that person shouldn't be allowed to get away with it. Don't you see?"

Tris yawned. "I haven't the slightest interest in the requirements of human justice, Simon. I dispensed with all that nearly two centuries ago when I became a vampire." He placed his pipe in the ashtray beside his chair and stood up. "If you will pardon me, Simon, I rather think I'll have a bit of rest now."

I wanted to scream at him in frustration, but I knew it would do me not the slightest bit of good. Tris would remain obdurate, and I would simply grow more and more frustrated.

"Very well, Tris," I said, getting up from the sofa. "Perhaps we could both do with some sleep. This has been a most peculiar day." I turned and headed for the hallway.

Before I had taken more than three steps, I felt Tris's hand on my shoulder. I stopped and turned to face him. He slid his arms around me and brought his lips to mine.

This is for you, Giles, I thought as I kissed Tris back with feigned enthusiasm. *Whether you would understand or not.* At that moment I would rather have sucked blood from a bat than kiss Tris, but I couldn't afford to let him know how much I distrusted him.

When at last he ended the embrace, he was the one with a dazed look in his eyes, I was amused to note. "Good night, Simon," he said, heading for the stairs. He paused on the bottom step and turned around to face me. "I don't suppose you would consider joining me upstairs?"

A kiss I could fake, but that was my limit. "Now, Tris," I said playfully, "remember that I'm going to play fair with you and with Giles. You're not going to get anything he isn't getting. Understand?"

Tris frowned, then shook his head. "Damnation, Simon! You'll end up driving me quite mad." He turned and walked loudly up the stairs and into the guest room.

In my office, I closed the door and leaned back against it. Talk about relief! I had managed to get through that confrontation in good shape. But it wasn't going to get any easier from here. There were plenty more bullets to dodge, until

I could come up with a solution that wouldn't bring harm to anyone.

In the meantime, until I came up with a scathingly brilliant idea, I would expend my mental energies on trying to figure out who had murdered Luc d'Amboise. I had the uneasy feeling that the killer was upstairs in my cottage right this very moment.

Tris might have no qualms about murdering someone if he felt threatened, but just because he seemingly had no conscience didn't mean that he was automatically guilty. He did have a compelling motive for getting Luc d'Amboise out of the way, but there were other motives, as I had discovered. There could be even more, once I really started digging.

I sat down at my desk and turned on the computer. Once it had completely booted up, I clicked on my word-processing program and started writing. I always found it helpful to record things, and if I put down everything I could think of that had anything to do with this murder, I might see something, some useful point to investigate further.

Once I had finished, I read it through a couple of times, making a few small additions here and there, but nothing jumped out at me. There were still too many gaps. I would be busy tomorrow, asking questions and hoping not to get caught by Robin Chase.

Frustrated, but too awake now to attempt even a brief nap, I worked on my current novel for a while. Finally, I tired my brain out enough that I felt able to go upstairs for a bit of sleep.

The ringing of a bell roused me from sleep some time later. I sat up on the bed and glanced at the clock. It was barely five-thirty in the morning. I grabbed the phone and said, "Hello."

"Simon," Giles said, "sorry to wake you, but I knew you'd want to hear what happened." He must have been on his mobile, because I heard a bit of static and, in the background, the sounds of a number of people talking.

"Where are you, Giles? What on earth is going on?" I asked before he could continue.

"That's what I'm trying to tell you, Simon," he said. "I'm at the encampment. Someone tried to kill the king last night!"

Chapter 17

—————•—————

"Someone tried to kill Harald Knutson?" I asked Giles, still a bit stunned.

"Yes, Simon," Giles said. "It happened early this morning, about three-thirty, apparently."

"Is he badly hurt?" I asked.

"He had a bit of a bang about the head," Giles said, "but that was all." He laughed. "Apparently His Majesty has rather a tough old bean."

"What on earth are you doing at the encampment at this hour of the morning, Giles?" I asked, glancing at the clock again.

Giles had moved away from the source of the chattering. "I slept well, Simon, but I woke up a bit early. About twenty minutes ago, I looked out of the window of my sitting room, and I could see the people down here were stirring around quite like a hive of angry bees. I came down to see what was going on."

The sun rose early here in the summer, so Giles would have had a pretty clear view of the meadow down below the Hall.

"Are the police there yet?" I asked.

"Not yet, Simon," Giles said. "I gather that His Majesty is dithering a bit about calling them. He doesn't seem to think this has anything to do with what happened last night." He snickered into the phone. "He persists in the belief that Luke's death was accidental. I wonder who it is he's trying to persuade."

"I'm beginning to think he's a dimmer bulb than I had even imagined," I said. "Tell you what, Giles. I'll be on my way in a few minutes. Meet me by that old oak near the entrance in about fifteen minutes."

"Righty-ho, Sherlock," Giles said cheerfully. "Watson signing off." His mobile went dead, and I hung up my phone, smiling.

Hastily I took my morning pill, made sure I had several doses in my spare pillbox, then donned my tunic, hat, and shoes for my day of snooping at the encampment. Before I went downstairs, I opened the door of the guest room as quietly as I could, but my care was for naught. Tris's bed was empty.

He was nowhere to be found downstairs either. Sometime while I had been asleep, he had slipped out of the house. I was used to his coming and going at his leisure, but I found this faintly disturbing. What was he doing, and where was he?

I sped through the village in my Jag, but very few denizens of Snupperton Mumsley were to be seen. At the encampment, however, a few minutes later, it looked like everyone was up and about, even at this hour. There was no one manning the guard post at the entrance, and I walked right in.

A few feet away, Giles waited patiently under the old oak. Dressed in his finery from the day before, he was young and handsome and incredibly appealing. Casting a quick glance about, wondering where the devil Tris could be, I took Giles in my arms and gave him a good morning kiss.

"Good morning to you, too, Simon," Giles said, smiling. "Whatever has come over you this morning, I approve most heartily."

"I'm simply pleased to see you, Giles," I said, adjusting my sunglasses, which had gone slightly askew. "Looking so much better this morning, that is." *And you don't know the half of it, my boy*, I thought.

"I feel fine this morning, Simon," Giles said as we left the tree and began walking into the encampment. "A good night's sleep was all I needed. I am becoming a trifle peckish, however. As I recall, neither of us had any dinner last night, and I certainly had no time for breakfast this morning."

Responding to that broad hint, I led Giles to Mistress Maud's bakery shop, where I had little doubt we would find something suitable for Giles to breakfast upon. While Giles helped himself to some of the victuals on display, I tried discreetly to avail myself of Mistress Maud's secondary specialty. "I hear that you all had a bit of a to-do here earlier this morning," I said to the proprietress.

Mistress Maud finished arranging some pastries in a basket upon the counter before replying. "Oh, my, yes. There was quite a commotion, woke up most of us, all that yelling and carrying on."

"What happened?" I asked.

She sniffed. "It's not all that unusual. Some of the lads get a bit het up sometimes, and they have to find a way to work off some of their excitement. There is usually a brawl or two before we all head our separate ways at the end of the week. But this was something different." She shook her head.

"I gather someone attacked the king," I said, prompting her when she remained silent.

"Yes, that's what they say," she replied. "I'm not one to bear tales, mind you, but our king has made a number of people angry of late. Perhaps one of them decided to get back at him for one of the underhanded things he's done."

"You'd think he'd be more worried about retaining his crown," I said mildly, "but if he's playing dirty, he can't expect people to put up with it for long."

Mistress Maud busied herself, fussing with some loaves of bread on the counter next to the pastries. Her back to me, she continued, "The only way Harald knows how to fight is dirty, unfortunately. He learned that in business in the mundane world, and he thinks he can continue to get away with it here."

"Oh, really," I said, glancing at Giles, happily munching on his third pastry. "And what kind of business is he in?"

"He's a glorified barrow boy, he is," she said, sniffing like she detected a sour smell. "Oh, he's very successful, quite well off, or at least he was, but he's still a grocer, can't get away from that."

"He's in the food supply business," I said to clarify what she had told me.

Turning back to face me, she nodded. "Oh, yes, he deals with lots of fancy restaurants." She grinned spitefully. "That's why he disliked our late duke so much, wasn't it? Poor Luke turned his nose up at Harald's attempts to get him to buy the food for his restaurants from him. Wouldn't have a thing to do with our king the grocer."

Well, well, well, that was mighty interesting. It certainly did help explain at least part of the deep animosity between the two men. Though why had Luke taken so strongly against Harald? Why shouldn't he have wanted to do business with the man, one of his fellow G.A.A. members?

I expressed that thought aloud to my amiable informant.

Mistress Maud glanced around, and since Giles was the only other occupant of her shop at that moment, she evidently decided she could speak freely. "I'm not one to bear tales, mind you," she said again, and I did my best to keep a straight face. "It was all really that woman's fault, you see. She's a bit of a flighty miss, that one, forever buzzing about the men. She doesn't stick with any one of them for long."

"I gather you're talking about Adele, Mistress?"

She nodded. "Oh, my, yes. What a flibbertigibbet that young woman is. A few years ago, she was flirting with Harald something fierce, and the idiot didn't have the wit to see that she was just stringing him along. She does it with any man, doesn't really matter how attractive—or not!—he is." She grinned maliciously. "Harald fell for it, and he thought she was in love with him. With Adele in his pocket, so to speak, he could sign a lucrative contract with her family, and make even more money."

"I take it that didn't happen," I said dryly.

"Not a bit of it," Mistress Maud chortled. "Not a bit of it. Luke would have nothing to do with him, or his food, and Adele had lost interest by that point. So Harald got snubbed by both of them, and ever since he's been hungry for revenge."

Her eyes widened as she realized what she had said. She leaned against the counter as the color bled out of her face. "Oh, my goodness," she said. "Do you think Harald could have murdered Luke?"

"Who said anything about murder?" I asked her curiously. From behind her, Giles raised one eyebrow eloquently.

"Well, it's all over the encampment," Mistress Maud said defensively. "Everyone seems to think it was no accident that Luke ate something that made him so ill he died from it."

"I'm sure the police are taking everything into consideration," I said piously. Giles struggled to keep from laughing behind Mistress Maud's back.

Before she could say anything else, I steered her back to the original subject of the conversation. "Tell me, good lady, what happened this morning? Was the king physically attacked?"

I braced myself for another rambling answer, but this time she went straight to the point. "Someone sneaked into his tent and tried to bash his head in." She collapsed with laughter, leaning against the counter and making it shake.

Giles and I exchanged glances. The woman seemed far more amused than the situation warranted.

"Pardon me, my good sirs," she said when she could finally speak again. "I doubt not you will think me totally without feeling." The laughter threatened to bubble forth again, but she made an effort to quell it. "He might have been badly injured, even killed, but whoever attacked him had no idea the man sleeps with his hair in big foam curlers and wrapped in a thick scarf." She hooted with laughter.

Exchanging startled glances, we waited a moment for the giggles to subside, then she continued. "From what I hear, the first blow stunned him but didn't hurt him, because whatever hit him bounced off his head. He was roused enough to start yelling, and the attacker ran out of his tent before anyone could see who it was. Then Harald ran out of his tent and started screaming bloody murder, until he realized everyone would see his head. He went back in his tent and has refused to come out ever since. After rousing the whole camp, mind you!"

Neither Giles nor I could restrain ourselves any longer. We joined Mistress Maud in picturing the ludicrous sight, and it was several minutes before we had exhausted our mirth.

"I take it no one has seen fit to inform the police?" Giles asked.

Mistress Maud shook her head. "My good husband, Master Ælfwine, was all for calling them, but Harald ranted and moaned about it so that everyone finally gave up trying to talk to him about it."

"And is the good king still sulking in his tent?" I asked.

She shrugged. "I doubt it not. The man is a flap-mouthed churl, and this proves it. As if we needed further evidence."

"Thank you, Mistress," I said, rising from my seat. "You have been most informative." I waited while Giles paid her for his breakfast. She was giggling yet again as we left her tent.

"A strange story indeed, don't you think, Simon?"

"Yes, Giles, it is. I wonder, though, if this whole thing might have been staged by Harald himself in order to divert suspicion away from him."

"It's possible, I suppose," Giles said, "but do you think he would go through this much embarrassment to do that?"

"It's possible," I conceded, "but perhaps not probable. From what I've seen of the man, he is very much upon his dignity, and he wouldn't embarrass himself lightly."

"What next?" Giles asked. "Are you going to let Chase know about this?"

"All in good time, Giles," I said, smiling roguishly. "But if the king hasn't seen fit to summon the constabulary, far be it for me to take it upon myself to do so. No doubt the police will be back here soon enough this morning. Someone can inform Robin then."

Giles laughed. "I doubt Chase will be very pleased, Simon."

"That's his lookout," I said. "Now, why don't we see if the bereaved sister is awake and stirring. I would like to question her, discreetly, of course. I have a feeling she might be the key to this whole situation."

Giles fell into step beside me as we made our way through the encampment toward the late Duke of Wessex's pavilion. Along the way people had gathered in small groups, and the buzz of conversation and laughter followed us. Occasionally someone would call out a greeting, and Giles and I returned it. No one seemed overly curious about our presence in the encampment this morning, but perhaps they thought we were merely new members of the group because we were appropriately dressed. If this investigation took many more days, however, I might have to invest in another costume. That might help with blending in even better.

We passed by the scene of the crime, and it was rather jarring to see the crime scene tape fixed about Totsye's tent. Talk about an anachronism!

As we neared the Wessex pavilion, I focused my hearing to detect signs that anyone was awake and stirring. Someone was definitely inside. In fact, there were at least two someones, because I could hear two different voices, one male and one female.

We were still about twenty yards away from the pavilion when a stumpy figure came hurtling out of the tent. His arms were crossed over his head, trying to protect it from the rain of utensils coming at him. Catching sight of us, he made a beeline for Giles and me.

"And don't ever come back here, you little piece of slime!" Adele de Montfort appeared in the opening of the tent, her chest heaving with exertion. She held an iron pot in her hands and was preparing to throw it when she became aware of Giles and me. She dropped the pot on the ground and vanished inside the tent.

"Don't go in there," Sir Reggie Bolingbroke advised, cowering safely behind Giles and me. "The woman has gone mad, completely mad!"

Chapter 18

Surveying Sir Reggie's appearance, I had my doubts about Adele de Montfort's madness, simply because she had chased her unwanted suitor from her tent. Good taste probably had more to do with it.

Sir Reggie was perspiring heavily, and his face had turned blotchy. One eye remained fixed, and the other goggled about wildly. When he had come running toward us, he was holding his leggings up to keep from tripping over them. Even as we watched, he struggled to pull them up to cover his undergarments and his jiggling belly.

"Just what were you doing in there, man?" Giles asked.

"Attempting to administer a little comfort in the woman's time of need," Sir Reggie said. His tights in place, he twitched his tunic about.

"With your pants down?" I asked, trying not to collapse with laughter. The man was truly a ludicrous sight.

"Everyone knows that hellcat will lift her skirt for anyone," Sir Reggie muttered. "And I've seen her come-hither glances, don't think I haven't."

"But not for you, eh?" I said, snickering. I couldn't help myself; the situation was completely farcical. Giles could no longer restrain himself either, and the two of us had some hearty laughs at old Reggie's expense.

Muttering something about poofters he doubtless considered scathing, he stalked away, much upon his severely bruised dignity.

When Giles and I could stop laughing, I saw Adele de Montfort peeking cautiously from the opening of her tent. "Adele," I said, striding closer, "are you okay? Did that buffoon hurt you in any way?"

She tossed back her hair and pulled her wrap closer around her shoulders. "I should say not, the bumbling fool. How he ever thought I would fall for his little act of seduction, I'll never know. The man's an idiot. An idiot!"

I forbore to enlighten her with the idiot's description of her reputation. "No harm done, then, I suppose. I apologize for calling on you so early in the day, but we took a chance you might be up and about, like the rest of the group."

"No thanks to another idiot," Adele said. Then she burst into laughter. "Oh, if only I had been there to see Harald in his curlers. What a sight that must be!"

"Yes, it must have been something," I agreed, following her as she waved Giles and me into the tent.

"You can see now why Luke was so eager to take this group in hand," Adele said as she indicated the chairs where Giles and I should sit. "Harald has grown increasingly incompetent of late, and Reggie, well, need I say anything more?"

"Your brother would certainly have made a far more impressive monarch, and no doubt a far more competent one, than either of them," I said.

Tears welled in her eyes. "Poor Luke! I still can't quite grasp the fact that he's gone and that I shall never see his dear face again. Who could have done such a horrendous thing to him? Who could have hated him so?"

"Then you are convinced his death was no accident?" I said.

"Yes," she said, and her tone grew hard. "It was murder. Deliberate and willful murder."

"Pardon me for asking in your time of distress, Adele," I said, "but do you have any idea who might have hated your brother enough to poison him?"

"It had to be Harald," she said, fairly spitting out the name. "He and Luke despised each other. Luke was everything Harald was not—handsome, dashing, successful."

"I've heard that Harald is actually a successful businessman himself," I said, "a grocer, I believe."

Adele emitted a most unladylike snort. "That's what he would have everyone believe, the nasty sod. He tried to get Luke to offer him a contract with our family business, but Luke turned him down flat. Harald was livid." She smiled with malice at the memory.

"Well, it does seem rather natural," Giles said, "his being a grocer and your family being in the restaurant business. You do need food for your restaurants, after all."

"Naturally," Adele said, "but Harald simply couldn't offer the quality that the Cuisine d'Amboise restaurants demand. His business has been in deep trouble for at least two years now, and apparently he was counting on a contract with us to get him out of it." She sniffed. "Luke didn't want to link an old and highly successful business with one teetering on the brink of bankruptcy."

"I can understand that," I said, "even if it is rather hard on poor old Harald. I suppose the kingship here is about the only thing he has left."

"And he won't have that for long," Adele said, her voice dripping with gleeful spite. "He has traded on his membership in this society long enough. We all try to help one another out, within reason, in the mundane world, but Harald counts too much on such loyalties."

Thus far she had made no mention of her own alleged relationship with Harald. Perhaps Mistress Maud had been wrong about that, but I somehow doubted she was. I could think of no delicate way to ask Adele herself about it.

"Then it does sound as if Harald had a motive to harm

Luke," I said. "But, pardon my asking this so bluntly, Adele, is there anyone else with such a strong grudge against Luke?"

Adele moved restlessly in her chair. "Could I offer either of you something to drink? Some tea, perhaps, or even coffee?" When both Giles and I had politely declined, she made a visible effort to be still. I could feel her mind working, and I could also feel the fear emanating from her.

What was frightening her, I wondered. What was it that she didn't want us to know? She was under no obligation to tell us anything, and I was surprised that she didn't suddenly ask us to leave her tent.

Finally Adele spoke. "Not really a grudge, I suppose, unless you count Reggie. He didn't care for Luke at all, for several reasons, but mostly because Luke was going to keep him from taking Harald's place as king. Reggie was campaigning for it when Luke suddenly decided, about six months ago, that he wanted to be king himself. When Reggie found out about it, at our winter gathering, he was livid."

"I see," I said. What was so worrisome about this? It had to be something else. "I hadn't realized that the kingship was such a highly prized office."

Adele laughed sourly. "To the outside world, I suppose it appears very foolish to expend such time, money, and energy on what is really nothing more than play-acting. I have never taken it all as seriously as my brother does . . . er, did. But you know how you men can be." She laughed coquettishly. "It's all a competition with you, isn't it, and you cannot *abide* the thought of someone else beating you at any game, even a game as foolish as this."

"I cannot disagree, Adele," I said, smiling. "Man is a very competitive creature, as you say. What matters is which of them will go to extreme lengths to get what he wants."

"Murder, you mean," Adele said bluntly.

"Yes, murder," I replied. "You say Harald would have murdered your brother, and you have given him two rather compelling motives. You've even ascribed a motive to that prat Sir Reggie. Anyone else? Did your brother have no other enemies?"

Adele thought for a moment. "He most definitely had some business rivals who will not be in the least grieved that he is gone. Though they may soon learn to their regret that I am not the weak-willed female they might think," she added almost as an afterthought.

"But are any of those business rivals here among the members of the G.A.A.?" Giles asked.

"No," Adele said. "I suppose one of them could have hired someone to do this, but that is not very likely. They didn't hate Luke that much." She shook her head. "No, the answer lies here, somewhere. I have no doubt whatsoever that Harald is responsible for my brother's death, either directly or indirectly."

"That may very well be," I said, "and I also have no doubt that Detective Inspector Chase will soon find out who is responsible."

"He did seem like a very competent man," Adele sighed. Her eyes had a dreamy aspect. "And, my, isn't he absolutely scrumptious?"

Giles coughed. He had no interest in discussing Robin's charms.

"I wonder, Adele," I said, "if I might ask you something else."

"And what is that, Simon?" she said.

"It's about what Harald had to say to Totsye Titchmarsh last night in her tent." I paused, trying to find a tactful way to rephrase Harald's accusation.

Adele needed no prompting. "Oh, you mean what he said about Totsye being so jealous over poor Luke?" She laughed. "Well, there is a certain amount of truth in that, I must admit."

"Oh, really?" I said leadingly.

"Oh, my, yes," Adele said, laughing again. "I do adore Totsye, I assure you. She's an amazing woman, and I have learned from her example as a professional businesswoman in a male-dominated world. Nevertheless, she has behaved very foolishly over my brother. She's a very bright woman, yet she has a blind spot where Luke was concerned."

"Did she not understand that he had no romantic or sexual interest in women?" I said. "As you say, she appears to be a bright woman, and surely she would realize she was wasting her time if she was hoping he would suddenly change."

Adele shrugged. "I can't quite fathom it myself. They appeared simply to be good friends until the past few months, and then suddenly Totsye came all over like a giddy schoolgirl. Giggling, blushing, you name it. It was all too, too Barbara Cartland for words."

"That does seem rather odd," I said.

"Perhaps she has begun menopause," Adele said. "Some women become completely unbalanced, and maybe that's what has happened to poor old Tots." She sniggered in a most unladylike fashion. "I mean, getting a pash for a gay man when you're over fifty and he's fifteen years younger is a bit unbalanced, don't you think?"

"It is perhaps not the most sensible thing one could do," I said, a tad pompously. "But when was love ever sensible?"

" 'Lord, what fools these mortals be!' " Giles quoted, smiling.

"I don't believe in love myself," Adele said. "There is little point in expending that much emotion on something that is more the stuff of make-believe than of real life. Life is too short to spend it all with one person. Variety is most definitely the spice of my life." She giggled in what she no doubt considered to be a completely captivating manner. Apparently she had forgotten, at least for the moment, that Giles and I were of her brother's persuasion.

"That's absolute rubbish," Giles said, almost coming up out of his chair in his anger. "Life is too short *not* to spend it with the right person, once you have found him. Anything else is unthinkable."

Ah, how romantic the young can be! I hid my smile from him, though I must admit that I was rather touched. He was trying so hard not to look at me while he so hotly defended his notion of romantic love to a laughingly skeptical Adele.

She stopped short of complete and contemptuous rudeness, however. "I see we must agree to differ on that issue, young sir! I'll not dissuade you from your feelings, and you'll not dissuade me from mine. But let us not part on ill feelings?" Very prettily, Adele held out a hand to Giles, and, ever the gentleman, he took it and did the mannerly thing.

Adele stood. "Now, gentlemen, if you will excuse me, I have ever so much to do today. I must get in touch with various members of my board of directors and attend to some rather pressing matters of business. I'm sure you understand."

"Certainly, Adele," I said, as I too stood. "And if there is anything either Giles or I might do to assist you, please ask. This is a very difficult time for you, and we wanted to be sure to offer you our condolences and our assistance. We knew your brother for only a very brief time, and we deeply regret what has happened." Giles had come to stand beside me, and he nodded in agreement.

"Again, thank you, gentlemen," Adele said. "Your sympathies are most gratefully noted." Her eyes told me, however, that she had not been in the least taken in by my words. I was being nosey, and she knew it.

After bowing slightly, Giles and I left the tent and began wandering back toward the main part of the encampment.

"A very interesting woman, don't you think?" Giles said.

"That's a rather tactful way of putting it," I replied. "She seems completely different from the woman we met yesterday. Much more forceful, certainly more outspoken and even aggressive, in some ways."

"A bit of a barracuda," Giles said. "I don't know that I would care to spend any more time with her."

"Under ordinary circumstances, I would agree with you,

Giles," I said. "But Adele bears further scrutiny. Just now she was trying very hard *not* to tell us something, yet she ended up telling me something entirely different, without knowing it."

"And what's that, Simon?"

"If that was the real Adele we saw just now," I said, "then she too had a motive for murdering her brother."

"I believe I see what you mean, Simon," Giles said. "She isn't quite the shrinking-violet, empty-headed type I first thought her to be."

"No, indeed." I laughed. "I'm beginning to think 'Voracious Violet' might be more appropriate. The rumors we have heard about the lady's dispensing of her favors perhaps have not been exaggerated."

"Using sex as a weapon, you mean," Giles said.

"Yes, exactly," I replied. "I also have begun to think that the pair of them, the d'Amboise siblings, were equally skilled at the game."

"I presume you noticed that there was something *unusual*, shall we say, going on between Luke and Professor Lovelace?"

I stopped dead in my tracks (and please pardon the unintentional pun). "What do you mean?"

Giles came to an abrupt halt beside me. "Come now, Simon, you must have been aware of it."

"I knew that they had once been involved," I said, wincing inwardly at the euphemism. "But I do not believe that they had resumed their relationship."

"No, I don't believe they had either," Giles said. "In fact, quite the reverse. Professor Lovelace positively hated Luke, and, well, ..." His voice trailed off.

"Yes, Giles, what is it? Go ahead and say whatever it is."

He breathed deeply and expelled the air before replying. "I think you cannot overlook the fact that Professor Lovelace could have killed Luke."

Chapter 19

Thinking we had better have this discussion with a bit more privacy, I led Giles a short distance away from the encampment to a line of trees that bordered the eastern side of the meadow. There we would be protected from the early morning sun. An apprehensive look on his face, Giles followed me. He leaned against one tree, and I positioned myself against the one next to it, a bare three feet away.

"Now back to what you said," I said slowly, drawing out the syllables and sounding very Southern. "I'm willing to entertain that thought." I had to tiptoe lightly through this little minefield.

"Good," Giles said, appearing vastly relieved. "And none of this has anything to do with our, well, the contest over you, Simon." He looked away from me.

"Yes, Giles," I said. "I understand that. Go on." All this time my mind was racing as I tried to figure out when, and where, Giles could have overheard something dangerous.

"Remember yesterday, when we had gone back to Laurel Cottage, and I was sleeping on the sofa?"

At my nod, Giles continued. "At some point I woke up, and I was very thirsty. You were in your office, tapping away at the keyboard. I stumbled into the kitchen to get some water, and once I had some, I decided a bit of fresh air might help clear my head." He grinned weakly. "I opened the back door and stepped out into the garden, and a moment later I heard a loud voice."

"Yes," I said, when he fell silent. "Go on."

"I didn't intend to eavesdrop," Giles said, shifting uneasily against his tree, "but I was still a bit groggy. The loud voice I heard belonged to Professor Lovelace. He had his back to me, and I suppose he was so intent upon his conversation that he hadn't heard me come outside."

"With whom was he having this conversation?" I asked. "Was there someone else in the garden with him?"

Giles shook his head. "No, he was talking on a mobile phone. I could hear only his side of the conversation, but I knew immediately who the other party was."

I had a sinking feeling. "What exactly did you hear?"

"Ordinarily I would have left immediately, Simon," Giles said with an earnest gaze. "But I'm afraid my reactions were rather dulled by the hangover."

"Yes, we've established that, Giles," I said, fear making me the tiniest bit testy with him. "What was it you heard?"

"The first thing I heard was Professor Lovelace saying, 'I know very well what you want, Luke, but no matter what you say, I shan't change my mind.' "

"Was that all?" I asked, hoping desperately that Tris had not been more explicit.

"No," Giles said. "There was a pause, while I suppose Luke responded to that, at some length. Then Professor Lovelace spoke again. 'Don't try to threaten me, Luke,' he said. 'I could easily arrange to give you half of what you want.' Then he laughed, and I felt very cold, suddenly. 'You'd be dead, but without all the fringe benefits.' That was the last thing I heard, because I decided I didn't want Professor Lovelace to catch me listening. I slipped back into the cottage and back to the sofa." Giles broke off, shuddering. "What on earth did he mean by that, Simon? What fringe benefits could there be to being dead?"

Oh, dear, I thought. *How do I dodge* this *bullet?*

I assumed a very puzzled look, which I made sure Giles noticed. "That is a facer, Giles, I must admit. Yes, it does definitely sound like Tris was threatening to kill Luke, but as to what he meant by 'fringe benefits,' I'm not quite sure."

"Maybe it has something to do with whatever Luke was trying to blackmail the professor over," Giles said. "Do you have any idea what that might be? What could Luke have wanted from the professor?"

"That's a reasonable assumption," I said airily, "but I'm afraid I haven't a clue. Maybe it was something to do with the time when the two of them were involved, as you called it. Some peccadillo of Tris's that Luke was threatening to make public." That sounded good. "Something that might embarrass Tris. Yes, that must have been it. But whatever it was, I haven't the foggiest."

"I don't know, Simon," Giles replied, patently skeptical. "I should think it would take more than a *peccadillo* to warrant a death threat. That would be quite an overreaction, and Professor Lovelace doesn't strike me as the type to indulge in such histrionics."

Giles was too shrewd by half. My attempt to weasel out of this was going nowhere fast.

"Then it must have been something more serious," I said. "But what it could be, I just haven't a clue."

"The whole thing seems absurd," Giles said, "and I might have thought it a joke. But the tone of Professor Lovelace's voice as he said that last bit, 'You'd be dead,' was anything but amusing."

"Why didn't you tell me about this before?" I asked.

Giles's face reddened. "Truth be told, Simon," he said, "after I woke up the second time, I thought for a while that I had simply dreamed it. Rather a bizarre dream, I grant you, but at first I was inclined to dismiss it as nothing more than that."

"Then what made you think it really happened? Could it

have been a dream after all?" I found myself in a quandary. I had no doubt that Giles really had heard the conversation as he reported it, but it would be to my advantage, temporarily, at least, to persuade him otherwise. I was simply not ready to tell him the truth about what Luke wanted from Tris, and thus about Tris's very real motive in wanting Luke dead.

Giles's eyes scanned my face. "Don't you believe me, Simon? It wasn't a dream, I'm certain of that."

"Of course I believe you, Giles," I said. How could I, in all conscience, respond otherwise? "But why are you now so certain you didn't dream it?"

"Because I remember it far too clearly," Giles said. "I hardly ever remember my dreams, Simon."

"I suppose so, Giles," I said, though I must have sounded skeptical.

"And if that isn't enough for you, Simon," Giles said, his voice turning frosty, "I found grass stains on the bottom of my feet. I had gone outside in my bare feet, and that's when I overheard Professor Lovelace. Satisfied?"

"Certainly, Giles," I said, "but I never really doubted you." I invested as much sincerity as I could into those words, and evidently it worked.

"Thank you, Simon," Giles said, thawing noticeably. "Now that we've finally settled that, what are you going to do about what I told you?"

"For the moment, nothing. I will keep my eye on Tris, and if I suspect that he did indeed have something to do with Luke's death, I shall take appropriate action. In the meantime, I think it's best to keep this between ourselves."

"Very well, Simon," Giles said. "I suppose you know best."

I thought he had forgotten about what Tris had threatened, but my relief was short lived.

"But what did Professor Lovelace mean about Luke being dead without the fringe benefits?"

"I really can't say, Giles." And that was the truth, because the complete truth would have complicated matters far too much at this stage.

"Can't, or won't," Giles said, sighing. "I suppose I shall just have to trust that you know what you're doing, Simon. Shall we leave it at that?"

"Yes, thank you, Giles," I said. "It's for the best, for now."

He pushed away from the tree, and I followed him as he headed back toward the encampment, away from the shade and shelter of the trees. "What next, Simon?"

"I really should go back and talk to Adele again," I said. "That is, if she'll take time to speak to me, and I am a bit doubtful that she will."

"Why do you need to talk to her again?"

"To find out what she knows about her brother's movements yesterday. Whom he saw, what he ate, and when. That kind of thing."

"She might balk at telling you such things, Simon."

"That wouldn't surprise me in the least, Giles," I said. "Adele has turned out to be far more shrewd than I had anticipated. Around her brother she was rather a nonentity, but now that he's gone, she seems quite formidable, in her way."

By this time we had reached the encampment again, and I paused, looking back toward the de Montfort pavilion. Should I try to tackle Adele again? Or should I wait and bide my time until a more appropriate moment?

Making a quick decision, I said, "Come along, Giles. Let's see if we can winkle anything more out of Adele." I turned back toward her tent.

"As you wish, Simon," Giles said, falling into step beside me. "I must say, however, I rather doubt you will find the lady very forthcoming."

"Perhaps not," I said, "but that, too, will tell us something, won't it?"

"You mean, if she has nothing to hide, she'll speak freely to you? And if she's covering up something, she'll be evasive."

"More or less," I said.

As we approached the tent, I could hear a lovely, lilting so-prano at a low volume singing the hauntingly familiar "Greensleeves."

"Can you hear that, Giles?"

He shook his head. I forgot sometimes that his hearing was not as acute as mine. We moved a few steps closer, and the singing became clearer. "A beautiful voice. Surely that can't be Adele," Giles whispered as we stood and listened for a few minutes more.

The song ended on a sigh, and after a moment of silence, Giles and I moved forward again.

"Hello," I called out. "Adele, are you there?"

"Begging your pardon, sir, but my lady is not here just now," said the owner of the beautiful singing voice as she stepped into view in the opening of the tent.

The speaking voice had the same lilt and lovely timbre. Its owner, however, was rather on the plain side, with a pale face and watery eyes. She curtsied. "Is there aught I could do to assist you, gentle sirs?"

"Perhaps," I said, quickly revising my plan. Maybe this young woman, clearly a servant in the de Montfort menage, had the information I wanted, and I wouldn't have to try to get it out of Adele after all.

"Was that you we heard singing just now?"

She nodded shyly.

"You have a very beautiful voice," Giles said, and she turned adoring eyes upon him.

"Thank you, sir," she said. But then a troubled frown ap-peared. "But I should not be singing when His Grace has died so sadly and horribly."

"I'm sure he would not mind," I said kindly. "With a voice like that, who could object?"

She blushed. "Thank you, sir," she said again.

"What is your name?" I asked.

"I am called Etheldreda, sir."

"A good Saxon name," I responded heartily.

She smiled.

"Perhaps we could wait inside the tent until your mistress returns?" I asked.

"Certainly, sir," Etheldreda replied, stepping back and allowing us to enter the tent.

"It is very tragic, though, Etheldreda, about the duke," I said as Giles and I sat down. I caught Giles's eye, and he understood my signal.

"Yes, terribly tragic," Giles said, looking up earnestly at Etheldreda, still standing before us. "I'm sure this must be very distressing for you, and for everyone in the late duke's service."

"Oh, yes," she said. "He was a good and generous master, and we shall miss him. Not like some I could name," she muttered. She sat down in a chair across from us after I had gestured for her to do so.

"And it's all very puzzling, too, don't you think?" Giles said in a tone that indicated he, too, was very puzzled by the whole thing. "Who could have done such a thing?"

Etheldreda shrugged. "It is a great mystery indeed. His Grace did hold strong opinions sometimes that angered some among us. But he was a good man for all that."

"I'm sure he was," I said. "You must have had plenty of opportunity to witness that, Etheldreda. How long have you been in service to the duke?"

"For three years now," she said proudly. "I hadn't the money to join the society on my own, but His Grace paid me well enough for serving his household at these gatherings that I could afford to."

"You must work very hard at these gatherings," Giles said.

"Oh, yes," she said. "But I don't mind. I don't mind hard work. This year His Grace appointed me his chief serving maid." Her homely face beamed with pride. "And he often asked me to sing for his guests."

"Then he indeed valued you highly," Giles said.

"Yes, certainly," I agreed. "But you must have had to be constantly in attendance when the late duke was here in his pavilion."

"Yes, sir," Etheldreda said. "His Grace was right popular, and there were always a lot of people coming and going."

"Yesterday was no different, I suppose," Giles said. Really, he had taken his cue well. Etheldreda had a hard time taking her eyes off him, and he continued gently to draw her out.

"Oh, no," she said. "There were ever such a lot of people here yesterday. I was busy filling and refilling cups and then taking them out to wash them and bring them back again."

"I imagine there were many who came seeking the duke's favor," Giles said. "Especially since it appeared that he very well might have been the next king."

Her face puckered so that I feared she might start crying. "And a fine king he would have been," she said, bravely holding back the tears.

At this rate we might never find out anything concrete, but it wouldn't do to rush her. I quelled my impatience and left Giles to continue his gentle interrogation.

"We have met the present king, of course," Giles said, allowing a hint of distaste to creep into his voice, "as well as the other candidate, I suppose you would call him."

Etheldreda's lip curled. "That fat little toad Sir Reginald Bolingbroke, you mean. What a prat! And a fat lot of good it did him, coming here with a basket full of pastries yesterday."

"Was he trying to curry favor with the duke?" Giles asked.

"Oh, yes," Etheldreda said. "He tried to make out like he was on the duke's side, but His Grace saw right through that." She laughed. "He sat right there and ate those pastries the little toad brought, then sent him away with a flea in his ear."

"What time was that?" Giles asked, a shade too quickly.

Etheldreda frowned, but when Giles smiled at her, she smiled back. "Mid-afternoon, the hottest part of the day."

This information was most interesting. Sir Reggie could have given Luke a poisoned pastry, and it might have taken the digitalis several hours to do its work. I longed to have access to the information from the postmortem, and if I were lucky, Robin Chase might be willing to share it.

Almost as if I had conjured him with that thought, Robin stepped into the tent, startling the three of us.

"Trying to do my work again for me, Simon?"

Chapter 20

❝Just chatting with this charming young woman, Robin,❞ I said airily. ❝You should hear her sing. She has a very lovely voice.❞

Robin laughed. ❝Actually, I've heard her sing quite often, Simon, though not for a couple of years as she's been living in London. She's the daughter of my vicar, and I've known her since she was a wee sprout. Hello, Beryl. How are you this morning?❞

❝Fine, Robin,❞ Etheldreda-Beryl said, smiling. ❝Is this the gentleman you were telling me about last evening?❞

Robin's face split in a huge grin. ❝Yes, Beryl, it is.❞

The girl tried unsuccessfully to stop a giggle before it escaped. She clamped a hand over her mouth as she blushed a fiery red. Giles turned his head away, but I could see his shoulders moving slightly.

❝Have a good laugh at my expense,❞ I said, pretending to pout. ❝I don't mind in the least.❞ I looked up at the handsome policeman. ❝This must be a first, Robin. Not only do you have a mole conveniently inside the household of the murder victim, you also have your ablest assistant on the job as well.❞ I beamed at him, and he commenced to stroking his moustache.

❝Yes, well,❞ Robin said, a bit uncertainly. ❝Too much help can be a problem, Simon.❞

"Yes, well," I said teasingly. "Am I too much, Robin?"

Beryl giggled again, and Giles sighed loudly. Robin simply stared at me, stony-faced. Oh, my, best not push him too far. He had been remarkably tolerant in the past.

"Strike that," I said. I stood. "Come along, Giles. I suppose we've outstayed our welcome, and we had best toddle along."

"Not so fast, Simon," Robin said, holding up a hand in a gesture that told me to stay put.

I sat back down, and Giles made a funny face at me that Robin couldn't see, as if to say, "This is a surprise!"

"As you've already put your foot in it, so to speak," Robin said, deadpan, "you might as well keep your foot where it is, at least for the next little while." He moved closer to stand in front of Beryl, to one side of me.

"Beryl," Robin said, "I gather Dr. Kirby-Jones here was inquiring, in his way, about who visited the deceased the day he died."

"Yes, Robin," she said, her eyes wide open and focused intently on his face.

I wondered whether Robin realized how deeply in love with him the girl was. He gave no sign of it in his avuncular manner, but perhaps that was for my benefit.

"Would you remind repeating what you told Simon here?" Robin asked. "Even though we discussed this last night," he added, forestalling her protest.

"Very well, then," Beryl said. With admirable conciseness she related to Robin what she had told Giles and me about the visit from Sir Reginald Bolingbroke.

Robin had pulled a small notebook from his pocket and appeared to be checking a few notes as Beryl talked. When she had finished, he asked, "Who else came to see the deceased yesterday?"

"His Majesty the King," the girl answered.

"Before or after Sir Reginald?" Robin asked, glancing at his notebook.

"After," Beryl said. "About a quarter of an hour after. I was laying out the clothes for the evening for both the duke and milady, checking to be certain they were in good nick, when I heard the king hail His Grace."

"Were you present for any of the king's visit with the duke?" Robin grimaced slightly as he spoke the two men's titles.

"Briefly, Robin," Beryl replied. "His Grace asked me to serve his guest some mead, and I did so."

"Were they talking at all while you were serving?"

Beryl shrugged. "Mostly chitchat, nothing of consequence." She paused. "I just remembered. The mead I served, well . . ."

"Yes, Beryl," Robin prompted. "What have you remembered?"

She looked sheepish. "I'm sorry, Robin, I suppose last night I was too dazed by what had happened to recall clearly." She paused for a deep breath. "And I don't know whether this has any bearing on anything, but the mead I served was from a jug that the king had brought with him. He said it was a gift for the duke. He makes his own mead, you know."

Robin scribbled furiously in his notebook, while Giles and I exchanged startled glances. Could King Harald have poisoned Luke with mead he had brought as an ostensible gift?

"Did you see both of them actually drink the mead, Beryl?" Robin asked.

Beryl thought a moment. "I know His Grace did. He quite enjoyed it and commented on the strong taste. But, come to think of it, I don't remember seeing the king drink any. At least, not while I was with them."

"Were you with them very long?" Robin continued his interrogation.

"No, only a few minutes," Beryl said, "just as long as it took to serve them, as the duke had asked. Then I went back to my work in one of the rear chambers." She pointed toward the chamber in question.

"But you could still hear what they were talking about?"

"Yes, Robin," she said, her eyes downcast. "One cannot help it. I did not mean to eavesdrop on their conversation, but there is no way to avoid hearing what goes on in the whole pavilion."

"What were they talking about?"

"Some business deal in the mundane world," Beryl said. "The king wanted the duke to give him a contract. It sounded like His Grace had already turned him down a time or two, but Harald, the king, I mean, sounded pretty desperate. He was begging the duke. He even said he would not fight His Grace for the kingship if the duke would grant him the contract."

"And what was the duke's response to that?" I spoke before I thought, and I earned a frown from Robin for my trouble.

"Go ahead, Beryl, you can answer him," Robin said.

Beryl's hands fidgeted in her lap, and she hesitated in her answer. "It was really rather awful, Robin," she said at last. "I had never heard the duke sound so cold or so cruel. The poor king was practically sobbing, and the duke laughed at him. He told the king he didn't need any help taking the kingship away from him, and he saw no reason to barter for it." She blushed. "Please don't ask me to repeat the word that the duke called him. But it was rather nasty, and after that the king stormed out."

"Did he have anything else to say to the duke before he left?" Robin asked.

I admired the delicacy of his question. He didn't want to lead his witness by asking whether the king had threatened Luke.

Beryl's face puckered up as she tried to hold back the tears. "He said he'd make the duke pay for this, somehow." A sob escaped her. "It was all so humiliating, Robin. I actually felt sorry for Harald, even though he's such an idiot."

"Yes, I can well imagine," Robin said. He pulled a handkerchief from his pocket and offered it to her. Her eyes shone as she accepted it, and Robin would have to have been blind not to understand their message. I looked away as Beryl delicately blew her nose.

"What happened after that?" Robin said, after giving the girl a moment to collect herself.

"I continued with my work," she said, "and I could hear the duke moving about in here."

"How long was it before you entered this chamber again?"

Beryl frowned, considering. "Perhaps another quarter of an hour, I suppose."

"And what did you observe when you came back in here?"

Shutting her eyes as if to aid her memory, Beryl concentrated. After a moment, she opened her eyes. "His Grace was busy with some paperwork at that table." She pointed to an area behind us, and we turned to look. Paperwork still littered the surface of the table.

"And?" Robin prompted her.

"And then I began to clear away the mead and the drinking cups," Beryl said. "The duke asked me to leave the mead and his cup with him, but I took the king's away to be washed."

"Was there any mead in the king's cup?" Robin asked.

Beryl shook her head. "No, it was empty."

"And you didn't see him drink anything from the cup?"

"No, Robin," she said. "I never did. But there was one odd thing." She paused.

"What was odd?" I asked, and this time Robin didn't bother to turn and frown at me.

Her eyes still fixed on Robin's face, Beryl responded, "I would have sworn that there was more mead in the jug than there had been when I had poured out for them earlier."

Again Giles and I exchanged startled glances. This could be potentially damaging for Harald, if the mead should prove to have been the method by which the poison had been administered.

"Where is that jug of mead now?" Robin asked.

"The duke drank it all," Beryl said, "and I washed the jug. It's still here, if you want it."

"Yes, I think I had better see it," Robin said. "Perhaps you could show me where it is."

Beryl rose from her chair, and Robin followed her into another chamber of the pavilion while Giles and I remained in our seats. "It's too bad that she washed it," Giles said, his voice low.

"Yes," I said. "That jug could prove to be quite significant. But she wasn't to know, of course, that the mead might have been poisoned." I shrugged. "The problem is, though, we don't know *how* Luke was poisoned. It could have been the mead, or it could have been those blasted fig pastries he loved so much."

"That's something the scientists will have to sort out," Giles said, sighing. "And I wonder whether Chase will tell you about any of it, Simon. I cannot quite figure him. One minute he complains that you're interfering, and the next he lets you (and me, which is even stranger!) sit in on an interview with a witness."

"Very odd," I said, "but Robin can be rather devious, as I have discovered. I'm not sure what his game is at the moment, but as long as he's being forthcoming, I'm certainly going to take advantage of it."

A few moments later Robin strode back into the front of the pavilion, all the while issuing orders over his mobile phone. He was arranging for some of the technical members of his staff to come and take charge of the jug that had once contained the potentially poisonous mead and to survey the whole pavilion for anything they might have missed on their first look around.

After ending the call and stowing the mobile away in his jacket pocket, Robin fixed a suspiciously friendly smile on

Giles and me. "I fear, Simon, Sir Giles," he said, "that I must ask you to vacate the premises, for, as you no doubt just heard, various members of my team will arrive shortly."

"And it wouldn't do to have them find us lolling about, is that it, Robin?" I offered a jaunty smile as I stood, and Giles did the same.

"You are a quick study, Simon," Robin said, offering a more genuine smile this time.

"I can take a hint," I said, "believe it or not." I turned as if to leave the tent, hesitated, then turned back. "One thing, Robin, before we leave."

"Yes, Simon?" Robin asked, eyebrows already half-raised in irritated inquiry.

"Have you any information you can share yet about the cause of death?"

Giles coughed beside me, but I waited with a patient smile. Robin made a show of reluctance over offering the information, but his heart wasn't really in it. He wanted me to know, whatever his reason might have been.

"We do not have conclusive results as of yet," he said pompously, "because the pathologist hasn't completed the postmortem and the tests. He won't make any statement as to cause of death until he has finished with his analyses." He shrugged. "But I can't ignore what Professor Lovelace said. It just might be digitalis poisoning."

"Very interesting," I said. "And was the pathologist willing to express any opinion as to just how the victim came to partake of the poison?"

Robin shook his head regretfully. "No, I did ask, but all he would say is that, if it were digitalis, it could have taken several hours to have acted."

"Which means that it was not present in anything he might have eaten or drunk at Totsye Titchmarsh's dinner party last night."

"Exactly. If it was digitalis," Robin said. "But that leaves a number of other possibilities."

"The mead he drank, which was brought to him by the king, or one of the pastries that Sir Reginald gave him."

"Yes, Simon, it could have been in either of those," Robin said. "Or in something else entirely. One of our tasks now is to trace, as closely as possible, every step the victim took yesterday. Discover everything he ate and drank throughout the day. When we have the complete results from the post-mortem, we'll know better what we're looking for."

"That should prove interesting," I said. "If I should happen to uncover anything on my own, naturally, I'll let you know right away."

"Naturally," Robin said, his tone devoid of inflection. "Now, Simon, Sir Giles, if you'll excuse me?" He held up a hand, indicating the opening of the tent, through which we could see several members of his staff approaching.

"Then we shall take our leave of you, Robin," I said, and without a backward glance, I glided out of the tent, Giles right on my heels.

Once we were out of earshot of Robin and his staff, I paused in the shadow of a nearby tent. Giles stepped close, sensing the need for privacy. "What would you like me to do, Simon?"

I smiled. "Good man, Giles." He dimpled. "Take your time and nose around the encampment, see what you can find out about the daily routine of the de Montfort pavilion. Where they get their food, how it's prepared, who prepares it, how many servants there are, and so on. Can you manage that?"

"Of course, Simon," Giles whispered with confidence. "What will you be doing?"

"I think it would prove very fruitful to talk directly to some of the suspects in the case," I said. "I have an idea what their various motives are for wanting Luke de Montfort dead, but I need to get a better sense of who hated him enough to kill him. Who was finally pushed so far that murder seemed the only way out."

"Just be careful, Simon," Giles said. "Whoever killed Luke was pretty ruthless, and I wouldn't want anything to happen to you."

I couldn't tell Giles that the possibility of the killer's harming me was practically nonexistent. Unless, of course, that killer were Tristan Lovelace.

In that case, both Giles and I could be in deadly danger. Though I felt confident in my ability to protect myself from Tris, I had no such assurance in being able to keep Giles safe from him.

That thought shook me deeply, and perhaps accounted for the fact that I gave Giles a long, lingering kiss before sending him off on his quest.

Chapter 21

After Giles left me, I dithered for a moment or two, trying to decide in what order to tackle my various suspects. I might as well deal with the most obnoxious and least attractive one first, so I set off to find Sir Reginald Bolingbroke.

I inquired of the first person I encountered, a cheerful elderly man dressed very plainly, where I might find Sir Reginald. His smile dimming appreciably, my informant directed me to my quarry's abode.

"You can't miss it," he assured me.

"Why is that?"

"You'll know it when you see it." He hesitated. I could see that he wondered what business I might have with Reggie, but I merely thanked him and continued on my way.

A few minutes later, I found Reggie's tent in one of the sections of the encampment I had yet to explore. I grinned. No wonder one couldn't miss Reggie's tent. Until this moment, I had thought Luke de Montfort's pavilion the most elaborate and colorful in the encampment, but Reggie's outshone Luke's by a mile. Bold designs in bright gold thread meandered all over the deep blue canvas, and numerous pennants fluttered in the light breeze from various points around the pavilion. How much money had the wanker spent on this outlay?

I approached the open flap at the front of the pavilion. "Sir Reginald?" I called.

"Come," a voice commanded me, and I stepped inside.

Removing my sunglasses, I peered with great interest around the tent. The furnishings were no less sumptuous and costly than the tent itself. I wondered idly whether the furniture I saw was actually real period stuff or costly reproductions. Either way, the man had spent a tidy packet on his medieval hobby.

"What do *you* want?" Sir Reginald demanded ungraciously.

I smiled disarmingly, trying to avoid looking him directly in his one good eye. "I heard about your beautiful pavilion and its contents, and I rather wanted to see it all for myself. I hope you don't mind." I paused to cast an openly admiring glance around. "This is quite an impressive collection you've got here."

He thawed enough to offer me a weak smile. "Yes, well, I've been collecting for years. Always had a thing for medieval furnishings."

"It's all pretty amazing," I said, moving a bit closer to where he sat on a chair that could easily have been mistaken for a throne. He even had it on a small dais. "How do you manage to bring all this with you?"

"I have a lorry specially designed for it," he said in a slightly boastful tone. "And men who are used to handling my lovelies."

I smiled inwardly at his unintentional pun. Or was it a Freudian slip? I must remember to tell Giles about it later, and we could both have a good laugh.

"I've been inside several of the pavilions here, and I haven't see anything like it. Not even in the de Montfort pavilion."

Sir Reginald preened at that. "Luke thought he knew what style really is." He waved a hand about. "This is how a medieval nobleman should live. But of course one couldn't expect a mere cook to know that."

"I suppose not," I murmured. "Luke came of rather plebeian stock, I take it."

"Most assuredly," Reggie said. "Thoroughly bourgeois, unlike myself."

"Oh, really," I said.

He nodded emphatically. "My grandfather was the seventh Earl of Morcaster."

I had never heard of that particular peer. Obviously a very minor earl, I decided, but I didn't share my opinion with the earl's grandson. Instead, I did my best to appear impressed that I was in such noble and exalted company. "Then you must not have encountered Luke socially very often, outside these gatherings, that is."

"I should say not!" Reggie huffed at me. "The very idea."

"But I suppose things are different in the world of the G.A.A. Anyone can be a nobleman, it seems. Or even king."

"More's the pity, if you ask me," Sir Reginald said. "When I am king, there will be some changes, you can be assured of that."

"One good thing about the Middle Ages," I said in a mild tone, "was that everyone knew his proper place in the scheme of things."

"Too bloody right!" Sir Reginald almost bounced off his throne in excitement. "There was none of this democratic stuff in the Middle Ages." He sighed longingly. "Ah, for the good old days."

I smothered a laugh. He really was a piece of work. "Ah, yes, back then you wouldn't have had to contend with jumped-up bakers' sons trying to run things, would you?"

He eyed me with suspicion, finally alert for any signs of mockery on my part. I gazed blandly back at him. Reassured, he allowed his features to relax into smug satisfaction.

"No, I wouldn't," he said. "I could have spit in Luke's face, and he couldn't have done a damned thing about it."

"Well, I'd say that someone has pretty much done that, don't you think?"

"What do you mean?"

I shrugged. "I should think deliberately poisoning someone is putting him in his place rather effectively. Wouldn't you agree?"

Sir Reginald stood up from his throne and hopped down from the dais. He took a couple of steps toward me, then thought better of it. He stepped back. "And just what do you mean by that?"

"Oh," I said, waving a hand about nonchalantly, "you know. Someone obviously thought Luke was getting above himself."

"He was," Reggie said. "But I didn't poison him, if that's what you mean."

"I didn't accuse you," I said, "but since you've mentioned it . . ."

"You don't dare!"

At this point I couldn't refrain from laughing openly at him. "Come now, my good man," I said, and nearly laughed again, watching him bridle at my condescending tone, "surely, after what you've been telling me, you can't expect me not to think you had a perfectly good motive for doing away with Luke."

He sputtered at me, nothing but nonsense syllables, while he grew so red in the face I feared his head would explode.

"Anyone could see you hated him," I continued, "and it was also fairly obvious that he was going to be elected king. You didn't stand a chance while he was in the running, did you?" I shook my head dolefully. "No, you didn't. You knew that, and you could easily have poisoned him. And with him out of the way, you could probably defeat poor old Harald pretty handily. Wouldn't you say so?"

Gasping for air, he collapsed in the direction of the dais. But he missed by an inch or so and sat down hard on the carpet in front of it. I almost took pity on him, he was so pathetic.

"Yes, you probably wouldn't have much trouble with Harald," I repeated. "Or should I say, 'you won't,' now that Luke is out of the way."

Sir Reginald at last found his voice, if not his dignity. "You pompous, interfering poofter! How dare you! I should throw you out of my pavilion this very moment." He struggled to get to his feet.

I regarded him with a smile indicating that we both knew how futile a threat that was.

Sir Reginald rearranged his gown with trembling hands. "It is true that I did despise Luke," he said, attempting a casual tone, "but I was not the only one. There would be quite a queue ahead of me, you know. There are others here who despised him as much as I."

"Come now," I scoffed.

"Oh, yes, indeed," he said. "And at the head of the queue would be that tart of a sister of his."

"She seemed like a lady to me," I said, "for all that she's a member of the dread bourgeoisie."

"Shows what you know," Reggie responded, ignoring the bait. "As if the likes of you would know a true, gently born lady." He snorted rudely. "That vixen is no better than she should be, you mark my words. Flirts with anything in trousers, she does."

"Or almost anything."

This time he knew he was being mocked. He reddened. "I wouldn't consort with such a woman. There's no telling what kind of pox one might get as a result," he said, but I'm not sure he convinced even himself.

"What possible motive could she have for murdering her own brother?"

"The basic thing that every woman wants," he said. "Power, pure and simple. Despite the fact that women are manifestly unfit to rule or to run large businesses."

"Don't let Queen Elizabeth hear you say that," I admonished him, shaking a playful finger in his direction, "or you might find yourself arrested for treason."

"Don't be ridiculous, man," he said. But he did look a mite worried.

"Have no fear," I said, "I won't report you to the Prime Minister's office. Or whoever it is you report treason to."

He glared at me. I knew he wanted me to leave, but he didn't have to courage to try to make me do it. Underneath the bluster quaked a raving coward.

"You say Adele wanted power," I continued. "That's not a very concrete motive. She might have wanted the power her brother wielded in their family business, but how could you prove that she would kill to get it? How would anyone be able to prove that?"

"Because I heard her, that's how." He smiled.

"Oh, really," I said. "What did you hear? And when?"

"Never you mind what and when," he said smugly. "I heard her plotting with her new beau, when she didn't think anyone could overhear her foul plans."

"I presume you mean Millbank." I paused for him to confirm that, but he didn't respond. "If you have heard something as potentially damaging as you claim, then you should go to the police with it."

"I'm not going to do the police's work for them," Sir Reginald said. "Let them find it out for themselves."

Really, the man was even stupider than I had first thought. "Then you have two options. I shan't hesitate to inform Detective Inspector Chase of our conversation, and I'm sure he'll be eager to question you."

Reggie's eyes widened at that. Clearly he hadn't thought things through.

"And if you don't tell the police yourself," I said, trying not to gloat, "you'll probably find yourself cast as the chief suspect. It wouldn't take a suspicious mind long to figure out that those pastries you gave Luke yesterday were filled with poison."

He started gabbling again, but nothing of any sense came out of his flapping mouth.

"Think about it," I said. "I'll give you a couple of hours to consider your course of action, and then I'll speak to the police myself." I bowed. "And now I must bid you good day, sir."

As I left his pavilion, I could hear him sputtering.

The man was as dumb as the proverbial dirt clod. If he had poisoned Luke with the fig pastries, he was stupid to think he could possibly get away with it. And if he withheld solid evidence of someone else's guilt from the police, he was equally stupid enough to get himself killed over it.

I walked a few yards away from Sir Reginald's pavilion and paused to take stock. Whom should I visit next?

Deciding that the king himself would be my next choice, I strode forward in search of the royal residence.

I hadn't gone far when I chanced upon Murdo Millbank in conversation with the de Montforts' young maid, Etheldreda-Beryl. I paused a few feet away and eavesdropped unashamedly.

". . . she has to," Millbank was saying in tones of desperation.

"I can tell her, sir," Etheldreda responded dubiously, "but I don't know as she'll listen to me. Begging your pardon, sir."

"But I simply must talk to her," Millbank said. "It's vital that I do so." His hands fidgeted with the long left sleeve of his houppelande. "I simply cannot understand it," he muttered, more to himself than to the girl in front of him.

"She's that upset about her brother, sir," Etheldreda said kindly. "I'm sure if you wait a wee while, she'll be happy to speak with you."

"Perhaps," Millbank said. He breathed in deeply, then exhaled as he stiffened his spine. "You tell her from me that I will call upon her in two hours' time, and I expect her to be ready to talk to me. Is that clear?"

Etheldreda shrank away from the fierce tone. "Yes, sir,"

she said. Then she grasped her skirt in her hands and scurried away from him.

Millbank was still glaring after her as I approached him.

"Good day, Master Millbank," I said.

Startled, he whirled to face me. "Who the devil? Oh, you. What do *you* want?"

Oh dear, oh dear. My second less-than-gracious greeting within the past hour. If I had been of a more sensitive nature, I would have begun to think some people didn't like me. Hard to imagine, I know.

"Me? I'm just out for a stroll through the encampment," I said in my breeziest tone. "How about yourself?"

"I'm too busy to enjoy myself by just wandering about," he said pointedly, then turned to walk away.

"I'm sure you are," I said, falling into step beside him. "I'm sure you have lots to do, what with your business venture falling apart like it has."

He stopped and turned to look up at me. "What the devil do you mean?"

"Oh, you know," I said, waving my hand about. "Your plans for all of this."

"Who have you been talking to?" he demanded.

"Well, not anyone in particular," I said. "But I was just thinking, with your principal partner dead, you can't proceed with your plans for the medieval restaurant and theme park, I guess you'd call it."

"Nothing has changed," he said shortly. "And it's none of your bloody business after all." He began to walk away from me again.

I matched him stride for stride. "I suppose Adele de Montfort aims to go along with the deal you put together with her late brother."

He made no response to that, no doubt hoping I'd take the hint and leave him alone. He didn't know me very well.

"I see," I said. "I gather Adele has changed her mind after all."

That stopped him. He glared up at me. "Have you been talking to her? What has she said?"

"Oh, you mean she hasn't said anything to you?" She certainly hadn't said anything to me, but he was too dense to see through my vague response.

He swore, loudly and fluently. "She's not going to get away with this. I have a contract, after all."

"Then you have nothing to worry about, I'm sure," I said, patting him on the arm consolingly.

Shaking off my hand, he said, "Too bloody right! No one crosses Murdo Millbank and gets away with it."

Chapter 22

———☠———

"Is that so?" I said, in a deceptively mild tone. "I think perhaps Detective Inspector Chase would be *most* interested to hear that. Shall we go and tell him together?"

Millbank stared at me, open-mouthed in shock.

"Come along now, there's a good chap," I said, taking him by the arm. "Let's go and have a chat with the nice policeman." I managed to lead him along about three steps before he recovered his senses.

"Take your bloody hand off me," he stormed. "I'll do nae such thing, man. You're bleeding crazy, if you ask me."

"Oh, really?" I said, dropping all pretense of good humor. "I'm not crazy enough to ignore the fact that you had a darn good motive for murdering Luke de Montfort."

"What the bleeding hell are you talking about?" Millbank was fairly hopping up and down, he was so angry. "We were business partners, and we were going to make a lot of money together. Now that he's dead, all that may fall through."

I laughed derisively. "Try that one on somebody else, why don't you?" I leaned forward and poked his chest with my forefinger, and he winced and backed up a couple of steps. "We all saw the way you were cozying up to poor Adele. The way I see it, you thought you'd get rid of Luke, marry Adele, and then cop the whole lot for yourself."

The color drained completely out of his face, and for a moment I thought the man was going to pass out in fear. "D-d-d-don't be r-r-r-ridiculous!" He finally managed to stutter at me. "I d-d-d-did no such thing."

"Are you denying that you and Adele haven't been getting rather chummy lately?"

A couple of interested spectators had gathered. Most everyone else had busily gone about their activities, ignoring us, but two men had stopped their work in a nearby tent to edge a bit closer. Seeing their curious gazes fixed upon us, I drew Millbank away, behind a tent a few paces away.

I repeated my question. Millbank frowned at me, and I could see his mind working, trying to figure out how to get around that.

Finally he gave up. "Yes, all right," he said. "Adele and I have become close. She's a damned attractive woman." His lip curled in disgust. "Not that the likes of you would know anything about that."

"Men have committed murder for less," I said, ignoring his attempt at insult.

"But not this man," Millbank said, thumping his chest. "Adele is a beautiful woman, but I'd not kill anyone for her sake."

"I didn't think you would," I said mildly, and he relaxed a bit. "But you very well might kill if you thought you could get your hands on a very lucrative business. A canny Scotsman like you knows the value of a million or so pounds, I have no doubt." I laughed. "Throw in a beautiful woman, and there you have it. A superb motive for doing away with Luke de Montfort."

Millbank howled in rage and launched himself at me. He was aiming to get his hands around my throat, but I deflected him easily. He was on the ground on his back before he realized what had happened.

"Don't try that again," I advised him kindly. "I'd really rather not hurt you, my good man, but I will defend myself."

He didn't move from the ground. Instead, he lay there cursing me and my forebears, accusing them of all manner of unnatural acts with one another and with a variety of livestock, until his breath gave out.

I leaned down and offered him a hand. He brushed it aside and got to his feet without any assistance from me.

"Now that you've got all that out of your system," I said with the utmost politeness, "perhaps you'll answer a question."

He regarded me with a murderous glint in his eyes, but he didn't try to get away from me.

"You're determined to make this difficult, I see," I lamented. "Very well. I suppose I shall just have to take this up with Adele instead. I cannot imagine how she will take the news that she has been a dupe in your little scheme at empire-building."

That drew a reaction, although not quite the one I had anticipated.

He laughed. When he stopped, he said, "Right, then. What's your question?"

"Were you present in the de Montforts' pavilion at any time yesterday?"

Millbank frowned. "Yes, I was there briefly in the late afternoon to discuss something with Luke. I had other matters to attend to, and after that I left the encampment entirely until it was time for Miss Titchmarsh's dinner party."

"And did you bring anything with you to the pavilion?"

"Nothing except some paperwork."

"Very well, then, Millbank," I said. "Thank you for your cooperation."

After insulting my forebears a final time, he stomped off. Had he seen the smile on my face, he would no doubt have been even more infuriated.

Altogether a most interesting, not to say, productive, interview. I congratulated myself. My forceful approach had yielded some unexpected results. Millbank was a sharp operator, but he hadn't been terribly clever in his responses to my little onslaught.

I was now more than ever convinced that his wooing of Adele de Montfort was all part of some scheme of his. Whether that scheme included the murder of Luke de Montfort was a very important question, and one I couldn't answer just yet.

A second question, and no less important, was whether Adele was in cahoots with Millbank or whether she was merely his catspaw.

From the way he laughed when I said I would confront Adele with his scheme I rather doubted that Adele was anybody's dupe. In fact it might be quite the other way round. Adele, playing at Lady Macbeth, so to speak, could have urged Millbank to murder her brother, promising him not only herself but her family's company as reward.

And if she turned her back on him once the deed was done, what could he do? In accusing her, he would open himself to a charge of murder. Stalemate.

If Millbank *had* murdered Luke, then how had he done it? How had he managed to get him to eat or drink something laden with foxglove? And when?

He could have been lying when he said that he had gone to the de Montfort pavilion only once yesterday and that he had taken nothing except some papers with him. Etheldreda the servant girl might very well know if he were telling the truth. It would at least be worth asking her.

Enough of that for the moment, however. It was time to move on to the next name on my list. His Majesty, Harald Knutson, in other words.

Moving from behind the tent, I walked down the lane and approached the first person I saw to ask for directions. He pointed in the direction I was already headed and said that I would find the king's tent a bit farther along.

"It's his time for hearing petitions," the young man advised me. "You can't miss the tent. There are several people in a queue outside it."

After thanking him, I wandered on down the lane. Sure enough, about fifty yards on, I found a tent outside of which waited four people.

Taking my place at the end of the queue, I listened idly to the chatter about me as I thought about the approach I should use with Knutson.

After twenty minutes, the person ahead of me had been admitted to the royal presence, and no one had come along to join the queue behind me. Just as well, I thought, because the king might not be in any frame of mind to listen to further petitions after I had finished with him.

Seven or eight minutes later, the tent flap opened, and the woman who had been ahead of me in the queue exited. An attendant, broad and stubby, beckoned for me to enter. I bent my head slightly to come inside, and when I straightened and removed my sunglasses, I nearly burst into laughter at what I saw.

I had thought Sir Reginald Bolingbroke's dais and throne a bit on the pretentious side, but Harald Knutson sat ensconced on a chair that made old Reggie's seem distinctly bargain basement in comparison. No wonder the man was having cash flow problems, if he spent money on accoutrements like this.

But, to be fair, I thought, perhaps the G.A.A. had footed the bill for this particular monstrosity.

Knutson hadn't been paying any particular attention to his latest petitioner, fiddling with some papers in his lap. When he finally deigned to notice me, however, his eyes widened in what looked very much like fear.

He stood up. "I'm afraid you must have been misinformed, Dr. Kirby-Jones," he said frostily. "These audiences are for members only."

"What about prospective members?" I asked. "Am I not allowed to speak with you about joining the group?"

He sat down again, eyeing me suspiciously all the while. "I suppose, if you are really serious about joining us, then I can spare you a few minutes of my time."

"Thank you, sire," I said, bowing.

Knutson waved a hand, and his attendant brought forward a chair for me. I sat in it, even though doing so left me at a distinct disadvantage. Or so it would appear to Knutson.

"Is there anyone else waiting?" Knutson asked his attendant belatedly.

"No, sire," the man answered.

"Then you may go," the king said.

Bowing, the servant took his leave, and I was alone with the king.

He immediately launched into a long and somewhat incoherent history of the society, taking the occasional detour to stress his own importance to the whole operation. I waited as politely as I could until he began to run out of steam.

Abruptly, he switched off the flow. "Did you really come here to talk about joining us?" Knutson asked.

"I *am* interested, actually," I said, "but you're right. I didn't really come here to talk to you about membership."

He stood up. "Then I have nothing further to say to you. I would very much like you to leave."

I remained seated. "This won't do, you know. You're not my king, and I haven't the slightest intention of going anywhere until I'm good and ready."

"Then I shall leave," he announced, stepping down from his dais.

"Without hearing me tell you how and why you murdered Luke de Montfort?"

He faltered, then backed up a couple of paces and plopped down on the dais. "What . . . what do you mean?" His voice came out thinly.

"You disappoint me, Your Majesty," I said, in tones of mock sadness. "I had expected you to deny my accusations forcefully, and yet you do not."

The sad excuse for a monarch breathed deeply. "And why should I bother to deny *your* accusations? Who the bloody hell are *you* to accuse *me* of anything?"

"That's better," I said approvingly. "Much more regal. The air of outraged majestic virtue might just work. On someone other than me, that is."

"You can go to the bloody devil," Knutson said. With his temper on the rise, he seemed to have regained his strength. He stood up from the dais and strode forward, shaking a finger at me. "Get out of here! You have no authority here, and I shall see to it that you are not allowed entrance here again. I *do* have authority."

"But for how long?" I said. "I should think, after the upcoming election, you won't have the authority to do much of anything."

His face darkened. "I said, get out!"

"Now, now," I replied calmly, "no need to get excited." Really, the man was much too predictable. He had behaved exactly as I had expected when I decided on this course of action.

"You still haven't answered my question," I continued. "Don't you want me to tell you how and why you murdered Luke?"

"You are completely, utterly, and entirely barmy, do you know that?" Like Millbank before him, Knutson was fairly hopping up and down in his fury.

"I'll take that as a 'yes,' " I said. "First, let me tell you how you murdered Luke." I waited a moment, and he stopped flapping about and paid attention to me.

"That's better. How did you do it? You put distilled foxglove in that mead you took him yesterday. Apparently he drank it all. Did you drink any of it?"

"Yes, of course I did," Knutson said, but I could tell he was lying. "And if I drank it, it couldn't have been poisoned, or I would have died myself."

"But you can't prove you drank any of it," I said. "The only person who might have seen you drink it was poor Luke, and he won't be answering questions."

He gaped at me. "But, but, that servant girl. She saw me."

"She says not."

"That's ridiculous," he shouted. "She's lying."

"No, I don't think she is," I said.

"She is," Knutson insisted. "But even if she didn't see me, then if it was poisoned, why didn't Luke die right then and there? Do you think I'd be stupid enough to poison him while I was right there?" He seemed very happy over his little feat of logic.

"Sorry to disappoint you," I said, trying not to laugh. "But since Luke may have been poisoned with foxglove, it would have taken several hours to act. Hence you could have poisoned the wine, knowing that he wouldn't succumb to the poison until sometime later, when you'd be safely out of the way."

"I didn't know that," Knutson said. "I don't know anything about foxglove, and you can't prove I did."

"I doubt I shall have to. That's a job for the police." I smiled at him. "Now, to the second part of the question. Why? Why did you murder Luke?"

Before I could continue, an interruption occurred, in the form of Knutson's servant, who erupted into the tent.

"Sire, sire!" He stumbled to a halt in front of Knutson, who took a moment to focus on him.

"Yes, yes, what is it?" His Majesty snapped.

"Someone's been attacked. You'd best come right away." The servant turned, expecting his master to follow him.

Knutson staggered forward. He seemed still dazed by our conversation. I stood up and grabbed his arm. "Come along, man, this could be serious."

Half-dragging the king, I followed the servant out of the tent. "Where did it happen?" I asked the man.

"Behind The Happy Destrier," he puffed as we ran down the lane.

Letting go of Knutson's arm, I pushed ahead of the servant and ran rapidly toward the tavern tent. Moments later, when

I reached it, I found a crowd gathered round the back. Elbowing a number of people aside, I quickly moved to the front of the crowd.

In shocked disbelief, I stared down at the crumpled body of Giles Blitherington.

Chapter 23

For a moment, everything was black. I could neither hear nor see anything or anyone.

Then my eyes cleared, and once again I saw Giles lying unconscious on the ground before me. He was on his back, his face turned slightly away from me and his arms flung out to either side.

I stumbled forward and fell to my knees. "Oh, Giles," I whispered. "Please be all right." I reached out with a trembling hand and caressed his arm.

In my shock at seeing him like that, I had failed to notice that he was breathing evenly and easily. At my touch, he stirred slightly.

"Don't move, Giles," I said, my voice gathering strength. "Lie still until the doctor comes."

I moved around to the other side so that I could see his face more clearly.

His eyes opened briefly, and when he saw me, his lips twisted into a smile. "Simon," he whispered.

"Don't try to talk," I said. I was afraid to touch his head. I couldn't see any obvious head wound, but I didn't want him moving about until a doctor had arrived.

"Has anyone gone for the doctor?" I said, looking up into the faces of the crowd around me.

My expression must have been more fierce than I realized, because those standing in the front began to press back a bit.

"Aye," said a voice from somewhere nearby. "She has been summoned."

Though it seemed an eternity, it must have been only three or four minutes longer before the doctor arrived, breathless, her Gladstone bag in hand. All the while Giles had continued to revive, growing increasingly restless under my attempts to keep him still.

I moved out of the way to let the doctor examine Giles. She probed his head carefully, and he winced as her fingers came into contact with the back of his head.

"A bit of a lump there," she said in a cheerful voice. "Not too bad though. Someone struck you on the back of the head. There doesn't seem to be any blood, just the lump."

"That's quite enough," Giles said in a brave attempt at humor.

She checked his eyes for signs of concussion, then asked, "Can you sit up?"

"Yes, I think so," Giles said. His voice had gained strength, and he sounded almost his usual self. Had I been able to breathe, I would have exhaled a huge sigh of relief.

"Will he be all right, doctor?" I asked.

"I believe so," she said. "A nasty knock on the head, and of course we have to be alert for signs of concussion. Confusion, nausea and vomiting, convulsions, any kind of muscle weakness, or even loss of consciousness. Keep him awake for the next twelve hours or so, and if you see any problems, get him to hospital right away."

"Do you think I should take him anyway, just to be safe?" I asked anxiously.

"Are you able to stand?" The doctor ignored my question, focusing instead on Giles.

"Yes," he said. "I'm feeling stronger now."

I bent down and grasped him under the arms. With extreme care I pulled him to his feet, and he leaned gratefully against me.

"I think he'll be fine," the doctor said, addressing me. "No need to take him to the casualty ward just yet."

"Thank you, doctor," I said.

"Yes, thank you," Giles echoed.

"You're quite welcome. Just take it easy." She smiled as she bent to retrieve her bag. She delved into it and rummaged around for a moment. At last her hand came out holding a small white envelope. "For pain," she explained as she dropped them into my hand. "One tablet every four to six hours as needed." Then she melted away into the crowd before I could offer to pay her. Still holding on to Giles, I tucked the envelope into a pocket. Then I glanced around at the curious faces surrounding us.

"Did anyone see what happened?"

There was a bit of muttering, but no one stepped forward as a witness.

"Very well, then," I said sharply. "The show's over. Get on with your business."

They dispersed very quickly at that.

Giles laughed, and I could feel his body shake slightly. "Oh, Simon, you're like the proverbial mother hen."

"You gave me quite a scare there, you know," I said.

He looked up into my face, and his smile grew wider. "No one is going to get rid of me that easily, Simon."

I wrapped my arms around him, and he laid his head on my shoulder. "When I find out who did this to you," I whispered, "I'll beat the crap out of him."

Giles drew back and grinned at me. "Not a very elegantly expressed sentiment, Simon, but I do appreciate it nevertheless. It's almost worth getting banged on the head to see you like this."

"Silly boy," I said tenderly. "If anything happened to you, I don't know what I'd do."

His eyes widened as the import of that statement dawned on him. "Simon?"

I nodded.

"Oh, Simon," he said, snuggling into my arms again.

"We have some things to talk about later," I said, feeling a bit light-headed, "when we can have some privacy. There are some things you need to know."

"Whatever you say, Simon," he said, then turned his face up to mine for a kiss.

After a few very pleasant moments I pulled away from him. Holding on to his hand, I led him around to the front of the tavern and across the lane to where someone had thoughtfully placed a long bench in the shade of a massive oak tree. Settling Giles on the bench, I sat beside him. Passersby glanced at us a bit curiously, but no one approached us. One quick glare from me, and no one would dare.

"Now, about this knock on the head," I said.

"Yes, Simon," he said. "And before you ask, I didn't see who did it."

"Very well," I responded. "What were you doing behind the tavern in the first place?"

Giles frowned in concentration. "I'm trying to remember," he said, "though things are a bit fuzzy. I know I had stopped in the tavern for something to drink, and there was someone inside. We were talking for a bit."

"Who?"

"I think it was Professor Lovelace," Giles said. He paused, his eyes closed. "Yes," he continued, opening his eyes, "it *was* Professor Lovelace."

"Did you talk with him for very long?" I asked.

"No," Giles said slowly, "I don't think so. I tried asking him a few questions, but he persisted in pretending to flirt with me."

"*Pretending* to flirt with you?" I said sharply. "What do you mean by that?"

"I'm not sure." Giles shrugged. "He was chatting me up a bit, but I didn't think his heart was in it. It just all seemed so insincere."

"And that's all he was doing?" I asked. Would Giles have realized it if Tris had tried to hypnotize him again?

"Yes," Giles said. "Although I did notice him glancing across the room a few times."

"What, or rather whom, was he looking at?"

"I believe it was a handsome young man, dressed in a scarlet tunic and hose. I had noticed him earlier, and he seemed terribly interested in what was going on between the professor and me."

I remembered seeing Tris chatting up a young man who fit that description. Tris was a fast worker, and perhaps the young man was so enamored of him, he was jealous of any competition. He could have perceived Giles as a threat and attacked him to discourage him.

I voiced these thoughts to Giles.

"Maybe," he said, "but that does seem a bit silly, don't you think?"

"Possibly," I said, "though where Tris is concerned, I wouldn't rule anything out." I watched Giles with some anxiety. "Now, are you sure you're all right? Would you like something to drink?" I stood up.

"Yes, Simon, I'm fine," Giles said. "My head is a bit sore and throbbing, but I'll do just fine. I wouldn't mind some water, however, and one of those pills the doctor gave you."

"Be back in a tick," I said, crossing the lane for the tavern. Moments later I returned with a tall pewter drinking vessel of cool water, and Giles quaffed it gratefully along with one of the pain pills.

"Thanks," he said. "That's much better." He set the water aside.

"Good. Now, before the tavern and the knock on the noggin," I said, "what had you been doing? Could anything you did or said, or anything you heard, have led to the attack?"

"If so, I'm really not certain what it could have been," Giles replied. "Until I decided to stop in at the tavern for something to drink, I was wandering around, eavesdropping on conversations, and occasionally joining in. As you might imagine, there's one basic topic of conversation today. By now, of course, most everyone knows who I am, and certainly who you are, and they know that I was there when it happened."

"And naturally they wanted to hear it from you. What you saw and heard, and all the gory details."

Giles grimaced in distaste. "Of course. I tried, whenever possible, to keep it as brief as possible, and that was usually just fine. These people love to gossip, Simon, and it wasn't very difficult to get them all going."

Particularly not if most of the people involved were female. A little attention from a handsome and charming young sprig of the nobility like Giles could work wonders on women who might otherwise appear reluctant to gossip. "Did you pick up any interesting tidbits?" I asked.

"Mostly the same things, with a few variations."

"Such as?"

Giles laughed. "For one, a number of the women had quite a bit to say about Totsye and her unrequited passion for the deceased. I don't think the poor woman realizes just how potty they all think she is." He shook his head, then winced. "It's hard to believe that a businesswoman as successful as she is could be so blindly infatuated with a man who would never return her affections the way she wanted."

"Yes, but where love is concerned, logic often flies out the window," I said.

Giles grinned. "May I quote you on that?"

I attempted a quelling glance, but Giles ignored it.

"Do these same people think Totsye could be the killer?"

"Not really," Giles said. "They do say she's smart enough to do it and get away with it, however. They admire her business acumen, even though they think she's a bit of a fool where romance is concerned. Would you believe that she and the king were once an item?" His eyes grew wide in mock astonishment.

"You can't be serious," I said dryly. "Surely the woman has better taste, and better sense, than that."

"One would think so," Giles said, "but apparently, once upon a time, as the fairy tales say, she was quite mad for Harald, and he was fair potty over her."

"What happened?" I asked. "Why didn't they live happily ever after?"

Giles grinned wickedly. "Because about that time, according to my sources, Luke and the fair Adele joined the group."

"I see," I said. "And poor Totsye can't hold a candle to the de Montfort wench."

"No, she can't, more's the pity," Giles answered. "Again, according to my sources, Adele made a dead set for old Harald. Apparently she specializes in going after men who are already attached to other women."

"Goodness gracious me," I said, "what a loathsome little quadrangle they were."

"Yes, quite the soap opera," Giles said, "as you would say in the States." He snickered. "Certainly better than the telly, if you believe what my informants were telling me. There were any number of scenes at previous gatherings over the past couple of years."

"And Totyse transferred her affections to Luke," I said. "Did she know from the beginning, I wonder, that he wasn't likely to be interested in her?"

"Apparently she knew and saw it as a challenge," Giles responded. He shook his head.

"She was going to be the woman who would change him," I said. I rolled my eyes.

"One of the women said she had talked to Totsye about it, trying to explain that it was useless, but Totsye refused to believe her. Even after she allegedly caught Luke *in flagrante delicto* with another man."

"What a scene that must have been," I said, trying not to imagine it. Instead, I stared unseeingly at the encampment before us. "The question is, does any of this have any relevance to Luke's murder?"

"I suppose one could work out some kind of motive for Totsye," Giles said.

"Yes," I agreed. "But what about opportunity? Unless it can be proven that she somehow gave Luke the poison earlier in the day, she's in the clear. She wouldn't have been able to do it."

"That's true," Giles said.

"But it was rather odd," I said, as a memory struck me.

"What was odd, Simon?"

"Hmmm? Oh, the police found a sprig of foxglove in Totsye's tent."

"Rather careless on her part, if she really is the killer," Giles said. "Even though she's in the herb business, I can't imagine that she would need to have foxglove with her."

"No," I said. "I doubt she would either. I rather think someone planted it there so the police would find it and keep Totsye on their list of suspects."

"Very likely," Giles said. "There's a lot of sympathy for Totsye, at least among the women I talked to, but they really despise Harald."

"Did they have anything interesting to say about him?"

"Other than that he made a right fool of himself over Adele de Montfort?" Giles asked sarcastically. "They had enough to say about that, I can tell you. But neither do they think much of his leadership. They were all looking forward to replacing Harald with Luke, but now they're not certain what will happen."

"Won't they just cancel the election for now, given the circumstances?"

"No, they won't," Giles said. "One of the women was quite certain about that. Because, according to her, a new candidate had been announced, just this afternoon."

"Well?" I demanded when he fell silent. "Who is it?"

His eyes sparkled with mischief. "Guess, Simon."

"Totsye," I said.

"No. Guess again."

"Giles," I said, "I hate guessing games. Who is it?"

He grinned. "Adele de Montfort."

"Ah," I said, leaning back against the tree while I considered this new wrinkle.

Had Luke de Montfort died so his sister could become queen?

Chapter 24

"Do you really think, Simon, that she would kill her brother simply to take his place in the election?" Giles asked. "Could she be that hungry for power?"

"Perhaps," I said. "Adele has proven to be a woman of unexpected depth. It seems to me that, while her brother was alive, she was always cast in his shadow. Maybe she got tired of that, frustrated with always having to take second place to her brother."

"And he wasn't exactly the type to step aside and let his sister move ahead of him."

"No, he wasn't," I agreed. I had a momentary pang when I thought of Luke, how vitally alive he had been, how attractive and how confident a man he was. And had Tristan Lovelace granted him his request, he would have been beyond the reach of poison forever.

Maybe that had been the answer all along and I just didn't want to face it. Tris had killed him, rather than grant his wish to make him a vampire. I glanced sideways at Giles. If Tris were guilty, my little talk with Giles would be even more complicated than I had anticipated. Just what I needed.

"What did the women think of Adele's chances to win?" I asked.

"They seemed to think that it would be practically no contest," Giles said. "Partly out of sympathy, but mostly because so many people in the group have come to loathe King Harald for his incompetence."

"So if Harald murdered Luke to keep from losing the election, it might not do him any good after all," I said, half in jest.

"Apparently not," Giles answered. Then he turned to me, his eyes wide. "But if Harald did kill Luke to keep from losing, mightn't he kill Adele, too?"

"It's entirely possible. I think the man's loopy enough," I said. "And desperate enough."

"This whole set-up seems rather loopy to me," Giles replied. "Would anyone really kill just to be the king or queen of this group?"

"That remains to be determined," I said. I stood, picking up the drinking vessel lent me by the tavern keeper. "Why don't you rest here for a few minutes. I want to ask a few questions in the tavern and return this cup. All right?"

Giles gazed up into my face, a slight smile hovering about his lips. "If you promise not to 'beat the crap' out of anyone on my account, as you so charmingly put it earlier."

I grinned back at him. "I reserve the right to wreak vengeance, young man, and no matter how you bat your eyelashes at me, I shall not be swayed from my purpose."

His laughter followed me as I strode across to the tavern. Stepping inside, I waited a moment for my eyes to adjust to the dimmer light inside. There were only a few customers seated here and there, and the tavern keeper was standing behind his bar, slowly sipping something out of a pewter tankard.

I approached the bar and set the cup down. "Thank you again, sir. The water was most appreciated."

"Ta," he said, taking the cup and putting it somewhere beneath the bar. I offered him a two-pound coin, and he tucked it into his apron.

"A moment of your time, if you don't mind," I said, as he started to turn away.

He waited patiently, tankard in hand.

Taking this as permission, I continued. "I'm sure you're aware of what happened to my young friend."

He nodded.

"Just before it happened," I said, "he had been here in the tavern, conversing with someone. Did you have occasion to notice anything? See anyone who was taking undue interest in my friend? Anything like that?"

The tavern keeper sipped reflectively at his tankard before replying. "He were chatting with that professor bloke, the dark-haired one. You know, the one who's the expert."

I nodded.

"The professor seemed to be getting a bit too chummy with your young friend, and there were someone who didn't seem to like that, not above half."

"And who was that?" I demanded, perhaps a shade too forcefully.

The tavern keeper frowned. I forced myself to relax and offer him an encouraging smile.

" 'Twas a youngish bloke, fancies himself as Will Scarlet. Fact, that's even what he calls himself. Allus dresses in scarlet too, head to foot, he does. I seen him earlier, coupla times, chatting in here with the professor and getting mighty cozy, if you understand me."

Again I nodded.

"Well, Will Scarlet didn't seem to take too kindly to the fact that the professor was chatting up another young bloke."

"Did he do anything about it? Did he approach them?"

The tavern keeper shook his head.

"Well, what happened?" I demanded.

"The professor up and left, that's what," the tavern keeper said, frowning slightly as if to rebuke me. "Your young friend sat there a few minutes longer, finishing his drink, then he left too."

"And where was Will Scarlet during this?"

"He was still here," the man replied. "I thought he might follow the professor out, but he didn't. He stayed here, watching your bloke. And when your bloke left, Will Scarlet followed him outside a moment or two later."

Just as I had suspected. This Will Scarlet fellow was jealous of Giles, thinking he was interested in Tris. So he followed Giles and attacked him, trying to warn him away from Tris.

I would certainly deal with Mr. Scarlet, as soon as I could get my hands on him.

"Thank you," I said to the tavern keeper, about to turn away. "You've been most helpful."

He merely grunted in response.

I reached into a pocket and withdrew my wallet. I found a twenty-pound note and fluttered it in front of him.

"I don't suppose you could tell me who else might have been in the tavern at the time?"

His eyes avidly following the movement of the twenty pounds, the tavern keeper nodded.

He began reeling off a list of names, most of which meant nothing to me. But two names did catch my attention. Murdo Millbank had been in the tavern, as had Guillaume, the soldier who was the henchman of King Harald. One of them could have attacked Giles just as easily as Will Scarlet.

"Tell me, then, Millbank and this Guillaume fellow. Did they pay any particular attention to my friend?" I watched him as he thought about it.

"Mayhap they did," he said. I brandished the twenty-pound note again, and his memory got sharper. "Guillaume was sitting at the next table, and I thought he was listening to them a bit."

I nodded encouragement.

"Not sure whether that Millbank bloke even noticed

them," he said. "He did seem to have something on his mind, though. He were muttering away to himself 'til I thought he was fair barmy."

"Did either of them leave before my friend left the tavern?"

The tavern keeper nodded. "They both did. Guillaume just before the professor fellow, and Millbank had left a couple minutes before that."

I dropped the twenty pounds on the bar, and more quickly than I could imagine, it had disappeared into the man's apron.

"You've been extremely helpful," I said. "Good day to you, sir."

His only response was another grunt as he turned away to serve a customer who had been waiting patiently at the other end of the bar.

Giles appeared to be dozing when I sat down on the bench beside him.

"Wake up, Giles," I said softly. "You're not supposed to sleep just yet."

He yawned and opened his eyes. "I'm not sleeping, Simon, just resting a bit." He sat up straighter on the bench. "Find out anything of use?"

"Perhaps," I said. I told him what I had learned from the tavern keeper.

When I finished, Giles pondered it all in silence for a moment. Then he shook his head gently. "Sorry, Simon, I still don't remember seeing anything before I was hit. It could have been anyone. Perhaps I might remember something more later."

"No flash of scarlet perhaps? Out of the corner of your eye, before you were struck?"

"No, I don't believe so," Giles said slowly. "You think it was this Will Scarlet fellow who was responsible?"

"Yes, I think he's the most likely suspect," I replied. "And when I find him, he will tell me, one way or another."

"Simon, you sound a bit grim," Giles said, half-jokingly. "As if you plan to torture the man if he doesn't confess." He poked me in the arm. "Come now, you're not going to do something silly, are you?"

I smiled at him. "No, I'm not. But he will certainly rue the day he ever laid a hand on you. If, indeed, he was the one who hit you."

Giles shrugged. "What if the king set his tame thug on me? What then?"

"Then I will take up the matter with both the king and his muscle man."

He laughed at that. "Come now, Simon, that Guillaume is pretty big and brawny. You don't want to tangle with him. Even for my sake."

"I'm stronger than I look, Giles," I said, smiling to make a bit of a jest of it. He would know, soon enough, that I was deadly serious (pardon the pun).

We sat in silence for a moment, then I turned to Giles. "How's your head? Feel like walking a bit?"

Giles touched the back of his head gingerly. "Still a bit tender, but that pill the doctor gave me is doing its job, Simon. My head has stopped throbbing, and I don't think a leisurely stroll will do any harm."

"Good," I said. I stood up and offered him my arm. He grasped it and pulled himself up off the bench. His hand on my arm, we began walking.

"Where are we going?" Giles asked. "Besides watching out for Will Scarlet and Guillaume, that is."

"Don't forget Millbank, though I can't quite see him bashing you over the head. I thought we might wander by Totsye's pavilion," I said. "See if she's there, and if she is, perhaps ask her a few questions."

"Won't the police still have it cordoned off?"

"Possibly," I said, "but even if Totsye's not there, Robin might be, and I have it in mind to ask him a question or two."

"Lead on, Macduff," Giles said grandly.

I turned my head slightly to offer him a raised eyebrow, and he chuckled.

As we moved in leisurely fashion toward our goal, I recalled what I had told him about our having some things to talk about. I repressed a shudder. Did we ever!

I couldn't bear to think how quickly it could all change when I told Giles everything about myself. What would I do if he never wanted to see me again?

Like another Scarlett, I would think about that tomorrow.

As we neared Totsye Titchmarsh's pavilion, I could see a few people milling about. Totsye was one of them, and she appeared to be in earnest conversation with the uniformed constable on duty. I focused my hearing to eavesdrop as we moved closer.

"But I simply must have access to my things," Totsye said in tones of great frustration. "I simply must, I tell you."

"I'm sorry, madam," the earnest young PC said, standing ramrod straight to appear more authoritative. "But I cannot possibly let you inside without a direct order from Detective Inspector Chase."

Totsye stamped the ground in anger, her foot narrowly missing the PC's boot. He moved back just a fraction.

"This is utterly infuriating!" Totsye stood, her hands curled into claws as if she were about to launch herself on the hapless PC who stood in her way.

"My dear Totsye," I said, coming to a stop just behind her. "Whatever is the matter? Might I be of any assistance?"

She shrieked and whirled around. Her right hand clutched at her ample, heaving bosom. "Simon! What a start you gave me." She breathed deeply to calm herself. "You naughty, naughty man. But I forgive you. You may be of assistance, my dear."

"How so?" I asked, inclining my head slightly.

She fluttered her eyelashes at me. "Can't you use your influence with the police and get this odious little man to let me inside my pavilion? There are things inside that I simply must

have, and he won't let me." Her lips twisted into an unat-
tractive pout.

I smiled gently at her. "My dear Totsye, perhaps you over-
estimate my influence with the police. I cannot countermand
the Detective Inspector's orders. I fear you must wait until
you can make a direct appeal to the man himself. I am sure
he will consider your request seriously."

Her lower lip poked farther out. "Oh, Simon, I cannot believe you are going to disappoint me like this. Surely there is
something you can do?" Again those eyelashes twitched in
my direction.

What on earth was the woman playing at? What possessed
her to behave in such a coquettish way with me? Had she tar-
geted me as her new beau, now that Luke was out of the
way?

No, that was too absurd even to contemplate. She was
simply using what she perceived as her feminine wiles to get
what she wanted. Unfortunately for her, those wiles were a
bit too unappetizing to appeal to any but the most desperate
of men.

I addressed the young constable. "Is Detective Inspector
Chase anywhere about? Perhaps someone could get in touch
with him and relay Miss Titchmarsh's request?"

The PC smiled gratefully. "Yes, sir, I believe he's still about
here somewhere. If you'll excuse me a moment, I'll see what I
can do about contacting him." He turned and moved several
feet away from us, pulling out a mobile phone.

"I'm sure you'll have an answer soon," I said soothingly.

"I should hope so," she snapped at me. "This whole situation is intolerable." Her eyes welled with tears. "Not only
was my poor, dear Luke horrendously and callously murdered right before my very eyes, now I cannot even get inside
my own pavilion to retrieve very personal items that I desperately need."

She sniffed loudly as she pulled a bit of linen from its hiding
place in the bosom of her tunic and dabbed delicately at her

eyes and nose. "And as if all that weren't horrible enough, I know they suspect me—*me*, of all persons!—of having done this to my poor Luke." She sniffed and dabbed again. "After all, it was at my table that he was poisoned."

I laid a consoling hand on her arm. "Perhaps not."

"What do you mean?" she demanded in mid-sniffle.

"If Luke was poisoned with foxglove," I said, "then he would have been given the fatal dose earlier in the day. It takes time to act."

"Of course," she said, her eyes widening. "What a silly goose I am! I should have thought of that myself." She heaved a huge sigh of relief, and her bosom trembled. "Then the dear man could not have been poisoned by anything at my table."

"Probably not," I said. "The only way you could have poisoned him would be if you had seen him earlier in the day and had given him something then."

Her eyes widened in horror. "Maybe I did kill him," she whispered. Then she toppled into my arms in a dead faint.

Chapter 25

Totsye's neighbor across the way, who had so kindly offered the use of her tent last night, stepped forward to suggest that I bring the stricken woman inside. I gathered Totsye in my arms and carried her in the tent.

Once I had settled her in a chair, I stepped back and let the neighbor see after her. Totsye's eyelids fluttered as the good Samaritan gently chafed her hands.

What on earth could the blasted woman have meant? I wondered. Was that a serious confession of guilt, or simply a neurotic bid for attention?

In the excitement I had momentarily forgotten Giles, but when I turned to see where he was, I found him in the tent just behind me. He leaned forward to whisper to me, "They've sent for Chase. He should be here any minute now."

I nodded as I examined him. He seemed to be fine, but nevertheless I pointed to a vacant chair and whispered back at him, "Sit."

Though he rolled his eyes at me first, he did as I told him. I turned back to focus my attention on Totsye Titchmarsh. She had come round and was now trying to sit up, despite the protests of her erstwhile nurse.

Totsye batted the woman's hands away, none too gently. "I

shall be fine, I tell you. I have no idea what came over me. I never faint. Never! None of those missish ways for me." She started to get up from the chair.

"Now, Totsye," I said sternly, "I really do think you should sit there for a few minutes, just to be sure your head is completely clear."

She simpered up at me. "Well, if you think it best, Simon, I'm sure I don't mind resting a moment longer." She held out a hand to me, and I could not refuse to clasp it without looking like an utter cad.

Her grip was surprisingly strong as she attempted to draw me closer to her. I stood my ground, however, and after a start of surprise, she let go my hand. Her smile faltered.

"Detective Inspector Chase is on his way," I informed her. "I'm sure he'll be most eager to speak with you, especially now."

"Whatever do you mean?" she said.

"Don't you remember what you said to me just before you fainted?" I asked.

Her eyes widened in alarm. "Oh, dear, oh, dear."

"Exactly," I said. "Now, precisely what did you mean when you said, 'Maybe I did kill him'? Was that a confession? If it was, perhaps you had better wait until the detective inspector arrives."

"I'm here," Robin Chase's voice announced from behind me. "What is it you need to tell me, Miss Titchmarsh?" He stepped closer until he stood right beside me.

Totsye quailed a bit, with the two of us towering over her. "Oh, dear," she whispered, "what a mess this is."

Robin cast about for a chair, but the only other one visible was the one Giles was occupying. Anticipating Robin's request, Giles stood up. "Be my guest," he said. He started to move the chair himself, but I intervened.

"I'll do that," I said, ignoring the rolling of the eyes yet again.

"Thank you, Dr. Kirby-Jones," Robin said calmly, though I could see that he was curious over what had just passed between Giles and me.

Seated in the chair, Robin faced Totsye at a less intimidating angle. "Now, Miss Titchmarsh, what is it you wish to tell me?"

After a heartfelt sigh, she spoke. "Oh, Detective Inspector, I might have provided the means by which poor Luke was poisoned. I might have killed him, though I did not mean to, you understand." Her hands fluttered restlessly in her lap. "I can never forgive myself, even though it was all done with the purest and most unselfish of motives. Oh dear."

"What was done, Miss Titchmarsh?" Robin asked, demonstrating more patience than I would have, had I been the one questioning her.

"Someone must have poisoned the tisane I sent to poor, dear Luke," Totsye said, her eyes puddling with tears.

"What was in this tisane?" Robin asked. "And when did you send it to Mr. de Montfort?"

"It was chiefly feverfew," she said. "It has a number of medicinal uses, you know, and it can be an effective remedy for certain kinds of headache. My poor Luke was prone to headaches, you see, and he quite relied on my feverfew tisane for relief."

"I see," Robin said. "Did he request this herbal remedy from you yesterday?"

"Oh, yes," Totsye said. "That serving girl of his, Etheldreda I believe she calls herself. He sent her to me in the early afternoon yesterday, asking whether I had any already prepared I could send to him."

"And did you?" Robin prompted when she failed to continue. "Have any already prepared, that is."

Totsye offered a wan and tragic smile. "Certainly, Detective Inspector. I am always prepared at these gatherings. There is quite a demand for my headache tisanes, and not just from poor Luke. Though naturally I made sure I reserved enough so that he would never have to do without."

"What was this tisane in?" Robin asked.

"I have some special bottles I use, of varying sizes," Totsye replied. "The one I sent Luke yesterday held about two teacupfuls of the mixture."

"Would that be one dose?"

"Oh, no, Detective Inspector," Totsye said. "Perhaps half a teacupful would be sufficient, unless Luke were having a really severe headache. Then he might want something even stronger."

"So it's possible that some of the mixture might be left," Robin mused.

"Yes, I should think so," Totsye replied.

"We shall check into it," Robin said. "And now, Miss Titchmarsh, could you tell me how you think Mr. de Montfort might have been poisoned with your tisane? Did you add any other ingredient to the mixture?"

"Oh, no, Detective Inspector, I didn't add anything to it," Totsye said adamantly. "It was the same mixture as always. At least, I'm fairly certain that it was." She frowned.

"What do you mean, 'fairly certain'?" Robin asked.

Totsye fluttered her eyelashes at him. "Well, you see, I do take a wee dose of digitalis now and again for my heart. I had distilled a bit of it yesterday, and I might have mixed up the bottles, you see." She drew a deep breath. "But I really don't think I did. I'm sure I sent poor Luke the bottle of feverfew. Yes, I'm sure I did. But that doesn't mean, naturally, that someone else couldn't have tampered with it."

"How so?" Robin asked.

I awaited her reply with interest. I had been studying her intently the whole time she had been talking to Robin, doing my best to get a clear read of her emotional state. Totsye didn't seem all that difficult to assess. She was anxious, naturally, but I could detect no emotion stronger than that, other than her grief at Luke's death.

"Most everyone in the encampment would recognize those bottles of mine," Totsye explained. "They are a very distinctive red, and anyone seeing one of them would know that it contained one of my tisanes. Not just of feverfew, you understand, but one of my little decoctions for various and sundry purposes." She lowered her eyes modestly. "I am quite well regarded as an herbalist, naturally."

"Yes, I see," Robin said. "Do go on."

"Isn't it clear, Detective Inspector?" Totsye demanded. "Someone could have seen Etheldreda with the tisane, or could have seen it in poor Luke's pavilion, and then added the poison to it."

"That is possible, I suppose," Robin said, "and we shall certainly investigate all the possibilities." He rose from his chair. "Thank you, Miss Titchmarsh, for your information. Now, if you will excuse me, I must get back to the investigation."

"You're most welcome, Detective Inspector," Totsye said, "but before you go, might I possibly have access to my pavilion? There are things I need quite urgently, and I cannot see that it would harm anyone for me to remove them. Please, Detective Inspector?"

Robin paused. "I don't see why not, Miss Titchmarsh. I shall give the proper instructions to the men on duty there. They will need to make a note of anything you remove from the tent, of course, and examine it all."

Totsye blushed. "If they must, they must, Detective Inspector. But when will you be finished with it completely?"

"I hope by tomorrow sometime, Miss Titchmarsh," Robin said. "Now, again, if you will excuse me."

Indicating to Giles that I wished him to remain inside the tent to keep an eye on Totsye, I followed Robin outside after a moment. I waited patiently until he had finished issuing the instructions that would allow Totsye to do as she wished, then moved after him when he began to walk away.

I cleared my throat, but before I could say anything, Robin spoke without turning around. "Yes, Simon, what is it?" He did not stop walking.

"Now, Robin," I said, catching up to him easily in a couple of strides. "Is that any way to behave, when all I want to do is help?"

"Simon, I don't really have time for any more taradiddles, if you don't mind."

My, but he was testy. "What taradiddles have you been hearing, Robin, if I might be so bold as to ask? Could you by any chance be referring to what Totsye told you just now?"

Robin halted, and I stopped beside him. "I don't know why I even attempt to argue with you, Simon. It's bloody useless. No matter what I say, you insist on thrusting yourself into the midst of my murder investigations."

I had never seen Robin quite this annoyed with me before. "Can I help it if these things happen around me, Robin? I don't think so. It's not my fault these people get murdered."

"No, I realize that," Robin said.

Suddenly stricken by a pang of conscience, however, I remembered what had happened to Giles a little while ago.

"What is it, Simon?" Robin asked, alert to the change of expression on my face.

"Someone bashed Giles over the head," I said baldly.

"Do you have any idea who, or why?"

I shrugged. "I think it might possibly have been a fellow who calls himself Will Scarlet. Apparently he goes around dressed in a scarlet tunic and hose all the time. Have you seen him?"

Robin nodded. "Yes, I've seen him about."

"I'm looking forward to questioning him," I said.

"Now, Simon, I wouldn't want to have to haul you to pokey for assaulting someone," Robin said, smiling slightly. "Why would this Will Scarlet have attacked Sir Giles?"

"Jealousy, perhaps," I said, but before I could explain further, Robin laughed.

"What's so funny?" I demanded.

"What were you doing flirting with this Will Scarlet, Simon? I thought you were quite potty about Sir Giles."

"I was *not* flirting with anyone, Robin," I protested hotly. "And certainly not with this Will Scarlet, whom I have yet to meet. What I would have told you, had you allowed me to finish my explanation, was that this Will Scarlet was jealous of Giles and Tristan Lovelace."

"Oh, so Sir Giles has now taken up with Professor Lovelace? Why, Simon, I'm surprised."

"Stop mocking me, Robin. It's not in the least amusing," I said shortly. "Giles hasn't taken up with Tris, but Tris has been chatting Giles up a bit lately. And I think he's also been chatting up this Will Scarlet, and perhaps Will thinks Giles is a rival. Though nothing could be further from the truth."

"I see," Robin said, making a valiant effort to suppress his amusement.

"But Will Scarlet is only one of the suspects," I said. "It's just possible that Murdo Millbank could have done it, or it might have been this Guillaume, who seems to be a henchman of the king's."

"And why would either of them want to hit Sir Giles over the head, might I ask?"

"Because," I admitted reluctantly, "Giles was nosing about a bit, at my request, and they might have overheard what he was doing. Maybe it was their way of telling him to mind his own business."

"I see," Robin said, and suddenly he appeared to take the matter a bit more seriously. "I've warned you before, Simon, that sticking your nose into these things can be dangerous, and now you see what I mean."

"Yes, Robin, I do see that," I responded, holding on to my temper by the merest hair. "And if I had thought that I would put Giles in any serious danger, I would never have suggested it. I wouldn't want him to come to any harm."

"No, I know that," Robin said. "Your feelings for him have been all too plain recently."

"Oh, really," I said, "and why would *you* take notice, Robin?"

"I'm simply observant," he said. "It's part of my job." He regarded me with a bland expression.

"I see," I said. "Well, if I find out who it was that hit Giles on the head, I'll let you know."

"You do that thing, Simon," Robin replied. "Now, if you will excuse me."

"Wait a minute, Robin," I said sharply. "You still haven't answered my earlier question, about that 'taradiddle' you mentioned. What were you talking about?"

Chagrined, Robin turned back to face me. "Almost got away with it," he said. "Very well, Simon. That story that Totsye Titchmarsh told me."

"What about it?"

He shrugged. "I don't think it has any bearing on the case."

"Why not?" I asked. "Until you determine how the poison was administered, don't you have to check every possibility?"

"Yes, I do," Robin said with exaggerated patience. "But I had an update from the pathologist a short while ago, Simon, and what he told me put a whole new spin on the case."

"Can you possibly share that information with me, Robin?"

"I suppose I'm going to have to," Robin said. "We were wrong about the poison, Simon. It wasn't foxglove after all."

"What?" I said, stunned. "What do you mean, it wasn't foxglove?"

"Once the pathologist ran the appropriate tests," Robin said, "he ruled out foxglove completely. It was cyanide, Simon. The murderer used cyanide."

Chapter 26

I stared at Robin in complete disbelief. Cyanide! What the bloody hell was going on here?

"Professor Lovelace was wrong," Robin said, watching me closely. "Although it's easy to understand his confusion. Under stress like that, it's not unusual for someone who isn't a medical professional to make a mistake."

"I'm not following you, Robin," I said. "What do you mean by Tris's 'confusion'?"

"Some of the symptoms of the two kinds of poisoning are similar," Robin explained. "Vomiting, nausea, for example, some respiratory problems. It could have looked like foxglove, or digitalis, poisoning to a layperson who knew a bit about foxglove or plant poisons. But cyanide causes some of the same symptoms. Others are quite different."

"I see," I said, still trying to process the information. "And what about the emergency treatment? Is it the same?"

"In some ways," Robin said. "Gastric lavage, in either case. With cyanide poisoning, if proper treatment doesn't take place within the first half hour, there's not much hope." He frowned. "What they should have done, according to the pathologist, was administer some amyl nitrite as quickly as possible, then do the gastric lavage."

"Did Tris's error in calling it digitalis poisoning contribute in any way to Luke's death?"

Robin eyed me curiously. "Perhaps, Simon. Cyanide acts far more swiftly than foxglove, and frankly I don't think there was much hope for de Montfort once he had ingested the cyanide. The dose was small but enough to be fatal. But no matter what poison they thought he had ingested, they were treating him as they would any victim of poisoning and doing their very best to save him."

"Of course they were," I said hastily. "I didn't think otherwise, Robin, I assure you."

"Surely you don't suspect that Professor Lovelace, of all people, deliberately misled the doctor?"

That was exactly what I did suspect, but for the moment, at least, I couldn't allow Robin to know that. "Certainly not," I said, investing those two words with every bit of sincerity I could muster.

It must have worked, because Robin appeared satisfied.

"You see the importance of the fact that it was cyanide, rather than foxglove," Robin said.

"Yes," I replied. "It means he was poisoned in Totsye's pavilion last night. The cyanide would have acted immediately, wouldn't it?"

"Yes," Robin said. "And that's the main reason I told you all this, Simon. What happened in that tent last night is more important than ever, and I need you to remember as much as possible about it all. Anything you might have seen or heard, no matter how trivial."

"Did the pathologist have any idea how the poison was delivered? Was it in something he ate, or something he drank?"

"The pathologist believes it was in honey. The fig pastries have honey over them, I believe."

"How recently had he eaten the fig pastry?" I asked.

"Within a short time of his death," Robin said. "And because the poison would have acted very quickly, that means he had to have eaten the pastry *after* he arrived for the dinner party."

I nodded. "That's what I originally suspected last night, before we were all sidetracked by the idea that foxglove was responsible."

"I'll have to go back over all the statements to check, but I don't believe anyone mentioned seeing the victim eat one of the pastries on his plate. And then there's the question of what happened to the second pastry," Robin said. "But I shall have to question them all again anyway, in light of the pathologist's findings."

"Yes, well, if anything occurs to me, Robin, I'll let you know right away," I said.

"Thank you, Simon," he responded. "I've no doubt you will." With that, he turned and walked away.

I stood where I was, staring blindly after him, as my mind worked busily. I didn't like some of the ideas I was getting. Was I trying too hard to see Tris as the villain in this piece, simply because I knew that he had a motive for wanting Luke out of the way?

This was absurd. I shook my head to clear it, then started back to find Giles. Tris was insufferably conceited, quite certain that he knew everything. It was just like him to make a pronouncement about the poison that had felled Luke, expecting everyone to fall right in line with him. Just because he happened to be wrong in this case didn't mean there was anything deliberate, or sinister, in the error. My imagination was running a bit too rampant.

Giles stood waiting for me in the shade of Totsye's helpful neighbor's tent. He turned to thank her as I approached, and he joined me in front of Totsye's pavilion.

I glanced inside, but I caught no glimpse of Totsye. If she were still here, she must be in the rear chamber of the tent. I wanted to question her again about last night, but perhaps it could wait for a bit. Glancing at Giles, I noticed he appeared a bit wan.

"Time to get you away from here for a bit," I said, slipping an arm around his shoulders.

"I wouldn't mind that," Giles said with a faint smile. "I am feeling somewhat tired, Simon."

"Then off we go," I responded. "You're more important than any murder investigation. Shall I take you to the Hall?"

"No, Simon," he said. "I'd rather go home with you to Laurel Cottage, if you don't mind."

The diffidence with which he spoke was charming. Of course, I couldn't blame him for not wanting his mother dithering about and causing all manner of ruckus over him.

"Of course not, Giles," I said. "I'd rather have you there with me anyway, so I can keep an eye on you."

He laughed a bit at that. "Surely, Simon, you don't think someone else is going to attack me. That's absurd."

"Very likely," I said, nodding at various passersby as we moved steadily toward the exit to the encampment. I kept an eye out for a handsome young man dressed all in scarlet, but I caught nary a flash of such a dramatic color anywhere about us. "But better safe than sorry, as the saying goes."

"I'm too tired to argue with you," Giles said. He yawned.

"None of that, now," I said. "The doctor said you had to stay awake, remember."

"Yes, I know," Giles responded, "and I promise I'll stay awake at Laurel Cottage. At least we can be more comfortable there, and have a bit of privacy. You can tell me whatever it is you need to tell me."

I almost jerked to a stop when I heard those words, but I covered it by pretending to stumble over something. "Sorry," I mumbled. "A hole in the ground there."

"Simon?" Giles said.

"Ah, yes, Giles," I replied. We had reached the exit, and I nodded to the guard as Giles and I passed through. "Yes, we'll have a chance to talk when we get to Laurel Cottage."

Slowly we made our way up the hill to where my Jag was

parked. Giles said nothing further, even during the short drive through Snupperton Mumsley.

The front door of Laurel Cottage was unlocked, which meant that Tris was probably inside. I wasn't looking forward to confronting him about his mistaken identification of the poison, but at that moment I'd rather have tackled him than have had that little talk with Giles.

"Hello? Tris?" I called, but there was no response. I shut the door behind us.

"Why don't you go into the kitchen and find yourself something to drink, Giles?" I said. "I think I'll go upstairs and change out of these clothes. I'll bring you a robe, if you like, so you can change out of yours."

"That's fine, Simon," Giles said. He disappeared into the kitchen.

As I climbed the stairs, I became aware of certain sounds issuing from one of the rooms upstairs. Frowning, I ascended the stairs more quickly.

I paused on the landing. As I had suspected, the sounds were coming from the guest room. I hesitated a moment, then thought, *what the hell*! It wouldn't be the first time I had caught Tris in the act.

I flung open the door, and there, in the afternoon sun streaming through the window, were Tris and his companion, merrily going at it.

After a moment, Tris turned to look over at me. "Care to join us, Simon?"

"Don't be disgusting, Tris," I said furiously. My eyes swept around the room, coming to rest on a heap of discarded clothing on the floor. A scarlet tunic and hose. So this was where Will Scarlet had got to.

I advanced on the bed. "I've been looking for you."

A sullen, handsome face glared back at me as Tris moved aside to recline lazily on the bed. "Wot the bloody 'ell do yer want with me?" Will Scarlet demanded.

"I want some answers," I said, "and if you're lucky, I won't rip your head off."

Evidently the look on my face convinced him, because he cowered back against Tris. Tris, blast him, merely looked on in amused indifference.

"Answers ter what?" Will said. He scrunched closer to Tris.

"A friend of mine was attacked today, around the back of the tavern at the encampment. You were seen nearby just before it happened."

" 'Tweren't nought to do with me," Will said, attempting a defiant tone but just missing.

"Oh, I think it was," I said. "My friend, in case you didn't know it, is Sir Giles Blitherington, of Blitherington Hall, and around here they take a rather dim view of louts who attack the local gentry."

Will's eyes widened in fear.

"Did you strike him?" I said, stepping closer to the bed.

Cowering, Will said, "If'n he be *your* friend, how come he were chatting up Tris here? Tell me that!"

"If anyone were doing the chatting up, as you call it, it was Tris, not Giles," I said. "How dim can you possibly be?"

" 'Ere now," Will protested. "Watch 'oo you call dim 'ere."

"Really, Tris," I said, "your taste has certainly declined."

Tris laughed. "Now, Simon, I don't pick them for their conversational skills."

Will scowled, aware that he had been insulted, but apparently not able to figure out just how.

"Now, look 'ere," he said, "I didn't mean no 'arm, I didn't 'it 'im that 'ard. Besides, 'e didn't ought to be messing around like that with me friend, 'specially when 'e's got one of 'is own."

"You hit him hard enough, you bloody idiot, and you're lucky I don't rip off your arm," I said.

At that, Will dove under the covers and commenced sniveling.

"I think you've frightened the poor lad enough, Simon," Tris said, patting the covers somewhere in the region of Will's rump. "I think he's very sorry that he struck Giles, and I'm sure he'll apologize nicely. Won't you, Will?"

The covers jiggled, as Will presumably nodded.

"This is ludicrous beyond words," I said, trying not to laugh. My anger had spent itself, and now I could see only the ridiculousness of the situation. "If Giles chooses not to prosecute you, Will, then we'll let the matter rest."

His head came out from the covers, and he glared at me suspiciously.

"Yes, I mean that, Will," I said. "I'm going to change clothes, and by the time I'm done, I expect you to be dressed and downstairs, Will, and making your apologies to Giles. Then you get the hell back to the encampment and stay there. Got that?"

He nodded, and I left before I was treated to any further glimpses of naked flesh.

In my bedroom, I changed out of my medieval garb and into my comfortable working clothes. I rummaged around in the closet and found a large flannel dressing gown for Giles. Throwing it over my shoulder, I went back across the hall to confront Tris.

He was still lounging in the bed, filling his pipe and looking completely at ease.

"Well?" I said.

"Well what, Simon?" Tris responded.

"I should think the very least you could do is to apologize."

"For what?"

I stared at him. He set his tobacco pouch aside and reached for his lighter. When he finally had his pipe lit to his satisfaction, he stared back at me through the plumes of smoke swirling about his head.

"Oh, very well, Simon," he said, his tone amused. "I apologize for what Will did to Giles. I had no idea he would behave so rashly. Really, jealousy is such a tedious emotion."

"To you it is," I said, "though, correct me if I'm wrong, you were jealous of Giles and me, at least for a short while. But you seem to have recovered from that, Tris. And that makes me rather suspicious of your claims to wanting me back."

In response, he exhaled more smoke in my direction.

"Was it all just an act, Tris?"

"No, Simon, it wasn't," Tris said, dropping his pose of indifference. "It bloody wasn't. But it didn't take me long to discover that it didn't matter. The only way I could change your mind would be to take an irrevocable step, and I realized that would have alienated you forever."

"You're bloody right it would have," I said. "If you had harmed Giles, I would have done my best to destroy you."

"I figured that out," Tris said, "though it seems to have taken you rather a bit longer to face up to your own feelings."

"You pushed me into it," I said.

"Yes, I did," Tris acknowledged. "I had to give you a push to get you to make up your mind. Sadly, I lost."

"Do you really mean that, Tris?" I asked.

"Yes, Simon, I do. It's my loss," Tris said with a wry smile. "Otherwise I wouldn't have been consoling myself, shall we say, with the likes of Will Scarlet."

"So what was behind all that hypnosis business?"

Tris fiddled with his pipe. "Oh, that. Well, I decided to find out whether Giles felt as strongly about you as you do about him. The only way I could do that was to get inside his head."

"You found your answer," I said.

"Yes," Tris replied. "I did. The young idiot is utterly and entirely in love with you. You had better do something about it."

"I will," I said, "but I'm going to have to tell him everything."

"That's a big risk."

"It is, but I can't have any kind of lasting relationship with him without his knowing the truth."

Tris nodded. "I'd expect no less of you, Simon. You and your confounded ethics."

"Thanks. I think." I hesitated to spoil this moment of accord between the two of us, but I had to confront him about Luke de Montfort's death.

"I had some rather interesting information from Detective Inspector Chase a little while ago, Tris. Information that I believe you will also find interesting."

"What was it, Simon?"

"You seemed so certain that Luke de Montfort had been poisoned with foxglove," I said. "But it turns out that it was really cyanide. Terribly cliché, I know, but there you are."

Tris shrugged. "I was wrong, it seems."

"Yes, you were," I said. "But you seemed very certain at the time. Why was that, Tris?"

He puffed on his pipe before answering. "I had occasion in the past to take note, shall we say, of the effects of foxglove and its uses as a poison, Simon. And it looked to me like Luke was suffering in the same way."

"An innocent mistake."

"If you like," Tris said, a shade too casually.

"I'll tell you what I think, Tris," I said. "I think you knew it wasn't foxglove at all. In fact, I'd be willing to bet you knew that it was cyanide."

"If I did, and I'm not saying that I did, why would I want to do something like that?"

"Because, Tris," I said, "you wanted Luke dead, but you didn't want to have to kill him yourself. When someone else poisoned him, you did your best to delay the proper treatment. Luke would most likely have died anyway, but what you did confused the situation."

Tris puffed on his pipe and regarded me calmly.

"You're not denying this, Tris," I said.

"Would there be any use?" he responded. "You've made up your mind. If you expect me to express any regrets over Luke's death, I'm afraid I shall have to disappoint you."

Sickened, I turned away from him and stood in the doorway for a moment. "I want you out of this house immediately, Tris, and I never want to see you again. Goodbye."

Tris did not respond. I hadn't really expected him to.

I walked slowly down the stairs, clutching the robe in trembling hands.

Chapter 27

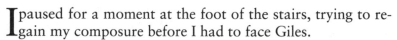

I paused for a moment at the foot of the stairs, trying to regain my composure before I had to face Giles.

The scene with Tris had upset me badly. I was closing the door on an important part of my life, and that was never easy. But it had to be done. I couldn't imagine myself forgetting what Tris had done or forgiving it, though I supposed I shouldn't be all that surprised. Tris was simply being Tris, looking out for Numero Uno, no matter the cost to others.

So be it. Tris had made his choice, and I had made mine. No regrets, no looking back.

My hands were steady now.

"Giles?" I called. "Where are you?"

"In your office, Simon," he responded.

I walked to the door of my office and looked in. He was seated behind my desk, idly doodling on a piece of paper.

"What are you doing, Giles?" I said.

"Just passing the time 'til you were back," he said. "What took you so long, Simon? I was beginning to think I would have to come upstairs after you."

Thank goodness you didn't, I thought. "Sorry, it took longer than I thought. I had a few things to sort out, as you probably gathered." I held out the robe to him. "Would you like to change into this? You might be more comfortable."

Giles got up from behind the desk and came around to where I stood. He took the robe from my arms and laid it across a chair. Smiling at me, he began to strip off his tunic and hose, and I watched, enjoying the view, until he made as if to take off his undergarments as well.

I cleared my throat, and he stopped. "I think that's far enough, Giles. After all, you don't want to catch cold." I picked up the robe and helped him into it. He grinned up at me, completely unrepentant, as he tied the belt into a loose knot.

"I don't think I'm in any danger of catching cold, Simon," he said, "at least, not so long as you're anywhere nearby." He wrapped his arms around me. "Though I must say, you do seem a bit on the cold side yourself."

"Oh, my body temperature is always a bit lower than normal," I said. I hugged him close to me, enjoying the feel of my arms around him.

We were still standing that way, minutes later, when Tris came clumping down the stairs. He glanced briefly in at us, smiled, then went out the front door, suitcases in hand.

"Where is he going?" Giles asked, pulling away from me.

"I asked him to leave," I said. "And he won't ever be coming back."

"Really?" Giles said. "That sounds rather drastic." Then he grinned. "Can't say that I'm too upset by the news, however. Good riddance."

"Yes, I do believe you're right," I said. Taking him by the arm, I led him into the drawing room. I made myself comfortable on the sofa, then drew him down so that he was sitting with his back against me, my arm around him and his head resting on my shoulder.

"I like this, Simon," he said, with a sigh of contentment. His warm breath tickled my nose.

"Me, too," I said. I reached my other arm around him and held him even closer.

We sat quietly for a few minutes, and I made sure that

Giles could feel my chest gently rising and falling, as if I were breathing.

"Giles," I said, and he stirred slightly in my arms.

"Yes?" he said in a drowsy voice.

"Did Will Scarlet apologize to you?"

"Who?" he said. "Oh, him. Yes, he did, Simon, and he was so pathetic I readily promised I wouldn't prosecute him. I told him he was welcome to his bloody Tris."

"Very well, at least we're rid of him," I said. "And we can forget all about him."

"Yes, indeed," Giles said. He shifted slightly against me. "Now, Simon, about that talk you wanted to have. What was it you wanted to tell me?"

I had hoped he would forget about that for a while, at least until I had given a bit more thought to how I would tell him. How should I do this?

The phone rang, and I was never more grateful to hear that sound in all my existence. Gently I eased from under Giles and went out into the hall to answer it, while Giles grumbled at being disturbed.

"Laurel Cottage," I said.

Lady Prunella Blitherington's voice squawked so loudly in my ear I winced in pain and held the receiver away from me. I waited until the spate of words slowed to a minor deluge, then tried to break in.

After several attempts at getting her attention, I gave up and set the receiver down on the table. Lady Prunella continued to chatter as I walked away from the phone.

"Giles," I said from the doorway. "It's your mother on the phone, and I think you had better come talk to her."

He groaned and sat up. "Dash it all, Simon, someone must have told her what happened."

"Yes," I said. "And until she hears your voice, she's likely to continue having hysterics over the phone."

He padded into the hallway and gingerly picked up the

phone while I watched. Lady Prunella had never stopped gabbling.

"Mummy," Giles spoke into the phone. "Mummy, I'm fine, really I am." He repeated this several times, but apparently to no avail. Finally, in desperation, he shouted, "MOTHER, I AM FINE. DO SHUT UP!"

Lady Prunella actually did as she was told. Rolling his eyes at me, Giles spoke in his normal tones, "Now, Mummy, I'm perfectly fine, and there is absolutely no need for you to take on this way."

She started squawking at him again. He listened for a moment. "Very well," he said. "I have no doubt that Simon will be happy to run me home, Mummy. Then you will be able to see for yourself that there is absolutely nothing wrong with me. We'll be there soon, I promise." He dropped the phone in its cradle without bothering to listen for a reply.

I half expected the phone to ring again at any moment, once Lady Prunella realized he had hung up on her. But the way she talked, that could take ten minutes or more, and by that time, I could have Giles safely back at Blitherington Hall.

"If I don't go," Giles said, "I haven't the least doubt that she'll turn up here."

For once I could have kissed his mother, thankful for the interruption. I offered a smile of commiseration as he went into my office to change back into his clothes. I then headed upstairs to do the same.

I decided I was tired of playing at being medieval, so I chose one of my more usual dark suits. I was back downstairs in five minutes, and Giles stood waiting patiently by the door.

"Trust my mother," he said as we walked to the car, "to ruin what could have been a very pleasant afternoon."

"Yes, it could have been," I said, "but it won't do any harm to reassure your mother that you're safe and sound, Giles."

"I know," he said, shutting the door of the Jag. "But her timing is deuced inconvenient."

"There'll be other opportunities, Giles," I said, turning the key in the ignition. "And soon, I promise."

"I'll hold you to that."

We accomplished the rest of the short drive in silence, and I parked the car in the forecourt of Blitherington Hall. The reporters who had been keeping vigil at the entrance seemed to have found somewhere else to wait.

"Want to come in with me?" Giles asked as he climbed out of the car.

"I think not," I said. "Things might go better if I'm not there for your mother to accuse, don't you think?"

"I daresay." He sighed. "Very well. Where will you be?"

I nodded in the direction of the encampment. "I might as well go along to see if anything new has developed."

"Be careful, Simon," he said. I came around the car to give him a quick hug and a kiss. I waited until he was inside the front door of the Hall before I traipsed around the side and down the hill.

Once inside the encampment, I paused, considering what I might do. Robin Chase would no doubt be even more annoyed with me for continuing to poke about, but I hadn't let that stop me in the past. I had met one person in this encampment who seemed to know quite a bit about the principals involved in the case, and I might as well see if I could dig up anything else of use.

Thankful that the day had turned cloudy, I sauntered down the lane toward the bakery shop and Mistress Maud. Her amiable nature and proclivity for gossip had been most enlightening before, and perhaps would be again.

In the bakery tent, I waited a few minutes for a couple to finish dithering over the choices of baked goods, but finally only the proprietress and I remained.

"Good day to you, sir," Mistress Maud said, beaming at me. "And what might you be wanting today?"

I stepped up to the counter and smiled back at her. "Oh, more of those wonderful fig pastries of yours, my good lady. I have developed quite a taste for them."

Her face fell. "Oh, sir, I mislike to disappoint you, but I have not a single one left. I shall have more tomorrow, however."

"That is a disappointment, Mistress, but I shall endeavor to overcome it."

She giggled at my gallantry, then waited patiently for me to make another choice. I pretended to examine the various wares on display.

"Such an appetizing array of choices," I said. "It really is difficult to decide." I glanced up at her. "Tell me, Mistress Maud, is this what you do in the mundane world? Pardon my curiosity."

"No, in the mundane world I have a much different life," she said. "Baking is something I dearly love, but I couldn't do it full time. No, I earn my daily bread"—she giggled a little over the pun—"as a financial journalist."

"How very interesting," I said, and indeed it was. That explained how she knew so much about the business dealings of some of her fellow members of the society. "In your professional capacity, you no doubt have run across some of the folk here this week."

"An occupational hazard," she said. "When we gather for our meetings, we do our best to leave the mundane world behind, but that isn't always possible."

I nodded encouragement, and she continued, "Take our late Duke of Wessex, for example. He was a very hard-headed businessman, with a reputation for tough dealing. Not many cared to cross him, and a couple of members of our group learned that, to their cost."

"Like your king, for example," I said.

"Oh, my, yes," she said. "Poor Harald. But he wasn't the only one. Totsye Titchmarsh came out the loser on a deal she tried with Luke." She shook her head dolefully. "The woman completely lost her head on that one. And she's lucky she didn't lose her business."

"And yet she remained enamored of him."

"So it would seem," Mistress Maud said. "She lost a pot of money in trying to open a chain of herb shops, and allegedly the late duke had promised some financial assistance. When that backing failed to materialize, Totsye was lucky she didn't have to declare bankruptcy."

"Most interesting," I said. "That reminds me of something else very interesting I heard, and perhaps you can confirm it for me."

Mistress Maud tilted her head to one side, reminding me of a bird waiting for an unlucky worm.

"I heard from somewhere," I said slowly, "that once upon a time, your king and Totsye were deeply devoted to each other."

"That's true enough," she said. "We all thought they'd make a match of it, but that was about the time that Luke and Adele joined the group."

"And that was the end of that," I said.

Mistress Maud nodded, her eyes gleaming with malice. "Adele made certain of that." She chuckled. "The two of them made a pretty formidable team. Divide and conquer, that's what they did. Neither Harald nor Totsye stood a chance, once Luke and Adele got to work."

A fairly powerful motive for revenge, I thought. Things were beginning to fall into place. Now I just had to figure out how it was done.

Thanking Mistress Maud, I departed rather abruptly. I wandered down the lane, glancing at the various shops as I went.

The honey was the key to it, somehow. The poison, presumably in the form of powder, had been added to honey, which would have helped disguise the taste and any smell. The fig pastries had a bit of honey poured over them, of course, and the killer could have sprinkled the poison into the honey somehow.

But that might have been awkward, to say the least. And what had happened to the second fig pastry on Luke's plate? I had seen one remaining on his plate after he collapsed, but later, it had disappeared. Why would someone have removed it from the plate?

And then it hit me. The fig pastries weren't the only item on Totsye's menu that used honey. Mead was made from honey as well, and what had Totsye been pouring into each of the pewter cups on the table?

Mead.

It was as simple as that. The poison had been in the mead, but how had it come to be there?

It had to have been put in Luke's cup before the mead was poured into it, or shortly thereafter. The murderer must have removed the second fig pastry to make the police think that both pastries had been poisoned.

But how? How had the murderer managed it without anyone catching on?

Without realizing it, I had paused in front of the tent of a jeweler. As my mind cleared, I focused on the rings, necklaces, and brooches laid out on velvet before me.

I began laughing and shaking my head, startling several persons milling about nearby. How could I have missed it? How obvious, and yet how simple.

Time to find Robin and get this thing finished.

Chapter 28

Hold on just a minute, I told myself sternly. *Better check out a couple of things before you go announcing to Robin that you've figured it all out.*

With my own warning in mind, I stepped into the jeweler's tent. I waited until he had finished chatting with a woman, already overloaded with jewelry, who couldn't make up her mind between a lovely pendant and an ornate ring. Finally she left without buying either, and the merchant stared after her with a sour face.

"Good afternoon, sir," he said, turning to me with a hopeful smile. "Is there anything in particular that catches your eye? I have some handsome rings that would well suit a gentleman of your stature."

I smiled back. "Actually, I *am* rather interested in rings." I pointed to a tray of them on the table in front of me. "These are all most attractive, but what I had in mind was something special."

"I'm certain that I will have something to suit you, sir. What is it you seek?"

I laughed, as if I were embarrassed. "Well, what I'd really love to have is one of those poison rings. You know, a ring like the Borgias or Catherine de Medici used to get rid of their enemies."

The jeweler beamed at me. "I know exactly what you want, sir, and I must say that I am often asked for such objects." He pointed to three different rings, all set with large single stones, on the tray in front of me. "Each of these has a special hollow chamber beneath the stone." He picked one up and deftly manipulated the stone open to show me the hollow space beneath. It was more than ample for the secretion of a deadly amount of prussic acid powder.

"That's quite striking," I said. "And I'm sure you must have ladies' rings like it." I waited for his enthusiastic nod before I continued. "In fact, I fancy that I've seen a couple of these rings already."

His head kept bobbing up and down as he beamed at me. "Oh, yes, sir, they are quite popular with the ladies." He winked at me. "You never know when a lady might need to add a little love potion to her lover's drink, naturally."

Or a little poison, I added silently.

"Did you make the one that Dame Alysoun wears?" I asked.

"Yes, indeed, I did, though that was several years ago. Does she still wear it, sir? I had feared it was lost, and she was too shamed to tell me."

"Oh, no," I said blithely. "She still has it." And before much longer, the poor man would discover to just what use Totsye Titchmarsh had put said ring. I doubted that he would welcome the news, though I could be wrong. Some people loved any kind of publicity, and the tabloids would have great fun with a medieval poison ring.

I decided that having such a ring might prove useful, and I tried all three of the men's rings he had shown me. One of them fit perfectly on my forefinger, and I liked the way it looked. I winced a bit at the price, but he was delighted to take my credit card. A few minutes later I was again on my way, ready to put the next part of my plan in motion.

As I had hoped, there was still a PC posted outside Totsye's pavilion. I explained that I needed to speak with Detective

Inspector Chase most urgently. He directed me to the area where Robin had set up a temporary headquarters, and luckily I found Robin seated at a desk, going over statements.

He looked up at me and without missing a beat said, "I take it you've got it all figured out, Simon. You look very much like a cat who's just had the canary for lunch."

"Quite right, Robin," I said, dropping down in the chair across from him. "I believe I know who did it and why, and for once, I don't think it should be all that difficult to prove."

"Go ahead, then," he said, dropping the sheaf of papers on the desk and leaning back. "Dazzle me."

"Totsye Titchmarsh in the tent with a poison ring."

"What?" Robin said, puzzled. Then his face cleared as he caught the reference. "This isn't a game of Cluedo, Simon. Do be serious."

"I am serious, Robin," I said. "Totsye Titchmarsh is your murderer. She put the poison in a ring like this." I paused to demonstrate my new trinket, and Robin stared at it.

"Ah, I begin to see," he said.

"The poison wasn't in the fig pastries at all," I said. "It was in the mead. Mead is made from honey, and Totsye dropped the poison into Luke's drinking cup before she poured in the mead."

"How can you be so certain?" Robin said. "Couldn't she have sprinkled the poison on a pastry?"

"No," I said. "She did it right in front of me, though I didn't realize it until a little while ago."

"Are you certain it couldn't have been put on a pastry?"

"Reasonably so," I said. "Were you able to find out how long the pastries had been on the plates?"

"The pastries arrived only a few minutes before she began to pour out the mead. She had her serving girl place the pastries on the plates, and I don't think she had a chance to poison one of them. But it does explain why the second fig pastry disappeared. She took it so that you would think it was the pastry that was poisoned. But it was in the mead all along."

"When did she take the uneaten pastry?"

"I'm not sure," I said, "but she probably managed to swipe it before she left the tent in search of the doctor. Once she had, it would have been easy enough for her to dispose of it somewhere along the way."

"It makes sense," Robin said. "But why? Why did she want to kill him?"

"Has anyone told you that, once upon a time, Totsye and Harald Knutson were an item?"

Robin shook his head.

"I thought not," I replied. "Apparently they were a couple until Luke and Adele de Montfort joined the group. Adele quickly enthralled Harald, and Luke inveigled him into a disastrous business deal. If you do some digging, I imagine you'll find that Luke and Adele had done that a few times before. Luke also involved Totsye in a bad deal, and she was lucky, according to my source, to escape without going bankrupt."

"Revenge, then," Robin commented.

"Yes," I said. "It's as simple as that. She was never in love with Luke at all. It always seemed ludicrous to me, and it was nothing more than an act. She's quite an accomplished actress, I'd say. She was biding her time until she could pay him back, and if she's not stopped, I imagine she'll try to kill Adele as well."

"This is all well and good, Simon," Robin complained. "I grant you that it's all very plausible, and I could probably charge her based on all this, but to make it stick, I need something a bit more concrete."

"I thought you'd never ask," I said, leaning forward in my chair. "Let's get Totsye in the same room with Harald and Adele, and even Millbank, if you like, and let me have a go at her. I don't think it will take long."

Robin rolled his eyes. "Not again, Simon. Haven't you tired of playing Poirot yet? Assembling the suspects in the drawing room is a bit much, don't you think?"

"Have you a better idea at the moment?" I said. "Do you want to run the risk that Totsye might try to do away with Adele de Montfort while you're trying to get your concrete proof?"

He shifted uneasily in his chair. "You win, Simon." He called for one of his subordinates and began issuing orders. His men would find Totsye and the others and get them assembled at the scene of the crime.

"Come along, Simon," Robin said. "Let's go."

Smiling, I followed Robin back to the encampment to Totsye's pavilion. It didn't take long for the group to assemble, and they all watched me and Robin warily.

Robin waited until Totsye, Adele, Millbank, and Harald had seated themselves, then he launched into his spiel. "I appreciate your cooperation in this, ladies and gentlemen. It will not take long, and no doubt you are all as anxious as I to get this matter settled. To that end, I have enlisted the aid of Professor Kirby-Jones, who will explain everything." He moved to one side, and I stepped in front of the group.

"Thank you all," I said. "As Detective Inspector Chase told you, this won't take long." I paused for the effect. "I am here to reveal to you the name of the murderer of Luke de Montfort, late Duke of Wessex."

I paused again, and three of the audience leaned forward, their faces alight with curiosity. Totsye did not move.

"I discovered rather quickly that a number of people had reason to dislike, even despise, Luke de Montfort," I said. "He was apparently a sharp operator when it came to his business dealings, and he wasn't above using the rather obvious physical charms of his sister to help him get what he wanted."

Adele hissed in outrage.

"I would beg your pardon, Adele," I said, "but I have little doubt that you were complicit in your brother's schemes. It's a bit late to pretend that Luke used you without your consent."

Harald Knutson spoke up. "You've got that right. That bitch did whatever her brother wanted. I learned that, to my cost. The two of them nearly put me out of business before I realized what they were doing."

I nodded. "Yes, they did. Unfortunately you were rather an easy mark, weren't you?"

Glaring at me, Harald shrank back in his chair.

"Luke and Adele went after you, Your Majesty," I said, "but that wasn't enough. They also went after Totsye. You dropped Totsye very quickly when you thought Adele was interested in you, and Luke tried to involve Totsye in one of his disastrous deals." I smiled. "But Totsye was a bit smarter than you, Your Majesty. She at least managed to get out of the mess with much of her business intact."

Harald shot a poisonous glance at his former love. She stared straight ahead, acknowledging nothing.

"Totsye had two reasons to hate Luke and Adele. First, they destroyed her relationship with you, and second, they nearly cost her her whole livelihood. She didn't forget that, nor did she forgive them. She put on an incredibly convincing act, of a woman hopelessly in love, and she even had me believing her. That's one reason it took me longer than it should have to realize that she was the most likely suspect the whole time."

I didn't say anything more for a moment. I watched Harald and Adele squirm. Millbank had the look of a man who would pay dearly to be anywhere but there.

"Totsye decided to revenge herself, and she did that by poisoning Luke."

I stepped forward and brandished my new ring in front of them. "See what I bought today? I found a jeweler here who sells very interesting rings. Watch." I demonstrated how the ring opened to reveal the cavity beneath the jewel, and Totsye paled. The others merely looked puzzled.

I snapped the jewel back into place and moved back a couple of steps. "It took a bit longer than it should have to get to the solution," I said, "because we thought at first that Luke had been poisoned with foxglove. That was a mistake, but if it had been foxglove, Luke could have been given the poison four to six hours, roughly, before he collapsed in this tent.

"Everyone knew how much he loved those fig pastries, and it would have been easy to give him a fig pastry laden with foxglove, and that would have been more difficult to prove."

"If it wasn't foxglove, what was it?" Millbank asked, his curiosity overcoming his discomfort.

"Cyanide," I said. "Prussic acid, in the form of powder. It acts almost immediately, which meant that Luke had to have ingested it very shortly before he collapsed."

I waited. No one spoke.

"You can all see the implications of that," I said. "He had to have been poisoned after he arrived here for Totsye's dinner party. I thought at first that he had been poisoned by a fig pastry, because the poison was in the honey, according to the pathologist. But as you all know, mead is made from honey."

"So she poisoned the mead with poison she had in her ring," Adele said wonderingly as she turned to stare at Totsye.

"Yes," I said. "I was even watching her while she did it, and I didn't realize, until this afternoon. She got rid of the second, untasted pastry on Luke's plate when she went to fetch the doctor. Very quick thinking on her part. Tell me, Adele, did you drink out of your cup?"

Wide-eyed in horror, Adele stared at me. "No, I didn't. Luke collapsed before I had a chance to taste it."

"I don't know for sure," I said, "but I wouldn't be surprised if your mead had been poisoned as well. She would have gotten rid of both of you at once, though that might have been more difficult to carry off."

Adele paled to the point that I thought she might faint, and Millbank got out of his chair to come and put a comforting arm around her shoulders. She leaned against him and closed her eyes.

"Do you have anything to add to this?" I addressed Totsye. "Have I left out anything?"

Dull-eyed, she shook her head. "No."

Suddenly she began to sob—a deep, wrenching sound. Her right hand clutched convulsively at her throat, and she twisted sideways in her chair.

As I watched in horrified fascination, she pulled her poison ring from her bosom, opened it, and swallowed the contents.

By the time Robin realized what she had done, she had slid out of her chair onto the ground.

Chapter 29

Totsye died in the ambulance on the way to hospital. It really was better that way, I supposed. Robin would be able to find enough proof, I had little doubt, to be certain that she really was guilty. The case could be closed, and everyone else could get on with their lives.

I waited around until I heard the news about Totsye, then left the encampment and walked slowly up the hill to Blitherington Hall. I figured the news would be better coming from me, since Totsye had been an old school chum of Lady Prunella's.

Lady P's reaction was not anything like I expected.

"I cannot claim to be *completely* surprised," she said, after the initial shock. "After all, she *was* a scholarship girl. It's not as if she had parents who could *afford* to send her to our school." She sniffed. "Her father was a *coal* miner, and her mother was a barmaid. *No* breeding whatsoever."

Giles and I exchanged glances over her head.

"Yes, breeding does tell," I said gravely, forbearing to remind Lady P that her own father had been a greengrocer. Or so someone had once told me.

Giles winked at me and followed me out of the drawing room after I bade his mother good night.

"Care for some company, Simon?" he said once the door

was closed behind us. "After all, you have something to tell me, don't you?"

"Are you certain you're feeling up to it, Giles?" I asked, trying not to betray my unease. "After all, you've had quite a day."

"You're not going to get out of it that easily, Simon," he said. "I've been patient long enough."

"Yes, you have," I said, capitulating. "Come along, then."

"Just let me tell my mother I won't be home for dinner," he said, grinning at me before he went back into the drawing room.

"I hope," I said softly. "But you just might be." I wanted to get it over with, and yet I wanted to put it off. I couldn't bear the thought of his turning away from me in disgust or horror.

Giles tried to engage me in conversation on the drive through the village, but he found me a dull companion. I was too busy thinking about what to say to pay much attention to his chatter.

Sensitive to my mood, he stopped talking when we got out of the Jag and watched me a bit apprehensively. I smiled briefly, attempting to reassure him, but his expression remained anxious. I retrieved my mail and sorted through it in the hall, nothing more than a delaying tactic, but I couldn't stop myself.

"Shall I get us something to drink, Simon?" Giles said.

"Whatever you like, Giles," I responded absently. "I'll be with you in a moment.

I stared down at one of the envelopes in my hand. It had not arrived through the mail, though it had been in the mailbox. I recognized the bold handwriting. It was a letter from Tris.

I was hardly aware that Giles had left me. I felt curiously empty as I regarded Tris's writing. *Should I even bother to open it?* I wondered.

Might as well, I told myself. I tore the envelope open and pulled the letter out.

"My dear Simon," I read, "perhaps some day you will forgive me. I realized all too quickly that my campaign to win you back was for nought, because I could see you held more fear for what I might do than deep affection for me. If it's any consolation, I will have a very long time in which to regret what could have been, had I offered you the same affection and loyalty you once gave me."

The words swam before my eyes, and I blinked to clear them. "But don't look back, only forward. Trust him, Simon, and don't worry. He won't disappoint you."

That was all, except for the signature, a bold *T.*

I folded the letter and went into my office. I dropped the paper on my desk and stood there, staring at the wall. It would take me a long time to sort out my feelings about Tris and what he had done. Could I ever forgive him? I didn't know.

I was surprised and touched by his letter. I hadn't known Tris ever to express his feelings in that way. It demonstrated generosity of spirit, and while Tris had always been generous with material goods, he had rarely been so in other ways.

"Simon? Is something wrong?" Giles said, and I turned to see him standing in the doorway. His concern was evident. "Is it bad news?"

"No, Giles," I said. "Not bad news." I accepted the glass of wine he offered me, and I turned him gently in the direction of the sitting room. "Let's get comfortable and have that talk."

I sat on the sofa, and Giles sat at the other end, facing me. He sipped at his wine as he waited for me to speak.

"You've been very patient with me, Giles," I said, "even though I know it was very difficult for you at times. You wanted something more than I felt I could give you, at least for a while."

"But now?" Giles asked.

"Now I don't want there to be any more barriers between us," I said. "I love you, and I can't imagine my existence without you."

He started to speak, but I held up a hand to forestall him.

"I know you love me," I said, "and I don't doubt for a minute the sincerity or the depth of your feelings for me. It's not that."

"Then what is it, Simon?" Giles said, an edge of anger in his tone. "Are you suddenly going to tell me you have a wife and kiddies tucked away somewhere in Texas? Or that you're not really a man, but a woman in drag? What is it?"

I laughed. "If only it were that simple. No, Giles, it's something else entirely."

"What, then?"

I found myself suddenly unable to look into his eyes. Instead I stared down into the wine in my glass. "Do you know what a vampire is, Giles?"

"Yes, Simon," he said. "And I know what werewolves and zombies are, too. What is the point of all this?"

"Because I am a vampire, Giles," I said, and I forced myself to meet his gaze.

Instead of the shock I expected, I saw merely curiosity. "I knew there was something different about you, but I could never quite sort out what it was." He frowned slightly. "You don't disappear during the daytime, Simon. How can you really be a vampire, if the sun doesn't affect you?"

"Because I take a certain medication that enables me to do so," I said. "I do better if I don't expose myself to sunlight for very long at a time, but I can tolerate it, as long as I'm well covered."

"I see," Giles said, drawing out the two syllables. "What about blood? Don't you need that, too?"

I shook my head. "Those same pills make it possible for me to exist without having to prey upon humans for blood."

Giles thought about that for a moment. "I've seen you in St. Ethelwold's, and you don't seem afraid of crosses. And I'm sure I've seen your reflection in a mirror."

"Yes," I said patiently. "Your idea of vampires is like everyone else's. Formed by old movies. All that nonsense was invented by Hollywood."

"I guess this means you can't change into a bat, and I'll bet you can't fly either," Giles said.

"No, I can't."

"Did you become a vampire by choice?"

"Yes," I said.

"Why?" Giles asked.

"It seemed like a good idea at the time," I said, a shade too flippantly.

"That's not funny, Simon," Giles said.

"No, it's not," I replied, "and I do apologize. You want to know why I became a vampire. Well, then." I looked straight into his eyes. "It was a choice, my choice, and something I very much wanted at the time. I don't really regret it either."

"So why did you do it?"

"Because I was afraid of what could happen if I didn't," I said bleakly. "Someone I loved dearly died of AIDS, and I lost a number of friends to it as well. I was terrified of that happening to me."

"Were you terribly promiscuous, Simon?" Giles asked gently.

"No, I never have been," I said, "but I wanted to cut out the risk. AIDS can't kill a vampire."

"So it's that simple."

I nodded.

"Well, I suppose I can understand that," Giles said. He was taking this all a lot more calmly than I had had any reason to hope.

He set his wine glass down on the coffee table. "How does being a vampire affect your abilities to, er, well, you know." He turned a bit pink.

"Not in the least," I said. "Everything works just as it should."

"I see," he said, his face even pinker. "Well, then."

"Well, what?" I said softly. "Does this change how you feel about me, Giles, now that you know the truth?"

He remained silent just long enough that I was preparing

myself for the worst, but finally he spoke. "Simon, have you ever seen the movie *Some Like It Hot?*"

Puzzled, I nodded. "Yes, many times."

"Do you remember the last line of the movie, Simon? What Joe E. Brown says to Jack Lemmon, when Jack tells him he's really a man?"

"Yes," I said, then I quoted, " 'Nobody's perfect.' "

"Exactly," Giles said, smiling at me.

He stood up from the couch and held out his hand. I took it, and I stood up beside him.

He moved away, and I watched him anxiously. He stopped in the hallway and turned around. Slowly he beckoned for me to follow him.

He turned and began to walk up the stairs.

In that moment, I felt like a vampire from the old days. I could have flown.

Afterword

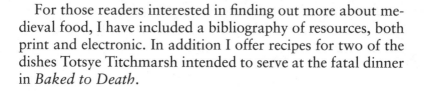

For those readers interested in finding out more about medieval food, I have included a bibliography of resources, both print and electronic. In addition I offer recipes for two of the dishes Totsye Titchmarsh intended to serve at the fatal dinner in *Baked to Death*.

Lamb Stew

(From Constance B. Hieatt, Brenda Hosington, and Sharon Butler. *Pleyn Delit: Medieval Cookery for Modern Cooks*, 2nd ed. [Toronto: University of Toronto Press, 1996], recipe 79.)

Ingredients

1½–2 lbs stewing lamb
2 medium onions, minced
1 tbsp minced parsley
1 tsp each fresh thyme, rosemary, savory or ½ tsp dried
¼ tsp each ground ginger, coriander
salt to taste

1½–2 cups chicken broth
1 cup white wine
1 egg
juice of ½ lemon (or 1 tbsp white wine or cider vinegar)
optional: pinch saffron

Cut lamb into pieces 2-inches square and put in an enam-
eled, pyrex, or nonstick cooking pot. Add onions, herbs, and
spices; cover with wine and broth. Simmer for 45 minutes,
covered. Beat egg with lemon juice or vinegar; pour a little of
the hot (but not boiling) sauce into this mixture, stirring,
then add this to the contents of the pot, off the heat. Stir over
very low heat to thicken, taking care not to let it boil after the
egg is added.

Fried Fig Pastries *(serves six)*

(From Maggie Black, *The Medieval Cookbook* [New
York: Thames and Hudson, 1992, reprinted 1999], pp.
66–67.)

Ingredients

450 g/1 lb dried figs, soaked, drained and minced (reserve
   the soaking liquid)
"Powder fort" mixture made with ⅛ tsp each ground ginger and cloves, pinch of black pepper
¼ tsp dried saffron strands moistened with fig-soaking
   liquid
¼ tsp salt
1 egg, separated, and 1 egg white
6–7 sheets filo or strudel pastry
Oil for frying
About 225 ml/8 fl oz/1 cup warmed clear honey (optional)

In a food processor combine the minced figs, spices and saffron, salt, and egg yolk.

Beat the egg white until liquid. Lightly brush the top sheet of pastry with egg white. Mark the short side of the pastry sheet at 7.5-cm/3-inch intervals. Then cut the sheet into strips 7.5-cm/3-inches wide. Put a dab of fig mixture on the end of one sheet and roll the strip up like a mini–Swiss roll. Pinch the ends to seal in the fig mixture.

Repeat this process until you have used all the fig mixture; remember to brush every pastry sheet with egg white before cutting it into strips.

Fry the rolls, a few at a time, in deep or shallow oil, as you prefer. Serve them with warmed honey spooned over if you like a very sweet sauce.

Bibliography

Books

Black, Maggie. *The Medieval Cookbook*. New York: Thames and Hudson, 1992, reprinted 1999.

Cosman, Madeleine Pelner. *Fabulous Feasts: Medieval Cookery and Ceremony*. New York: George Braziller, 1978.

Henisch, Bridget Ann. *Fast and Feast: Food in Medieval Society*. University Park, Penn.: University of Pennsylvania Press, 1976.

Hieatt, Constance B., Brenda Hosington, and Sharon Butler. *Pleyn Delit: Medieval Cookery for Modern Cooks*, 2nd ed. Toronto: University of Toronto Press, 1996.

Websites

http://www.regia.org/main.htm
   Regia Anglorum: Anglo-Saxon, Viking, Norman and British Living History
http://www.sca.org/
   The Society for Creative Anachronism, Inc.
http://www.godecookery.com/
   resources on medieval cooking

http://www.medievalcookery.com/
   recipes and resources for medieval cooking

   In general, searching any of the Internet search engines for "medieval cookery," "medieval cooking," or "medieval food" will yield a number of interesting and useful results.